USA TODAY bestselling author **Katherine Garbera** writes emotional, sexy contemporary romances. An Amazon, Barnes & Noble and iBooks bestselling author, she is also a two-time Maggie Award winner and has sold more than seven million copies of her books worldwide. She loves to hear from readers via her website, www.katherinegarbera.com.

Andrea Laurence is an award-winning author of contemporary romances filled with seduction and sass. She has been a lover of reading and writing stories since she was young. A dedicated West Coast girl transplanted into the deep south, she is thrilled to share her special blend of sensuality and dry, sarcastic humor with readers.

RANCHER UNTAMED

KATHERINE GARBERA

THE BOYFRIEND ARRANGEMENT

ANDREA LAURENCE

MILLS & BOON

First Published in Great Britain 2018
by Mills & Boon, an imprint of HarperCollinsPublishers,
1 London Bridge Street, London, SE1 9GF

Rancher Untamed © 2018 Katherine Garbera
The Boyfriend Arrangement © 2018 Andrea Laurence

ISBN: 978-0-263-93623-0

1018

MIX
Paper from
responsible sources
FSC™ C007454

This book is produced from independently certified FSC™ paper to ensure responsible forest management.

For more information visit: www.harpercollins.co.uk/green

Printed and bound in Spain
by CPI, Barcelona

RANCHER UNTAMED

KATHERINE GARBERA

This book is dedicated to all believers in happy endings and the power of true love.

One

Diego Velasquez felt foolish as he stood in the wings waiting to be announced in the Five Families Country Club bachelor auction. He'd give anything to be with his horses on his ranch, Arbol Verde. He had tried to get out of participating in the annual charity event by making a huge donation, but his mom, a formidable morning newscaster on a Houston station, was on the committee and wanted to see her sons—all four of them—married. So there was no getting out of it, even though every year he and his brothers tried.

"What do you think, Diego? Got it in you to land a huge bid?" his youngest brother, Inigo, asked.

Diego was pretty sure Inigo had toyed with the idea of making one of the women who followed him on the F1 racing circuit his temporary bride to avoid the auction. But since their beloved mama was a devout Catholic, a temporary marriage was a no-no, so he'd flown in on his G6 this morning from Japan. Luckily for Inigo the F1 was racing in Austin in two weeks' time. Or maybe unluckily, because it meant there was no excuse not to be here, he thought as he watched Inigo messing with his bow tie.

Diego turned to his other two brothers, the twins. Alejandro did some sort of social media management that had made him a millionaire and he wasn't even thirty. And Mauricio had the golden eye when it came to spotting property in neighborhoods on the cusp of becoming "it" places to live and work.

Diego was proud of them. They were all the kind of bachelors that the charity auction should be promoting. Sure, it was annoying that Mama was competitive and wanted to see the Velasquez name at the top of the fund-raising leaderboard. But at the end of the day, it was a good cause, wasn't it?

"You look like you're thinking of bolting," Mo said.

"I am," Diego admitted. But before he could make good his escape, there was a commotion on stage.

"Ethan Caruthers is making a fool of himself over some woman. He just proposed to her," Inigo said, from his spot near the curtain leading to the stage.

"Crissanne Moss," Diego said, coming over to join his youngest brother. "While you were touring the world, this has been the big news in town. Ethan and Crissanne were living together and the Carutherses thought it was leading toward marriage. But then Crissanne's ex came back from the dead. Literally. People thought he'd died in a plane crash until he showed up in town, very much alive, wanting to know what was going on between his best friend and his ex-girlfriend."

"*Dios mio*, Diego, you sound like the town gossip," Alejandro said, coming up behind him and slinging his arm over Diego's shoulders.

"Don't remind me. I had dinner with Bi and Derek last night and Ma Caruthers was there spilling the dirt," Diego said.

"Ah, well, it looks like they might be getting back together," Inigo said.

"Yeah, it does," Diego said. He'd never met a woman he'd make a fool of himself over. Not like Ethan was doing right now. But as he watched Ethan go to Crissanne and embrace her…well, it made him wonder what it would be like to find one special person to settle down with.

"You're next, Diego," the stage manager said.

"Damn," he said. His chance to run was gone.

He heard Mo chuckling evilly behind him and turned to punch him in the shoulder, only softening it at the last moment because if he started a brawl with his brothers his mom would never forgive them.

"What are you afraid of?" Mo asked. "It's just harmless fun."

Yeah, it was. But as he got older, it felt like he should be retiring from this auction, not settling in as a permanent fixture. "Nothing. You're right. It's fun."

All four brothers watched the crowd as Diego's name was announced. Alejandro elbowed him, pointing to Kinley Caruthers's nanny, Pippa. She was close to the front of the crowd, a look of anticipation lighting up her heart-shaped face.

She'd caught his eye before. The cute blonde had come to Cole's Hill two years ago when Kinley moved here. Her hair was a honey blond and she usually wore it in a ponytail, but tonight it fell to her shoulders in soft waves. Her eyes were gray, but not icy at all. It was sort of a soft gray color that made him want to tell her things that he didn't even want to admit he thought about. Which made her dangerous. Her lips were full, and normally she wore only lip gloss—yeah, he'd spent a lot of time thinking about that mouth of hers. Tonight she'd used a red lipstick that made it impossible for him to look at anything but her mouth. Which was the last thing he needed because he already thought too much about what it would be like to kiss her.

She wore a figure-hugging dress in a deep blue jewel tone that made her creamy skin look even smoother than normal. He'd known her legs were long and slim because she tended to wear leggings around town, but tonight with a pair of fancy heels on they seemed longer, endless.

He groaned.

"Stop being a baby. I swear, Diego, you are the worst at this. I know they are women and not your beloved horses, but it's not that bad," Mo said.

He glanced at his brother. "I know that. I'm not exactly afraid of women."

"Your reputation proves that," Mo said. "So what's the deal?"

Mo leaned toward the curtain with him and followed Diego's gaze.

"Oh, it's like that."

"Yeah. But she's not interested and I'm—"

"Out of time," Mo said.

"Mr. Diego Velasquez," the emcee repeated.

And Diego, with a shove from Mo, walked out onto the stage.

Pippa Hamilton-Hoff rarely went out and certainly didn't get dressed up all that often. But here she was, seated at the Caruthers table for the Five Families bachelor auction. Among the descendants of the original five families who'd founded Cole's Hill, there was a friendly competition to see which one could raise the most money.

Given that all of the Caruthers brothers were married except for Ethan—and he now seemed engaged—that family's chances were slim this year. But Pippa had already had other ideas. It certainly helped that she was twenty-five today and would soon have access to her fortune. She knew exactly who she wanted to spend this birthday with.

Diego Velasquez—a long, tall Texan who looked as comfortable in his tuxedo as he did on the back of a horse. Though if she were being totally honest, she preferred to see him riding his stallion Iago. She'd been out to visit him twice with Penny, the little girl she nannied. Penny was a horse-crazy four-year-old, the daughter of Nathan Caruthers, and Diego was her de facto uncle now that his sister, Bianca, had married Dr. Derek Caruthers.

The long road that she'd been on for the last four years was almost up. She no longer had to hide who she was—an English heiress who'd run away from her controlling father and had become a nanny while on the run, trying to figure out what to do next. Now that she was twenty-five her inheritance was hers to claim and do what she wanted with. For this one night she still wanted to be young and free. To be with a man who didn't know about her fortune, who would be happy enough with Pippa the nanny.

She'd run into him enough times in town to know that it wasn't coincidence. The owner of a large ranch on the outskirts of town with an internationally acclaimed breeding program didn't have to drive into Cole's Hill at 10:00 a.m. every Monday, Wednesday and Friday to get coffee, but he did. They always chatted, and she'd been careful to not let it be more than talk, but in her heart… she wanted more. He had the kind of chocolatey-brown eyes that reminded her of drinking hot chocolate, so rich and comforting. Yet at the same time he made her feel alive…feel things that she hadn't allowed herself to even think about since she'd walked out of that party in New York City four years ago and gotten on a bus.

Since then, her life had been a lie. One big deceit where she had to keep moving, keep thinking and never let her guard down.

Until now.

Tonight.

Ethan Caruthers had done the romantic thing and

now he and Crissanne were in the corner snogging. Meanwhile, Pippa was sitting here with access to her fortune and looking up at Diego Velasquez. He wore his tuxedo with an easy grace that spoke of manners and class, but when their eyes met, she felt that zing. That sexual awareness that reminded her she was more than an heiress on the run. She was a woman with a plan tonight.

Not the one who'd hidden away for four years or the one who was afraid to claim things for herself.

No, she wanted Diego and was determined to have him.

The bidding started, and she raised her hand, increasing the bid. She just kept on until she and one of the women who worked with Diego at his ranch were the only ones left. Chantelle, Pippa thought her name was. Did Chantelle wish for a relationship that was more than boss/employee?

Pippa knew she was leaving. That as soon as the board of her family's company, House of Hamilton, read her email and accepted she was who she said she was, Cole's Hill, Texas, would be a distant memory. But she'd put aside so many things for the past four years. She'd denied herself for too long and she wasn't going to anymore. She raised her paddle and doubled the current bid, which made the emcee squeal with excitement and Diego raise his eyebrows as he looked right at her.

"I think someone definitely wants you, Diego, and unless there is another bidder who wants to top that bid…" The emcee glanced around the room, but she'd pushed the bid so high no one else raised a paddle.

For the first time since Diego walked onto the stage she was truly aware of the room and that everyone's eyes were on her. She started to sit back down, but Kinley put her hand on Pippa's butt. "Get your man, girl."

She had to smile at the way Kinley said it. Despite the fact that they had grown up in two very different worlds, Kin was a soul sister. Pippa had always believed that something stronger than coincidence had led them to meet on that Vegas bus the day Kinley went into labor. Pippa had been riding the bus trying to figure out her next move, since she was out of cash, and Kinley had been on her way to work when her water broke.

"I guess I will," Pippa said, carefully placing her paddle on the table and going up to claim him.

It was only for tonight, but then again, she felt tonight was all she'd had. She'd had four birthdays on her own in Texas, each of them fraught with tension and confusion. Only her determination had brought her to this moment, and as she climbed up the stairs at the side of the stage and went to him, she didn't worry about any of that. As she got closer, she noticed his smile, how tonight it wasn't as bold as it usually was. But it was still sexy and charming, and she admitted to herself she was smitten.

What an old-fashioned word, but it suited her and her emotions.

She hadn't really been paying attention to the other winners, so she had no idea what to do, but Diego caught her hand and pulled her close to him. "With a bid like that, I think you deserve my everything."

Up close she realized that his brown eyes had flecks

of gold in them. His lips were full, and he winked at her as he dipped her low in his arms and then brought his mouth down on hers. She stopped thinking and just let go.

Diego stood in the line at the bar watching Pippa talking to Kinley and Bianca. His sister was a former supermodel, but Pippa outshone her in his eyes. He wasn't sure what they were saying, but he noticed that Pippa smiled and laughed easily. He ordered two margaritas and then made his way back over to her.

"So I guess we shouldn't wait up for you," Kinley said as he approached.

Pippa's gaze met his and she blushed, the pink tint moving up from her décolletage to her neck.

"You'll see me when you see me," Pippa said in her very proper British accent.

She reached around Kinley and took one of the margaritas from him. He lifted his glass toward hers and took a sip before he moved to stand next to her. Kinley hugged her and went to join her husband across the room.

"Mama is very proud of the Velasquez family tonight," Bianca said.

"She should be. She did a good job raising us," Diego said. "And we are all home tonight, which you know always makes her happy."

"She's not the only one who's over the moon," Bianca said. "Benito can't wait until tomorrow morning for our family brunch. He loves his *tios*."

His nephew was four years old and had seen a lot in

his short life. His father had died while racing, something that had made Diego's own mother more determined to try to find another career for Inigo. But his youngest brother had the legendary Velasquez hardheadedness.

"We adore him," Diego said.

"Of course you do. Now, I am going to try to claim a dance with my husband. He's got early surgery tomorrow, so we can't stay late," Bianca said, leaning over to kiss his cheek. Then she gave Pippa a hug before she walked away.

He glanced over at the woman who'd been shutting him down in town but tonight had made the highest bid to spend the evening with him. "You could have saved yourself some money if you'd said yes when I asked you out a few weeks ago."

"Oh, well, then the charity wouldn't have made as much tonight. Somehow, I think that makes it all worth it," she said.

There was something different about her tonight. She was more confident. She'd always seemed to be a little bit on edge, her eyes frequently going to the door of the café where they'd met. It used to bother him when he'd first started running into her in town, but now he'd gotten used to it.

"Was that what brought out your wallet? The charity?"

She flushed again. "It is a very good cause. Children are so vulnerable and really at the mercy of the adults in their lives."

"Were you?" he asked. He couldn't help but be curious about her past. And how could a nanny afford the generous bid she'd placed? Maybe it was because she didn't really have any expenses living in her own house on the Rockin' C ranch. And she'd told him at the coffee shop that her daily lattes were her only indulgence. But still. No one knew much about her. She never mentioned her last name, and he knew from Nathan—Kinley's husband—that Pippa had met Kinley on a bus in Las Vegas, of all places.

But she was a British woman with no apparent connection to her homeland. And Diego, who was proud of being American, didn't understand that.

"I had everything a child could wish for," Pippa said. "The best toys, a first-class education and a stable with horses that even the legendary Diego Velasquez would envy."

"Legendary?" he asked, ignoring the sadness that underpinned her words. So she had been born with money, but when she'd come to the United States, she'd left that behind. He'd seen the way she lived. *Frugal* was one word for it. But it was deliberate.

"Don't let it go to your head, but you are sort of a superstar with horses. I mean, when I've brought Pippa out to your stables to ride, I've seen the way the rowdiest stallion settles down for you."

"I get horses," Diego said.

"But not people?"

"Some people," he admitted. Mo had warned him to not talk about his horses or breeding program around women and bore them when he was in his early twenties. Diego had seen his success with the ladies increase after his brother's advice and still followed it now.

The DJ had gotten set up, and as the drinks from the open bar flowed, more people were moving toward the dance floor. Pippa finished her margarita.

"Do you want another drink?" he asked.

She shrugged. "I'm not a huge fan of tequila."

"What would you prefer?" he asked.

"Something sparkling. I want to celebrate."

He raised one eyebrow and took the margarita glass from her. "I'll be right back."

He went to get them both some prosecco and then returned. "How's that?"

"Much better," she said, lifting her glass toward his.

"What are we celebrating?" he asked.

"My birthday," she said. "I'm twenty-five today."

"Happy birthday, Pippa."

Twenty-five. She was five years younger than him, but the way she said it made him realize there was a lot more to the story. She took a sip of her drink and he did the same, making small talk until they had finished. The band was playing "Despacito" and Pippa was swaying to the music.

"So, Pippa, what are we going to do?"

She tipped her head to the side. "I'm not sure what you mean. What are we going to do about what?"

"This night," he said. He put his hand on her waist and drew her closer to him.

"I'm not sure," she said softly.

Her breath smelled sweet like the prosecco, and her face was so close that his lips tingled. He remembered how soft and succulent they had been beneath his earlier.

"Well, I'm yours…for tonight," he said out loud to remind himself that it was only for this night. "Tell me what it is you want me to do."

She tipped her head back and their eyes met. Her lips parted and he felt her hand come to rest on his shoulder. "Show me a good time, cowboy."

Two

Once the auction was over and the winners collected their bachelors, it was as if all the tension left the room. Pippa felt freer than she'd felt since…well, ever. Her whole life she'd felt the burden of her inheritance and knew that she'd have to make the right choices when she became an adult. Her mother had coached her and told her to take her time. Not to marry young, as she had, because even though she loved her family she felt she'd missed out on so much of life.

Her father was a different story. Having married into the House of Hamilton fortune, he had wanted to do everything to make his own mark on the legacy jewelry company. But instead he'd always come up short. She knew this from a frank discussion two of her cousins had had with her when she'd turned twenty-one. She had been at that odd age where she was both an adult and also not yet allowed to take over her inheritance, which she couldn't do until she was twenty-five. Her father had full power over many things including voting her shares and her position on the board.

"Another prosecco?" Diego asked, interrupting her thoughts.

"Uh, that, or champagne will do. I'm a sucker for anything sparkling," she said. Now that she'd won the man she'd been eyeing around town for the past two years she had to admit that she didn't know what to do with him.

Her life with Kinley and Penny had been quiet and sheltered. She knew all of Dora the Explorer's little friends but really felt awkward with a man. That was sad. She aimed to fix that tonight.

He snagged two champagne glasses from a passing waiter and handed one to her. "To a glittering night."

She clinked her glass to his and then took a sip. She loved the bubbles in champagne and how they felt on her tongue. She closed her eyes and let the sip stay in her mouth awhile before she swallowed. When she opened her eyes, Diego was watching her and the look in his eyes made her feel…well, not awkward anymore.

The DJ was playing a good mix of dance tunes and slower ballads, along with some standards that got the older generations up on the dance floor, but all Pippa could think about was that she was free. After staying hidden so long, and that being the focus of her every day. Hoping she wouldn't be found before she could claim her inheritance…and now that fear was gone.

She'd known her father had private detectives searching for her. And she'd been careful to keep the Hamilton-Hoff name hidden. Not that she couldn't trust Kinley, but if she had to lie, that was her responsibility. Lying was her choice and not one she wanted to force her friends into. All she had to do was wait for her claim to be validated and then…her new life would begin.

"So do you dance?" he asked. Diego's voice was low and smooth. She'd spent way too much time thinking about the way he said her name. He lingered on the last vowel as if he liked the way her name sounded on his lips.

"I do, but mostly with Penny, and that little imp pretty much just jumps around and strikes crazy poses. I'm sure you're not going to want to see me do that," she said.

"I wouldn't rule it out, but maybe not in this venue," he said with a wink. "My nephew is a big fan of lying on the floor and spinning around when the music is on."

"Penny does that, too. I'm pretty sure that's a classic toddler move," she said.

"Can't recall it from my own past, but I hope I had a little more style," he said as the music changed and Justin Timberlake's "Can't Stop the Feeling!" came on. "Want to give it a try? See if you can control the urge to jump around and pose?"

She smiled and nodded. "This song is from the *Trolls* movie."

She groaned internally. She didn't even have a kid and yet kid stuff was all she could talk about. She'd turned into an old lady without even realizing it was happening.

"Please pretend you didn't hear that," she said. "Starting right now I'm going to be young and wild Pippa."

"No arguments here," he said, taking her hand and leading her onto the dance floor.

She'd expected him to let go of her hand, but he didn't. Just held her as they swayed to the music. She didn't have a hard time getting into it and remembered the last time she'd danced like this had been years ago when she'd gone to the winter formal at her boarding school before her mom had died and everything had changed.

After a period of grief, the board of the House of Hamilton had informed her father that he was no longer an official partner and would only be voting Pippa's shares until she came of age at twenty-five. Her relationship with her father changed after that. And when she turned eighteen, he had become obsessed with who she would marry and determined that she should choose a distant cousin of his who was his protégé.

Unexpectedly she felt the sting of tears and she shook her head until she could shove the emotion back down. She twirled away from Diego, who looked as if he were going to ask a question, and continued dancing with her back to him until her emotions were under control.

So much of her journey had been fed by her mom's death, but she was cool now. She was in control and she knew exactly what she was going to do.

The song ended.

"We've had a lot of requests for this song and I think it's about time I played it. 'Save a Horse' by Big & Rich, so, ladies, grab your cowboy and enjoy," he said.

She knew the song well as it was one of her favorites, but until tonight she hadn't had a cowboy of her own. She did now. She took his hand. All around them on the dance floor, there was laughter that soon turned into close embraces and kisses. But Diego just smiled and kept his eyes on hers as she sang and danced with him.

The crazy surge of emotion she'd had earlier changed into something else as she realized just how long it had been since she'd let her hair down and just danced.

At the end of the song, Diego pulled her close and their eyes met moments before he lowered his head and kissed her. Unlike the embrace on stage earlier, this one didn't feel like it was for show.

Diego and Pippa stayed on the dance floor for the next three hours. Some couples disappeared, then came back looking…well, like they'd enjoyed themselves. But Diego remained where he was. He drank champagne, which hadn't escaped Mo's notice. His brother gave him a look and Diego knew he was going to hear about it later. Alejandro was dancing with someone Diego didn't know, but he was pretty damned sure she wasn't his longtime girlfriend. According to the gossips at the coffeehouse, they'd had a fight about Alejandro's inability to commit and she'd dumped him about six weeks ago.

Pippa stuck close to his side and hadn't mentioned the kiss he'd been unable to stop himself from giving her. He knew that it was a bachelor auction, and all in good fun, yet as he'd held her hand and danced her around the floor, he'd wanted to be hers. He'd wanted her to have really claimed him.

"I don't want this night to end," she said as the DJ announced that there was time for only one more song.

"It doesn't have to," he said. "Wait here."

He went to the bar for a bottle of champagne and two plastic flutes before leading Pippa away from the party to one of the patios that overlooked part of the golf course. It was quiet as they moved away from the party.

"One of the things I really love about Texas is how big the sky is," she said, putting her hands on the railing and looking up. There wasn't that much light pollution out here, so the stars were visible.

"Me, too," he admitted. "Where are you from? I mean, you're obviously British."

"Caught that, did ya?" she asked as she turned and leaned back on the railing.

"Yeah, I'm smart that way," he retorted, pouring her a glass of champagne and handing it to her.

He poured another one for himself as she took a sip.

"I was born in Hampshire, but we mainly lived in London except when I was at boarding school," she said.

"I have to admit I have no idea where Hampshire is," he said.

"That's okay. I had no idea where Cole's Hill was until Kinley moved here," Pippa admitted.

"Why did you come with her? Las Vegas is way more exciting than this," he said.

"I had nothing holding me there. My job as Penny's nanny is important to me," she said, taking a sip of her drink. "I made Kinley a promise when Penny was born that I would stay as long as she needed me."

"You were there when Penny was born?" he asked.

This was the most she'd told him about herself since they met, and he was curious.

"Yeah. We were on a city bus when Kinley went into labor. I just stayed with her when she was taken to the hospital because she was scared and alone and we'd been chatting before her water broke… I think we both needed a friend in that moment," Pippa said. There was a note in her voice that hinted there might be more to the story, but she shook her head and looked over at him. "We've been friends ever since. What about you? Who's your oldest friend?"

He took a sip of his champagne. It was never going to replace Jack Daniels as his favorite drink, but the taste was growing on him. "If I'm honest, my brothers. Maybe Mauricio, since he's younger than his twin, Alejandro, by several minutes. Inigo is five years younger than me and closer to my sister, Bianca. He's a Formula One driver like Bianca's first husband was."

Why was he telling her all of this? But he knew. He didn't want to make any moves that would send her running away from him again. Even though she'd bid on him tonight, every other time he'd tried to connect with her she'd shut him down. And he didn't want to let this end.

Not now.

Not until… Well, not until he figured out the secrets behind those gray eyes. She always seemed so calm and controlled, but tonight there was a fire and passion in her gaze that he wasn't going to walk away from until he uncovered its source.

"You have such a big family…like the Carutherses. Is that a Texas thing?" she asked.

He had to laugh. "Well, they do say everything is bigger here. The families in Cole's Hill certainly are."

"I guess that's true," she said. "I do like this area of Texas. So lush and pretty with the green rolling hills. I mean, it's a bit of a stretch, but it does remind me of our country houses in England."

"Country houses?" he asked.

She shrugged. "You know, big old Georgian mansions that have been in one family forever."

"Then why are you here in Texas and not with your family?" he asked. "Sounds like legacy is important to you."

"It is and it isn't," she said. "This champagne is really good."

He knew she was changing the subject and he was tempted to let her do it. But the moon was full, and she'd claimed him for her own, at least for this night, and that meant he had nothing to lose.

"It is good, but what did you mean about your family legacy?" he asked. "You don't have to tell me, but I want to know everything there is about you, Pippa… I don't even know your last name."

"Do you need to?" she asked.

"If I'm going to kiss you again, I think I might want to know it," he said. "It's only fair. You know mine."

She was nervous to let him know her last name. It was silly. She'd reached out to her cousins and the board of directors to let them know she was very much alive and ready to claim her seat on the board. Yet here in the moonlight standing so close to Diego, she knew that she didn't want to tell him, because if he knew she was the House of Hamilton jewelry heiress it would change the dynamic.

He thought she was a nanny—

"Is it really that hard to trust me?" he asked.

"Yes. I've been keeping my identity secret for so long that I… Sorry, it's not you. It really is me," she said.

"Why are you hiding it?" he asked.

His voice was silky smooth, wrapping around her senses and making it hard to concentrate. "My father has a plan for my future and I want to choose my own path."

"Fair enough," he said. "So you are on the run?"

"Yes."

He came to stand next to her, leaning against the railing so they were facing the river rock exterior of the Five Families Country Club. "Then just be Pippa for tonight. I promise you have nothing to fear from me."

She reached out without really thinking about it, put her hand on his thigh and squeezed. "I know."

But the electric tingle that ran up her arm made her wonder if she was close to getting in over her head. She wanted Diego. That wasn't a surprise. She'd been dodging him in town and trying to limit their contact for that very reason. It was one thing to hook up for a night but something else entirely to start anything with him knowing she was leaving.

And she was going to have to work really hard

to prove herself once she was back in England. She wouldn't have time for anything else.

She groaned.

He turned his head to face her and in those deep brown eyes she saw desire. He quirked one eyebrow at her and she felt the brush of his exhalation against her cheek. He smelled faintly of expensive cologne and the outdoors. She closed her eyes and took a deeper breath. He smelled like everything she wanted. And tonight he was hers.

She had made a few missteps. Talking about herself and her past. She needed to keep those things quiet.

She opened her eyes and he was still staring at her.

Without saying a word she lifted her hand and ran it over the light stubble on his jaw. It abraded the skin of her fingers, but in a pleasant way. She ran her finger back and forth, and he caught his breath as his pupils dilated.

He reached out and touched her face in return, sending chills spreading down her neck and arms. Her breasts felt fuller and she felt the hot pulse of desire between her legs.

She wanted him.

Her lips parted, and he slowly cupped the side of her face with his fingers, rubbing his thumb over her bottom lip. The sensations intensified, spreading through her body in sync with her heartbeat.

She mirrored his gesture. He had a strong-looking mouth, but it was soft to the touch. And his breath when he exhaled was soft and warm. He'd kissed her twice, but both times had been restrained because there'd been so many people around. This time they were wrapped in a cocoon of intimacy with only the moon and stars to witness their closeness.

And that made this feel more real.

It wasn't just that he'd asked her for honesty and she'd changed the subject. It was that he wasn't deterred by her half-truths and evasions. He wanted her, she thought again. Just her.

Pippa.

She didn't need the Hamilton fortune or her family connections for him to see the woman she was and be attracted to her, and that felt…well, like something she'd never expected to find.

He leaned forward and she removed her fingers from his lips, putting her hands on either side of his face. She needed to do this. He'd kissed her before, but she wanted to be the one kissing him.

She needed this for herself and the self-doubt that had driven her from the only world she'd ever known. In a way, kissing Diego was her way of reclaiming the parts of herself she hadn't meant to discard along the way.

Reclaiming her womanhood.

She wasn't the nanny or a runaway or even the key to the Hamilton-Hoff future. She was just Pippa.

"Diego." She whispered just his name as their lips brushed.

He caressed her, his fingers lightly wrapping around the back of her neck, one of them brushing the sensitive spot behind her ear. Her eyes were half-closed as her lips met his, and she felt his power. But it was tempered. He was letting her take what she wanted from him.

She parted her own lips and felt the heat of his mouth against hers as her tongue darted out and she tasted him. Just one little taste of this cowboy on this big Texas night would be enough to satisfy her.

Not.

Oh, my God, definitely not.

She thrust her tongue deeper into his mouth for a better taste of him. He tipped his head to give her greater access and she leaned in closer, felt her breasts brush against his chest. His hand on her neck was still light, but the pattern with his finger was driving her forward. Increasing that need to have more of him. To taste more of him.

His tongue tangled with hers and she heard him groan. The vibration filled her mouth and she shivered again as another pulse of liquid desire went through her.

She shifted closer, losing her balance against the railing, breaking the kiss. The air felt cold against her lips and she straightened. Her fingers went to her own mouth as she shifted away from him.

Their eyes met.

"I want to take you home with me."

Three

Diego took her hand in his. His voice was rough and husky, but he couldn't control that. He'd been turned on by her kiss. Just her kiss had gotten him hotter and harder than he'd anticipated. But she'd said she was on the run…something that he'd suspected, along with most of Cole's Hill. And he didn't want her to feel pressured to go home with him.

"I'd like that, too," she said. There was a look in her eyes that made him even harder and he stood, putting the champagne glasses on one of the tables that lined the patio.

He turned back to her and held out his hand.

She licked her lips and closed her eyes for a second. "You taste really good, you know?"

"I think it was you."

She walked toward him, her hips swaying with each step she took, and he groaned deep in his throat. Damn. She was hot, and she knew it. She kept eye contact with him, but he broke it, letting his gaze skim down her body. He didn't care if she saw how much she affected him.

He wasn't going to pretend she didn't have him hotter than a tin roof in July.

"We'll have to do it again and again until we figure it out," she said. Her voice was husky with a note of teasing in it.

"Sounds like my kind of plan," he said. "I have a town house I keep here in the Five Families neighborhood. Will that be okay?"

"Sounds good. I live out at the Caruthers Ranch and I'm pretty sure we don't want to drive all the way out there. I don't really want to wait that long to touch you again, Diego," she said. Her words adding kindling to the fire that was already burning out of control in his body.

"Good," he said, lacing their fingers together and leading her down the patio walkway toward the path around the golf course. "I hope you don't mind walking, but I've had too much to drink to feel safe driving even just through this neighborhood. It's only a ten-minute walk."

"I don't mind walking at all," she said.

He held her hand in his and tried to concentrate on getting back to his place. But her perfume smelled slightly of spring and she kept humming "Save a Horse," distracting him. Filling his mind with images of her naked, on top of him, riding him. He groaned again.

"Are you okay?"

"Sí," he said, falling back on Spanish. His family had been in the United States for generations—their original homestead had been a land grant from the Spanish King back in the 1700s—but their family had always been multilingual.

"I know a little bit of Spanish, but it's not the Mexican dialect that a lot of people speak here," she said. "I had a very funny conversation with Isabella about that the other day. She's one of the new hires that Kinley brought in to work in her wedding and event planning office in town."

Diego didn't really care about all that. But he liked the sound of her voice, so he just made a hmming sound and she kept on talking. Finally, he saw the cluster of townhomes and his own front door.

"This way," he said, leading her off the path and across the street to his place. These townhomes were only about five years old and had been built from the same river rock that had been used in the country club. The path leading up to the front door was made of smaller stones but smoothed out so that it was comfortable to walk on.

He reached into his pocket for his keys, which drew his trousers tighter against his groin, and he realized that even walking and talking about nothing for ten minutes had done nothing to cool him down. But that wasn't surprising. Pippa had had him tied in knots for the last few weeks.

"This is it," he said. "Still want to come in? If not, I can arrange for someone to take you home."

"Diego, I want you. I want this. I'm not going to change my mind," she said.

"You've kept me at arm's length for a while now and I know that there has to be a reason. I don't want you to regret this," he said. He never wanted that. This night felt like…well, a dream, and he didn't want anything to ruin it.

She threw her arms around him and hugged him close. "Oh, Diego, I don't deserve you, but I certainly want you."

"Of course you deserve me," he said, lifting her off her feet and lowering his mouth to hers. Her lips tempted him; the entire time she'd been talking, all he'd thought about was kissing her again.

He set her on her feet and led the way to his front door. He unlocked it, pushed it open and beckoned for her to enter first. They stepped into the foyer. He was a pretty traditional guy, so it was decorated with solid dark wood furniture, and the floor tile was a terra-cotta color that reminded him of the mane of his favorite stallion. He tossed his keys in the bowl on the large chest to the left of the entrance and then undid his tie, tossing it on the table, as well. In the round tile-framed mirror he caught Pippa's gaze.

She watched him with the stark, raw need that he recognized in himself. She moved closer, putting her hand on his shoulder and walking her fingers up toward his neck to slowly pull his tuxedo jacket down his arms and off.

* * *

Pippa was glad she'd left her heels on because Diego was taller than she'd realized—at least six-one. She reached around him from behind and slowly removed the studs that held his dress shirt together. It had been a long time since she'd been with a man and she wanted to make every moment of this evening last.

"Hold out your hand," she said, her voice huskier than she meant for it to be.

He did as she asked, and she dropped each of the studs into his upturned palm. She watched him in the mirror as her fingers moved down his chest. It was sexier than she thought to see her manicured nails so close to Diego's tanned chest as each tiny strip of his skin was revealed. Finally, she had the shirt undone to his waistband. She deliberately rubbed her fingers over his erection. His hips jerked back for a moment and then canted forward into her touch. She undid the button that fastened his pants before tugging the tails of his shirt out. It hung open, giving her a few tantalizing glimpses of his rock-hard stomach and the muscles of his chest in the mirror.

"How are you so muscly?" she asked.

He gave a half laugh, half groan sound. "I spend all my day working with horses that I charge a lot of money for other breeders to use as studs."

"So?" she asked.

"I want the entire operation to project strength and prosperity and success. That means I can't look like a schlub when they show up," he said.

"I like it."

She bit her lip to keep from just shoving her hands underneath his clothes and touching him.

Patience.

She could do this. She'd spent years waiting to claim her inheritance. By now she should be very good at waiting.

She reached for his free hand and undid the cuff link, dropping it in his palm with the shirt studs. Then he poured them into his other hand, the small studs and cuff link making an almost musical sound as he did so. She smiled.

Then she undid the other cuff link and dropped it with the other shirt studs. He closed his hand around them and shoved them into his pants pocket. She focused all her attention on Diego's body.

She pulled the sides of his shirt open and he rotated his shoulders, making it easier for her to take it off. His shoulder blade rubbed against her right breast, sending a hot pulse of desire through her.

He tossed his shirt on top of his jacket and she put her hands on his chest. Diego worked outdoors but didn't have a farmer's tan. It was clear to her that he had spent a good amount of time in the Texas sun without his shirt on. She ran her hands down his chest. There was a tattoo in roman-type lettering that curved around a scar right below his ribs. She suspected that the scar was old as she ran her fingers over the ridge of it. She put one hand on his waist and the other on the small of his back as she leaned around to read the tattoo he had on his chest.

Courage is being scared to death and saddling up anyway.

"What does this mean to you?" she asked.

"Just a reminder that getting knocked down doesn't mean I need to stay down forever," he said, putting his hand over hers and rubbing it up and down his torso.

There was a thin line of hair that disappeared into the open waistband of his pants. She traced the line with her finger as she straightened back up, but he stopped her. He took her wrist in his hand and drew her fingers back to his chest.

"I like the way you touch me, Pippa," he said, his voice that low growly sound that sent shivers through her body. Shivers that seemed to pool between her legs.

She wanted him.

It had been a long dry spell for her and she'd done her share of masturbating and fantasizing about men. Diego had figured prominently in those fantasies since she'd moved to Cole's Hill. She figured there was no way he could live up to them. She'd never had a sexual encounter that had. But there was a heat in Diego's eyes that turned her on. Way more than in her daydreams.

"I like touching you," she admitted, pushing her hand into the open fly of his pants and stroking the hard ridge of his erection through the cotton fabric of his boxer briefs.

He groaned and reached for the zipper in the left side of her dress.

He'd done this before. She knew from the talk she'd overheard in the coffee shop after he'd left that he was a player. There were a lot of women who had either dated him or wanted him in their bed.

"I'm lucky I got you tonight," he said.

"I got you," she pointed out.

"Yes, you did," he said, raising both eyebrows at her as he ran his finger down her side, touching her skin as the zipper opened and the fabric parted.

He slipped his hand in and around to her back and drew her toward him, swaying along as he sang a popular Blake Shelton song under his breath. She closed her eyes, wrapping her free arm around his shoulders while keeping her hand on his erection.

He leaned down, his lips brushing the shell of her ear as he whispered, "This is what I was thinking about each time I held you close to me tonight."

"Really?" she asked, opening her eyes and tipping her head back. Their eyes met and that dark chocolate gaze of his held secrets and passion. She wanted it all.

"Yes, ma'am."

She fumbled around the elastic at the top of his boxers and reached inside to touch his naked flesh. "I was thinking about this."

He didn't say anything. His pupils dilated, and he brought his mouth down hard on hers. His tongue thrust deep into her mouth as he lightly drew his fingernail down her back, stopping at the small of her back. He dipped his finger lower, pushing aside the fabric of her thong panties.

An electric pulse of heat went through her as he cupped her butt and lifted her off her feet. She knew he was moving, but hardly paid any attention to it until he put her back down on the floor and lifted his head. They were in the master bedroom. She could tell by the deep, masculine colors and the large king-size bed behind her.

He disappeared for a minute and then was back with a box of condoms that he put on the nightstand. She was glad she hadn't had to bring up protection, that he'd just taken care of it.

"Now, where were we?" he asked, putting his hands gently on either side of her head and tipping it back. Their eyes met again and he brought his mouth down on hers.

And she forgot about everything.

She let her hand fall from his face to his chest. He was warm. She rubbed her fingers over the scar under his tattoo and then down his abdomen. He shifted his hips and his trousers slid down his legs.

"Impressive," she said.

He wriggled his eyebrows at her. "Thanks. I save that move for special occasions."

She couldn't help smiling at the way he said it. Of course, Diego wasn't like any other man she'd had sex with. He was at ease with his body and with her. There was no pressure to get to it and get it over with. She had the feeling that he wanted her to enjoy this night and that he intended to take his time. There was something sexy in his confidence.

His trousers were pooled around his ankles, but his dress boots kept them in place. His erection was a hard ridge straining against his boxer briefs and his lips were slightly swollen from their kisses. She felt that pulsing between her legs again and knew that she'd never seen anything more erotic in her life. He wasn't posing or pretending. He wanted her and he didn't have to put on moves to impress her.

He lifted the hem of her dress up over her thighs and then all the way over her head, tossing it aside. She stood there in just her tiny panties and no bra.

He groaned, and when he reached out to touch her, she noticed his hand shook slightly. Then he was cupping her breasts with both hands, his palms rubbing over her nipples.

He caressed her from her neck down past her waist, lingering over each curve and making her aware of places on her body that she'd never thought about before, like the bottom of her ribs. His fingers dipped between her legs, pushing her panties down her legs until she stepped out of them, placing her hand on his shoulder to keep her balance. He dipped his hand between her legs, rubbing his finger over her clit until she felt her legs go week.

He put his arm around her waist and lowered her back on the bed, coming down over her. She drew her hand down the side of his body, wrapping her hand around him, stroking him from the root to the tip. On each stroke she ran her finger over the head and around to the back of his shaft. He shivered each time she touched him there.

He ran his hands all over her torso, cupping both of her breasts this time. She shifted, keeping her grip on him but moving so that he could touch her the way she liked it.

She pushed her shoulders back and watched as

he leaned forward. She felt the warmth of his breath
against her skin and then the brush of his tongue. He
circled her nipple with it, then closed his mouth over
her and suckled her deeply.

She stroked him until she felt his hips lift toward her,
moving in counterpoint to her hand. She reached lower
and cupped him, rolling the delicate weight of him in
her fingers before squeezing slightly. He groaned and
pulled his mouth from her breast. He gripped the back
of her neck and brought her mouth to his.

As he drew her against him, she didn't move her
hand except to guide the tip of his erection to enter her.

He slid a little more into her and she reveled in the
feel of his thick cock at the entrance of her body. But
then he lifted his head and took her nipple in his mouth
again, biting down lightly on her nipple, and she shuddered.

She tried to impale herself on him, but he wasn't
about to let her have him now. He held her where she
was with just enough connection to drive both of them
mad.

"Are you ready for me?"

"Yessss," she said with a sigh.

A second later he thrust into her, filling her completely.

She rocked her hips, forcing him deeper into her
body. He hit her in the right place and she saw stars
dancing behind her closed eyelids as he pulled out and
thrust back inside her.

He held her with his big hands on her ass, lifting her
into each thrust, and soon she was senseless. She could

do nothing but feel the power of his body as he moved over her and in her.

She held on to his sides while he continued to drive her higher and harder, and then she felt everything inside clench as her orgasm surged through her. She cried out his name as he tangled one hand in her hair and drove into her even harder and faster, and then she felt him tense and groan as he climaxed. He thrust into her two or three more times before shifting to rest his forehead against hers.

She looked into those dark eyes of his and knew that everything had changed. She had thought this night would be just sex. Just some fun. But Diego wasn't just a fantasy—he was a real, flesh-and-blood man.

He rolled to his side and disposed of the condom before settling back into bed and pulling her into his arms. "Thank you for tonight."

She nodded against his chest, unable to find the words she needed to say. He drifted off to sleep, but she lay there thinking about her future, which was so much more complicated now.

Four

Pippa stretched and rolled over, slowly opening her eyes. It was Monday morning. Usually Penny had her up before this, but then she remembered she'd stayed over at Diego's. She sat up and looked around the empty room. The house was very quiet and, if she had to guess, empty.

"Crap."

She hadn't meant to stay out all night. She put her hand on her head, thinking of walking back to the country club in her dress from last night while parents were making the school run.

She wasn't embarrassed by what had happened. She had woken up exactly where she wanted to be, but at the same time she had to face those moms and dads when she picked Penny up from preschool this afternoon.

She glanced at the nightstand. It was only seven. So not that late, but still. She saw there was a piece of monogrammed stationery with bold masculine handwriting on it. She reached for the note and rubbed her eyes before she read it.

Good morning,
I had to leave early to do the morning chores on the ranch. We have a mare coming in to be covered later today and I need to get things ready. I'd love to see you for lunch or dinner. Text me when you wake up. I had your car brought to the house and I've laid out some sweats and a T-shirt in the bathroom. Sorry I wasn't here when you woke.
Diego

"What am I going to do?" she asked the empty room as she fell back on the pillows. Diego was her one-night hookup. Her bit of fun before she left Texas and went back to her real life. She could just say no and never see him again. There was nothing stopping her from doing just that.

But she didn't want to.

She grabbed her phone to text Kinley and saw she had two messages. The first was clearly from Penny. The four-year-old used the text-to-talk feature on Kinley's phone all the time. The message just said Pippy, where are you?

Kinley's message said:

Ignore the scamp's message. I told her you had the

morning off. I assume you are with the hot rancher you
outbid everyone for last night. I want deets.

Ugh.
Double ugh.

She tossed her phone on the nightstand without responding, made her way to the bathroom and took a
quick shower, avoiding looking at herself in the mirror until she was clean and wearing Diego's sweats.
They were huge on her but super comfy. She took a
deep breath. If she had a cup of coffee, she'd start to
feel human again.

She went downstairs to find her clutch and found a
coffee mug next to the Keurig machine. She made herself a cup and then went back up to the master bedroom
to gather her stuff. Diego had even laid out a duffel bag
and a pair of flip-flops near the foot of the bed. She had
to smile. He'd thought of everything.

Which shouldn't really influence her decision to see
him again, but it did.

Heck, everything about Diego made her want to see
him again. It would be easy to say that waiting four
years to have sex would have made any partner seem…
well, better than they might really be… What the hell
was she thinking? She could have had sex a week earlier with someone else and Diego would have wiped that
from her memory. Her body ached to have him again.
She remembered the way he'd felt between her thighs
and craved more of him.

But he wanted… Well, it seemed like he wanted to
get to know her. And until she reclaimed her inheri-

tance, she really needed to lie low and stay off her father's radar.

In Texas…

It had been the perfect spot for her to hide out until she came of age. But now that the time had come, starting something with Diego, all the while knowing she was leaving in a few weeks… Was that a dick move?

She felt like it might be.

She saw a message flash on her phone and went to pick it up. Kinley again.

At the office, stop by if you are still in town.

Pippa knew Kinley would be brutally honest with her about the situation with Diego. Her friend was just always that way with everyone.

She grabbed the duffel bag, her phone and Diego's note and went downstairs to collect the rest of her things.

She found the alarm code on a Post-it on the inside of the front door and entered it to let herself out. She walked to her car without glancing at the street and got in, sitting there for a moment before starting the engine.

She drove through town to the bridal shop that Kinley ran as a satellite to her boss Jacs Veerling's Vegas bridal operation. It was through her work that Kinley had first come to Cole's Hill. She'd been sent here to plan former NFL wide receiver Hunter Caruthers's wedding. Of course, she hadn't wanted to come, given that Hunter was her baby-daddy's brother and said baby-daddy had no clue he had a kid. There had been a bit of a rough patch where Nate hadn't realized that Penny was his child, and when he found out, he blew up at Kinley. But after the family drama had died down they realized how much they loved each other and got married.

Pippa groaned as she noticed that all of the pull-in parking spaces were taken and she'd have to parallel park. When she was done about five minutes later, she walked into the bridal showroom. It was an elegant space that had been designed to suggest understated opulence. Classical music played in the background. Pippa knew that she'd take some of the design elements from this small bridal shop with her when she returned to London and claimed her place on the board of House of Hamilton. The royal jewelers needed to attract a younger crowd and Pippa was determined to do that.

She sighed, realizing she already knew the decision she would make regarding seeing Diego again.

It had to be a no.

She wanted the chance to prove herself to her family and the world more than she wanted a new lover.

Diego hadn't expected his younger brother to be waiting when he got home to Arbol Verde, but Mauricio was sitting in the breakfast room enjoying huevos rancheros that had been prepared by Diego's housekeeper, Mona. And he was drinking a Bloody Mary, unless Diego was mistaken.

"No need to ask how your night was," Mo said as Diego entered the room.

"Same. Struck out?"

Mauricio shook his head. "You don't even want to know. Breakfast or shower first?"

"Shower. I assume you're going to still be waiting when I get out," Diego said.

"Yes. It's business. I have a line on a piece of property on the outskirts of town that is exactly what you're looking for," Mauricio said. "Go shower. I'll wait here."

Diego started to turn away, but Mo had that look like he'd been rode hard and put away wet, which wasn't how Diego wanted to see any of his brothers.

He walked over and pulled out one of the ladder-back wooden chairs, spinning it around and straddling it. He reached out and snagged a piece of the maple and brown sugar bacon that Mona always had on the breakfast table.

"What happened last night?"

"Hadley was there," Mauricio said.

Of course she was. "I thought she moved to Houston."

"She did. But she came back for the auction," Mauricio said before he took a long swallow of his Bloody Mary.

"You broke up with her," Diego reminded his brother as gently as he could. Hadley and Mo had been a couple since high school. He'd followed her to the University of Texas, and when they'd come back to Cole's Hill, everyone expected them to marry, including Hadley. After waiting five years—longer than most women would, according to Bianca—Hadley had given Mo an ultimatum and he'd balked.

Hadley had packed up and moved out of the town house they'd shared and started dating again. Since then, if gossip was to be believed, Mauricio had had some wild hookups out at the Bull Pen.

The Bull Pen was a large bar and Texas dance hall on the edge of Cole's Hill. It had a mechanical bull in the back and live bands performed there nightly. It was respectable enough early in the evening, but after midnight things started to get rowdy.

"I know that, D. I didn't mind it when she was flirting with men. I knew she wasn't taking any of them seriously. But she was with Bo Williams. Sure, according to Mom he's one of the most eligible bachelors at last night's charity auction. But that guy isn't right for her. You know he's just using her to get back at me."

Diego knew the guy and understood his brother's anger. The two men had been fierce rivals all of their lives. They'd competed on opposing Pop Warner football teams during their youth, both bringing their teams to the Super Bowl more than once. And the rivalry had continued in middle and high school. But Diego had hoped now that both men were in their midtwenties, it was a thing of the past.

"Possibly."

"Whatever," Mo said. "I thought you'd be on my side."

"On your side? What did you do?"

Mauricio turned his head and mumbled something that Diego hoped he heard wrong.

"I couldn't hear that."

Mauricio stood up. "I told her that guy was just using her to get to me, and then he punched me, so I punched him back—"

"Where did this happen?"

"At the Grand Hotel bar. They walked in while I was there with Everly—just talking. You know, she's Mitch's gal. The evening didn't end well."

Everly was Hadley's sister and probably not a huge fan of Mo. "Ya think? Mo, do you want Hadley back?"

"I don't know," Mauricio said. "But I don't want anyone else to have her, either."

Diego stood up and put his hand on his brother's shoulder. "Dude, I know it's hard, but you can't have it both ways."

"I know that. I just need time," he said. "I told her that."

"Then she's the one with the reins," Diego pointed out as delicately as possible. He knew his brother had to understand deep down; he was a smart, considerate man who really cared for Hadley.

"I'm screwed."

"Why? Move on."

"I can't. It's complicated. If I give in, she'll know she has me. That I care more for her than she does for me," Mauricio said.

"Love doesn't work that way," Diego told his brother.

"How the hell would you know? You've never been in love," Mauricio pointed out.

"True," Diego said as an image of Pippa spread out underneath him last night danced through his mind. "I just don't think couples should keep score. No one wins in that scenario."

"You're right," Mauricio said. "But I keep doing stupid things and she pushes my buttons, too. I mean, why did she bid on him?"

Diego had no idea. It would be so much better for

Mauricio to have this conversation with their sister. Diego almost pulled out his phone to text her but knew that Bianca would want to know what had happened last night with Pippa, and he wasn't ready to talk about that yet. And Bianca wouldn't let it go the way Mo had.

"Women are a mystery. I mean, Pippa has been flat-out turning me down every time I've asked her out for the last three weeks, and then she bids on me last night. How does that make any sense?"

Mauricio shook his head and started laughing. "Damned if I know. I wish women were as easy to read as real estate."

"Never say that to a woman," Diego warned his brother. "I have some new horses coming this morning if you want to hang around and get your hands dirty."

Mauricio nodded and then went back to eating his breakfast. Diego got up, heading toward the hallway, ready for that shower.

"D?"

He glanced over his shoulder at his brother.

"Yeah?" he asked.

"Thanks. I know I'm being an ass where Hadley's concerned, but I can't help it."

"It's okay, Mo. You'll figure out how to let go and then things will be back to normal," Diego said with a confidence he wasn't sure was justified. Where his brother and Hadley were concerned, he doubted that anything would be that simple.

"So spill," Kinley said as she hung up the phone and turned her brown eyes on Pippa.

She flushed. "What exactly are you hoping to hear?"

"Something that will take my mind off Nate," Kinley said, shuffling papers on her desk.

"Uh, you bid on him and then pretended to lasso him on the dance floor before you led him out of the country club," Pippa pointed out with a smile. "Did you get to ride your cowboy? Maybe you should spill."

"Fair enough, but I need some more coffee. What about you? I assume you didn't stop at the coffee shop dressed like that," Kinley said, giving Pippa the once-over.

"No. I didn't want to get out of the car in Diego's sweats." She felt the heat creeping up her neck. She had no reason to be embarrassed that she'd slept with Diego last night. Yet somehow…she was. She knew it was because she liked him and she also knew she wasn't going to sleep with him again.

It was so complicated.

And she could even argue that she was the one who was making it so.

"Pip?" Kinley asked.

"Mmm-hmm?"

"I asked if you wanted an extra shot of vanilla in your latte this morning," Kinley said.

"Yes. Sorry. I'm trying to figure out Diego and everything and it's…complicated."

She had to come up with another way of describing this thing with him other than just saying it was "complicated." Kinley didn't even know that Pippa was leaving. She hadn't wanted to say anything to anyone—even Kinley—until she was in the clear. Old enough to inherit without any restrictions. She couldn't let a man throw her off course. True, it wasn't like this was the first time a man had thrown a wrench in her plans, but it definitely was different this time.

Diego made her want to stay and let him continue to interrupt her plans, while her father had made her chafe and eventually left her no choice but to run.

"Why? Also, two pumps of vanilla?"

"Yes. Two pumps," Pippa said. Normally she had only one because she liked to watch her sugar intake, but this morning she needed the boost of sugar and caffeine. "I have a lot to tell you."

"I've heard that Diego is a good lover," Kinley said.

"Not that, Kin. He is, but I'm not talking about that right now," she said.

"Why not?"

"I don't know. What do you want to know?" she asked.

Kinley waggled her eyebrows at Pippa as she handed her the coffee mug and then went back to make her own. "Everything. I told you about that hot night I had with Nate when we were on his balcony."

"You did. That was hot. Well, Diego was a very good lover. He likes to wait for my reactions and he made me feel like I was the only woman in the world that he wanted in his bed."

"Sounds perfect. How is that complicated?" Kinley asked, taking her own mug and coming to sit down on the love seat next to Pippa.

She took a deep breath and turned to face the woman who was closer to her than any blood relative. She hoped that Kinley wouldn't be upset when she told her the truth of her past.

"I— Well— I'm— That is to say—"

"For the love of God, what the heck are you trying to say?" Kinley asked. "Whatever it is, I've got your back, girl. You know that, right?"

"I do know it," Pippa said, hugging Kinley with one arm. "That's what makes this harder to say. You know how I ran away from home and have been hiding since?"

"Yes," Kinley said, hugging her back. "Did they find you? Nate and I will protect you. And Ethan is a damned good lawyer, so he can get involved, too. Just tell us what you need."

"You are the best, Kinley," Pippa said. "I am so lucky I was on that city bus in Vegas when you went into labor."

"I feel the same way. So let me help you out. You've done so much for me," Kinley said. "What's going on?"

"Um, I ran away when I was twenty-one because I had no control over my inheritance or my life. My father was pressuring me to marry a man who he wanted to take my place on the board of our family company."

Kinley arched both eyebrows. "That's interesting. Who are you?"

"Um…well, Pippa is my name. I mean, everyone calls me that, but my given name is Philippa Georgina Hamilton-Hoff. My family owns the House of Hamilton jewelers by royal appointment of the Queen."

"Shit. Are you serious?"

"Yes."

"So what's changed?" Kinley asked.

"I turned twenty-five. That's when my shares in the company and my inheritance becomes mine to control. They are a legacy from my mother. My father had hoped by marrying me to one of his distant cousins that he would be able to bring his family into the business and take it over."

"That's a lot to take in," Kinley said. "You're leaving us, aren't you?"

She nodded. "I'm sorry. But you and Nate and Penny are a family now. You don't need me the way you used to."

"That's so not true. But I want you to have your inheritance and stop running, so I am not going to be mad about this," Kinley said. "How long do we have until you leave?"

"I'm not sure. I contacted my mother's solicitor in London yesterday—"

"Because of your birthday?"

"Yes. I mean, I could have waited, but I've been watching the company and they have a big board meeting at the end of November and I want to be able to vote my shares this time," she said.

"Okay. So has he gotten back to you?" Kinley asked.

"Yes. He has to verify I'm who I say I am," Pippa said. "So I'm still in limbo until I hear back from him."

Five

Diego resisted the urge to pull his cell out of his pocket and check his nonexistent text messages again. He had work to do to get the ranch ready for the sire that was being brought in later in the day. They had their own prize-winning sires and mares, but he liked to experiment with other lines to see if he could breed stronger horses. Diego, as the eldest son, had always been expected to take over the Velasquez stud farm. He'd worked closely with his father and later their foreman to develop his skills at spotting the signs when a broodmare would be ready for a sire. The signs seemed instinctive to Diego now; he found horses so much easier to read than people.

The fifteen hundred acres in Texas Hill Country had been in the Velasquez family since the late 1700s, and Diego and his father worked hard to maintain the ranch's clear roots in its history. The Arbol Verde operation of today encompassed the former Velasquez Stud and Luna Farm, legendary breeding operations whose decades of prominence ensured their bloodstock's continued influence on the modern thoroughbred. Through Diego's careful stewardship of the land, Arbol Verde had grown in the last ten years.

He loved the ranch that spread out before him as he sat on the back of Esquire, a retired stud who'd sired three champions, including Uptown Girl. He patted the side of Esquire's neck and then tapped him lightly with his heels to send him running over the grass-covered hills toward the barn. Diego had always had a connection to this land and today it was serving to take the edge off while he waited to see if Pippa was going to text him.

He unsaddled Esquire and brushed him before putting him back in his stall. The ranch was busy and he heard the voices of his other grooms. One of them— Pete—asked for everyone to talk more softly when he noticed that Diego had returned.

His phone pinged and he used his teeth to pull his leather work gloves off before reaching into his pocket to retrieve it. He glanced at the locked screen. It was his sister.

Not Pippa.

Bianca wanted to bring his nephew out to ride later in the day. And given that he had no other plans—and wasn't about to contact Pippa first and seem to be more into her than she was into him—he texted back to come on out.

When he was finished working, he walked up to his house. He stopped for a minute to look around the land that had been in his family for generations. Originally his ancestors had been part of the royal horse guard of Spain. His father liked to say that they had been born with an innate horse sense. Diego didn't know about that, but he had no problems with his horses. They made sense. They behaved the way that nature intended for them to. Unlike women.

He rubbed the back of his neck. He wouldn't change his life for anything, but there were times when he wanted…well, things that shouldn't be important. The ranch was his life. His focus should be here.

He saw Bianca's BMW sitting in the circle drive and knew he had to push all thoughts of last night from his mind. His sister would jump on any perceived weakness, and while having a conversation with Mauricio had been one thing, talking to Bianca would lead to him admitting more than he wanted to about Pippa.

He entered through the mud room, taking time to shower off the dirt and put on the clothes that he'd left there. He entered his house and heard a song by Alejandro Fernández and Morat playing and smiled. Bianca had lived in Spain during her brief first marriage and brought back some new influences for their family. Alejandro Fernández was hugely popular there.

"Tio," Benito, his four-year-old nephew, called out as he came running down the tiled hallway toward him, his cowboy boot heels making a loud noise with each step.

Diego scooped him up and hugged him. "So, you want to ride this afternoon?"

"*Sí*. I have to practice every day because Penny lives on a ranch now and she rides more than me," Benito said.

"Why does that have anything to do with your riding?" he asked. But he knew his nephew and Penny were best friends.

"I like her," Benito said, as if that was the only explanation needed.

And since he seemed to be developing a crush on a girl who wasn't texting him, Diego got where his nephew was coming from way too well. "You are always welcome to come and ride. In fact, *Tío* Mauricio and I are looking into opening a riding center closer to town. Maybe you and your friend can ride there."

"Is that true?" Bianca asked, coming out into the hallway and joining them.

"Yes. He was here this morning discussing it," Diego said.

"Really? That's odd. I thought I saw your truck parked in front of your town house this morning," Bianca said.

"What were you doing up that early?" he asked. Bianca was five years younger than him, and as the only girl in a family dominated by boys, she'd learned to hold her own. In fact, Diego would rather get in a rowdy fight with all of his brothers than have a one-on-one conversation with Bianca.

"Derek was on call, so I went over to have breakfast with Mama and pick up *changuito*," Bianca said as she ruffled Benito's hair. She'd called him "little monkey."

"I had a bit to drink last night, so I figured I'd sleep in town," Diego said, hoping his sister would let it drop.

"We can talk about P-I-P-P-A later," Bianca said, spelling out the name so that Benito wouldn't know what she'd said.

"That's none of your business," Diego countered.

"As if that's going to stop me from asking," Bianca said.

Benito squirmed down from his arms. "What is P-I-P—"

"Nothing. Let's get you out to the barn and saddled up. Are you riding, too?" he asked his sister.

"Yes. I guess I can't keep spelling things around this little one," she said as they all donned straw cowboy hats and went to the barn.

"What else did he spell back?"

Bianca blushed. "You don't want to know. Derek thought it was funny, but it was embarrassing."

Diego didn't need any further explanation. He guessed it had something to do with sex and just shook his head.

He accompanied his sister and nephew to the stable, where he kept a mare she liked to ride. As Bianca started to groom her, Diego took his nephew out, distracted for the afternoon from his phone.

Kinley had a meeting with a bride who'd come up from Houston. Jacs Veerling was one of the top three bridal and event planners in the world and having Kinley running her operation in Cole's Hill was a coup.

Many brides who didn't want to fly to Vegas to see the showroom or talk with Jacs were happy enough to come to Cole's Hill. With its close proximity to Houston it was very convenient.

Pippa was at loose ends while Penny was at her four-year-old prekindergarten program and Kinley was working. It gave her too much time to think and hit refresh on her email again and again waiting for a response from the House of Hamilton solicitor. Simon Rooney hadn't given her a timeline for when to expect his response, but because she'd kept close tabs on the company over the years, she knew that her twenty-fifth birthday coincided with a couple of crucial board changes. One of them was that her great-uncle Theo was retiring. He had no heirs, and though Pippa had some second and third cousins who were on the board, she was the only direct-line heir to the company.

And their charter expressed that a direct-line heir, male or female, had the first right to the chairmanship. And Pippa had been studying for the role. She knew that if House of Hamilton wanted to stay a top luxury brand they were going to have to be relevant in the modern world. She'd been researching the marketing strategies of brands like Tiffany and had focused on that topic in her online courses, earning a master's degree in business. She'd also taken classes in jewelry design in Vegas and Cole's Hill. She'd worked hard for this and was impatient to claim her rightful place at the company.

Though she hadn't used her real name in a long while, she'd prepared a prospectus that she'd sent to

Mr. Rooney along with her birth certificate, passport and details of her identity.

"Okay, that's done," Kinley said from the doorway. She wore a slim-fitting skirt that had a slit on one side ending just above the knee. She also had on a pair of ankle boots and a thin sweater. Though it was September there had been a dip in temperatures that signaled fall was just around the corner. "Any news from jolly old England?"

Pippa had to smile at the way Kinley said it with her fake British accent.

"No. I'm jumpy, so I don't want to head back to the ranch. I hope you don't mind me just hanging out here," she said.

"Of course I don't mind. Tell me more about your family business," she said, then giggled. "I'm sorry, but when I hear family business, I think of the mob, and you are so far from that mafia princess image."

Pippa smiled back at her friend. "I'm not a princess, mafia or otherwise. The House of Hamilton—"

"My God. I still can't believe you're going to inherit that company! They're huge. Jacs is going to die when I tell her we have an in there. She's been trying to get them to allow her to use some of their designs for her wedding tiaras."

"I'm not even sure they are going to acknowledge me," Pippa said.

"They have to, right? I mean, you are the heiress," Kinley said. "I should call Ethan…he's the only lawyer I know. He could help you."

She shook her head. "Not yet. Let me see what I hear

back from the family solicitor first. What kind of tiaras does Jacs want?"

Thinking about bringing in a new line of business was a nice distraction. It kept her mind from Diego. And she had to admit her thoughts drifted to him far too often. He'd told her to text him and she was ignoring that instruction. She didn't need another complication in her life, but at the same time, he was already distracting her.

She kept remembering how nice it had felt to sleep in his arms last night. To put her head over his heart as she cuddled at his side and listen to it beating. She'd been alone for a long time. Of course, she had Kinley and Penny, but that was different. Last night, for a few moments, she had almost felt like Diego was hers.

It was tantalizing, but at the same time she wanted to handle her situation with House of Hamilton on her own, and she had to wonder if it was a tiny bit of fear that was driving her to think of him as anything more than just a bachelor auction hookup. Fear of facing off with her father had her imagining what it would be like to stay here and pursue something with Diego.

He was a rancher. He was as much a part of Cole's Hill as the Grand Hotel, the quaint shops on Main Street or the mercantile. He belonged here and he would never be able to leave. And after watching her father and mother, and the manipulation and struggle for power between the two of them, Pippa knew she was afraid to ever let herself commit to a man who would try to control her the way her father had.

And Diego was safe that way.

He was never going to leave Texas.

"What are you thinking about?" Kinley asked. "You have the oddest look on your face."

"Diego."

"Ah. Are you going to text him?" Kinley asked. "I think you should. Why not enjoy your time left in Cole's Hill until you hear back from the lawyer?"

"Because I like him."

"That stinks. I swear if I didn't love Nate, life would be so much easier," Kinley said, then shook her head. "I'm joking. Having Nate makes life so much richer."

She wanted that, yet at the same time it scared her. Then again, it wasn't as if she had a kid with Diego, so she and Kinley were looking at relationships through different lenses. But a part of her wondered what it would be like to have a man who she could be herself with. She quickly shut down those thoughts. Of course, that man couldn't be Diego, because his life was here and she'd told him only half-truths about herself.

Facing the prospect of dinner alone and plagued by the constant temptation to text Pippa, Diego told the housekeeper to take the night off and texted his brothers and Derek to see if anyone was available to head to the Bull Pen. He got two yeses. Mauricio couldn't make it; he was on his way to Dallas to meet with someone who had a portfolio that included some high-end property in the Cole's Hill area. He wanted a chance to be the agent on the listing. Inigo was due to head back to his team for the next stop on the Formula One tour, so tonight would be their last night together.

Diego needed to blow off steam. He pulled up in his Ferrari and got out just as Derek Caruthers pulled up. He waved at his brother-in-law. Derek looked tired— Bianca had mentioned that he'd had an early surgery this morning, which explained why.

"Thanks for the invite," Derek said. "I think Hunter and one of his former NFL buddies are going to join, too. The women are having a girls' night—did you know?"

Of course they were. He could even stretch his imagination and pretend that was why Pippa hadn't texted him back, but he knew when he was getting the brush-off. He'd done it enough times himself.

Yeah, karma was a bitch.

He'd known that forever, but he'd never expected to be on this end of it. Plus, he was nice to the women he slept with and for the most part always called when he said he would. Why would karma be coming for him?

To be fair, Pippa had never said she wanted more than last night. More than what she'd bid on.

"Nah, I didn't know. It's Inigo's last night in Cole's Hill for a while, and I thought we should give him a proper send-off. It's time for some payback for when he put me on a plane in Madrid with a massive hangover the last time I was there."

Derek clapped him on the back. "That's little brothers for you. I'm happy to do my part. It's been a long day for me."

"Bianca mentioned you had early surgery," Diego said. It seemed like Derek wanted to talk, but Diego didn't know the right questions to ask. And he knew a lot of things were private thanks to the HIPAA laws.

"Yeah, it was a tough one. Touch and go for a while. I just need to blow off some steam. And your sister is sweet as hell, so I can't let my temper out at home."

"Do you have a temper?" he asked. Derek had always struck him as calm, maybe a little arrogant, but not someone with a temper.

"I just get short when I'm tired. It's better if I get that out of my system before I go home. I don't want to say anything to Bianca or Benito that would hurt them," he said.

They entered the bar, which had a mechanical bull in the back and was frequented by the astronauts and technicians from the nearby Mick Tanner Training Facility. The joint NASA and SpaceNow project was focused on training and preparing candidates for long-term missions to build a space station halfway between Earth and Mars. When they did come into town, they tended to get rowdy.

"I'm the same way, but it's just me, the horses and my housekeeper," Diego said.

"You need a woman, Diego," Derek said.

He had a woman. Or at least there was one specific one he wanted, and she hadn't texted him all day.

"I'm good. I like being a bachelor."

"Every guy says that when he's single, but the truth is we are all just waiting to be claimed," Derek said as they found a large high-top table in one of the corners.

"I can see I got here just in time," Inigo said, coming over to join them. "Don't let a Caruthers talk you into monogamy. They are all chained now and won't be happy until every guy in Cole's Hill is, too."

"I'm going to tell Bi you said I was chained to her," Derek said.

"Uh, I'm going to deny it, and I'm her baby brother, so she'll probably believe me," Inigo said with a grin. "Beer or whiskey, boys?"

"Beer for me," Derek said.

"Same," Diego said. It was always better to start slow when he was drinking with Inigo.

When Inigo turned and walked to the bar, Derek took a seat and said, "That one is trouble."

"He is. He's always been wild, and then something happened when Jose died," Diego said. "He's more out of control than he was before. Like he's trying to prove something to someone."

"Bi is worried about him, too. She wants him to stop driving, but there's no way that's going to happen," Derek said. "He's third in the point rankings, right behind his teammate and rival. He wants to beat Lewis. He's not going to stop until he does."

"One thing about the Velasquez boys is we are stubborn," Diego said.

"It didn't skip Bianca as much as she might want to think it did," Derek said. "And I'll deny I said that if you mention it to her."

Diego just shook his head. He felt something that could be a pang in his heart but wrote it off as heartburn from his late lunch. He didn't want to admit that he wanted what Bianca and Derek had. He was happy with his life. A woman wasn't a necessity for him.

But that didn't mean that he didn't wish that he was going home to Pippa tonight.

Six

Kinley was at her book club with Bianca and the other Caruthers wives. She'd kindly invited Pippa to join, but Pippa had declined. She wasn't sure she was ready to come face-to-face with Diego's sister. Not because Bianca was anything but kind; it had more to do with her own insecurities. She was trying damned hard to convince herself she wanted nothing to do with the long, tall Texan, but in reality she had done nothing but worry about her future, and a chunk of that worry had included him.

So she'd left the Jacs Veerling bridal showroom and driven toward Famous Manu's BBQ to get an early dinner. It had opened less than six months earlier and was a popular spot in town. The owner was retired NFL special teams coach Manu Barrett, who'd bought a second home in the Five Families neighborhood to be closer to his brother Hemi, who was part of the astronaut training program.

Pippa had found that the Southern pork sandwich, without the coleslaw, reminded her of the pork baps she could get back home. She'd placed her to-go order and now sat in the car waiting for her food to be ready, staring at her phone and the text message she'd written, deleted and rewritten a hundred times... Okay, that was a slight exaggeration, but it felt like she'd done it a hundred times.

Sitting in her car in a designer mother-of-the-bride dress made her feel silly. But not as silly as wearing Diego's sweats.

There was a rap on her window and she glanced up to see Diego standing there. *Speak of the devil.* What was he doing here?

"Saw your car and decided to come out and say hello." He was carrying a take-out bag.

"What are you doing here?" she asked.

"The food at the Bull Pen isn't as good as this place, so we walked over to eat, and then my brother noticed your car," he said. She could smell the hoppy scent of beer on him and she realized that Diego had already had more than a few drinks.

"I was going to text you," she said.

"Sure you were," he said.

Feeling defensive, she lifted up her phone so he could see the message she'd just retyped before he'd shown up.

He looked at it and then back to her. "So you weren't lying."

Not about this, she thought. Because now that she'd reached out to her family back in the UK, she probably should talk to Diego about who she really was.

"No. I just… I wasn't sure if you were being nice and I'm not sure if I'm staying in Texas and last night was perfect and I didn't want anything to ruin that," she said in a rush of words. *There.* She'd finally admitted out loud what had been dancing around in her brain for most of the day.

"Perfect?" he asked, leaning against her car. "I think I could do better."

She shook her head. "I doubt it."

"Challenge accepted."

"I'm not talking about sex," she said. "Well, not just the sex. The entire evening was like something out of a dream."

"I wasn't just talking about sex, either," he said, leaning into the window. His black Stetson bumped the top of the door and was pushed back on his head. He reached up, impatiently took it off and hit it against his thigh. "I like you, Pippa. I had a lot of time to think about it as I waited for you to get in touch today."

His words were heartfelt and so sincere she knew that she had to be careful with him. She liked him, too, of course, but most of that attraction was purely hormonal. He cut a fine figure of a man with his muscular shoulders and whipcord lean body. He was wearing faded jeans that clung to his thighs. She was intrigued by his strength. She remembered the way he'd lifted her onto the table in the hallway of his condo.

"Me, too," she admitted. "I know you are out with friends, but do you want to go someplace and talk?"

"Yes. Hell, yes. Let me go tell those yahoos I'm not coming back. Where do you want to go?"

"I don't know. I have my own cottage on the Rockin' C, but that's a little far out of town and you aren't in any condition to drive," she said.

"I'm not. I'll ask one of my ranch hands to come pick my Ferrari up in the morning. Dylan is always hot to drive it, so he'll be happy to do it," Diego said.

She nodded. This would be good. They could talk. She could put on her own clothes, and then maybe she could figure out what she wanted from Diego. She hadn't been lying to herself earlier when she acknowledged that she wanted more than sex. But she also knew she was in no position to ask for more than that.

She was leaving. It wasn't like she was going to fall in love with him and give up her heritage. She'd waited too long for this chance.

She got a text that her food was ready. "Let me go pick up my sandwich. Do you want me to order you anything else?"

"Nah, I'm good," he said. "Meet you back here in a few."

He opened her door for her, and when she stepped out of the car, the slim-fitting dress fell around her thighs. She smoothed her hands down her sides, aware that she was way overdressed for barbecue.

"Damn. You keep getting better looking every time I see you," he said.

She shook her head. "I feel stupid in this."

"You shouldn't," he said. "Come on, I'll walk in there with you."

He held open the door to Famous Manu's and then put his hand at the small of her back as they entered the restaurant. People turned to see who was coming in and one woman muttered under her breath, but loud enough for Pippa to hear, "A bit overdressed."

Diego arched one eyebrow at her. "Mandy, be nice."

It was a small thing, but for the first time she felt like a man had her back. She was probably reading way more into it than she should, but it made her feel good deep inside.

They barely spoke on the drive to Pippa's cottage on the Rockin' C. She had the radio turned to Heart FM, which played soft rock music. The buzz he'd had going was starting to fade, but as usual just being in the same vicinity as Pippa was having a pronounced effect on him.

His skin felt too small for him and every breath he took smelled of her perfume and something that re-minded him of sex. It was just her scent, but he couldn't smell it and not be turned on. He shifted his legs, mak-ing room for his growing erection as she drove. She was a careful driver, going just below the speed limit and signaling way before she got to the turn-in for the Rockin' C. They were about ten miles from the entrance to Arbol Verde, where he lived most of the time.

She pulled to a stop in front of a mason stone cottage that had a rough-hewn wood front porch. The motion-sensor lights came on as they got out of the car. On her front door hung a wreath that as he got closer he could tell had been made out of toy Breyer horses.

She noticed him looking at it as she shifted her bag of barbecue and fumbled for her keys. He took the food from her so she could unlock the door.

"Penny made it for me for my birthday," she said by way of explanation. "I'm sure you know that she's horse crazy."

"I do know that. Benito was out at my place earlier today getting riding lessons so he can keep up with her," Diego said, but a part of him suspected that his nephew was always going to be chasing after Penny.

"They are too cute together," Pippa admitted. "I missed seeing them today."

"I want to know more about how you came to be a nanny," he said. "Last night you mentioned you were on the run."

She led the way into the small entry hall. There was a tiled mirror and a table with a wooden bowl and a bud vase containing a single gardenia. She threw her keys into the bowl and flipped on a light as she continued into the great room. He saw a set of stairs to the left that led up to a loft. He guessed it was her bedroom.

Immediately an image of her lying naked in the middle of his bed sprang to mind and he shoved it aside. He'd been serious when he said it was more than sex he wanted from Pippa. Now if he could only get his body on board with that.

The far wall was made of river stone and had a fireplace and hearth dead center. There was a rough-hewn mantel that matched the wood on her front porch and a large clock above the fireplace with a swinging pendulum that ticked off the seconds. Two recliners with a side table between them faced the fireplace, and a large leather couch sat opposite an armoire that he suspected housed the television. The great room led to a breakfast nook with a round table and four chairs.

She led the way to the table. "Let me grab some dishes and cutlery and we can eat."

He set the food down next to a white bowl filled with oranges and continued to look around the house. He noticed there was a small office area in the kitchen with a laptop computer and a notepad. Yesterday's date had been circled several times in red on a calendar.

He saw that next to the calendar was an older-looking silver frame that had a distinctive patina. As he moved closer, he noticed it contained a black-and-white photo of a woman who bore a striking resemblance to Pippa, and was holding a little girl who looked just like Pippa, too. They both were smiling.

"That's my mum and me," she said as she moved past him. "My auntie took the photo."

"What happened to make you leave home?" he asked as they sat down. She'd set the table with place mats, cloth napkins and Fiestaware dishes in a turquoise blue. She had also poured them both glasses of water.

It was the fanciest setting he'd ever seen for pulled pork sandwiches, but at the same time it just sort of felt right considering he was with Pippa.

"Um…well, Mum died when I turned fourteen and

my father took over the guardianship of me and my inheritance. He had a different idea for my future, including me marrying someone he'd chosen."

"Are you married?" he asked. He'd never thought she might belong to someone else. Then immediately he realized that he didn't think she was the kind of woman to sleep with one man when married to another. He knew it had been his own insecurity at realizing how much he didn't know about her that had prompted the question.

"No. Obviously not, given what you and I have been up to. I ran away the night he was going to propose," she said.

Diego leaned back in the chair, feeling like a fool as he watched her carefully. She hadn't been kidding when she'd mentioned that it was complicated. He couldn't imagine his father ever trying to control him. If he had, Diego would have done something similar to what Pippa had.

"I'm sorry for asking that. I knew you weren't married. It's just a shock to hear all of this… I mean, I knew you were more than a nanny, but this is bigger than just inheriting some jewelry, isn't it?"

"Yes, it is."

"So what's next? Can you return to England?"

"I have started the process," she admitted. "But they have to verify that I am who I say I am first."

"Is there some doubt?"

"Not really, but there will be questions, and my coming back will make things awkward for my father, who has been managing my assets while I've been missing," she admitted.

"I take it you two don't get along," Diego said. "Stating the obvious, right?"

Her relationship with her father was complicated. Over the last four years she'd spent a lot of time waking in the middle of the night and thinking about how much she hated him. Especially when Kinley was having a hard time making ends meet when she'd first started working for Jacs. If she weren't having difficulties with her father, Pippa knew if she'd walked into the bank and made a withdrawal she could take care of Kin's finances and let her give Penny the financial stake they needed to make a good life.

But at the same time, she'd be giving up her freedom.

Because her father had final say in practically everything she did with her money and her time until she turned twenty-five. And he got to vote her shares on the board as he saw fit. The only recourse she'd have had was to lodge an objection, which was virtually the same as having no power.

But she also remembered how broken he'd been after her mum had died. How the two of them had sat in their home mourning her. She knew that part of the reason why he had wanted to control so much of Pippa's life was due to losing her mum. But she hadn't been able to understand why his grief had taken this particular form: to control Pippa.

And time had brought her no closer to understanding him.

"I can't say if we got along or not. I had a typical lov-ing child's view of my father before my mum died. But then when I turned twenty-one he gave me an ultima-tum, which was the wrong thing to do. I mean, I know I look all sweet, but I'm really very stubborn," she said.

"*Sweet* isn't the first word I'd use to describe you," Diego said. "I've seen signs of that stubborn streak."

She arched one eyebrow at him. She wasn't going to ask what word he would use. Really, she wasn't. "When have you seen me stubborn?"

"When I paid for your coffee and you insisted on paying me back," he said. "You didn't want to owe me anything."

"Oh, that… Well, I didn't want to lead you on," she said at last.

"By letting me buy you coffee?" he asked. The amusement in his voice invited her to have a laugh at the situation, but she couldn't.

"Yes. I have been waiting to turn twenty-five since the moment I walked away from my old life and I didn't want to give you any encouragement that we could have anything other than—" She broke off, realizing she had admitted to him that she only wanted sex. That hooking up was fine, but anything deeper scared her.

Of course it did. But she hadn't meant to say it as bluntly as she had. "I didn't mean that."

"You did," he said. "Let's be honest with each other, okay? I'm not going to lie. I do want to do more than just burn up the sheets with you. So if we are going to have any chance of making this work, I think we have to both be honest with each other."

She nodded.

Honest.

She could do that.

She thought she could. She wasn't lying to him. She'd told him the truth.

"Fair enough."

"So where does that leave us?" he asked after a few long moments.

She stood up and started to clean the table. Diego helped her out. He rinsed the dishes and put them into the dishwasher without saying anything. She suspected he was giving her time to figure out what she wanted to say.

But like the text message she'd struggled to send earlier, she was still confused when it came to him.

"I'm waiting to hear back from my family attorney," she said, using the American term. "I can't do anything, make any real plans until then. Even my money is tied up until my identity is confirmed. So I'm planning to continue to help out with Penny and live here until that's sorted."

Diego wiped his hands on the dish towel and leaned against her kitchen counter. She tried to concentrate on what he was saying, but his voice was a deep rumble that reminded her of last night when she'd lain on his chest and he'd said good-night to her. The sound had rumbled under her ear.

She knew that she wanted Diego. Wanted to somehow figure out a way to have him and her inheritance. Like one of the fairy tales she read to Penny before bedtime, she wanted a happy ending of her own.

But she'd never been good at trusting others. If she had been, maybe she wouldn't have run away in the first place. Because she could admit that when she'd first come to the States, it was her temper and her stubbornness that had driven her from the upscale Manhattan hotel to the bus station with only a haute couture dress on her back and the cash in her wallet.

She could have tried to speak to her potential fiancé, but she hadn't known if she could trust him. She'd just felt like everything was out of control.

But in this kitchen with Diego watching her as if she were in charge, she realized she was exactly where she wanted to be.

"Pippa?"

"Hmm?"

"I asked how long you thought you had until they confirmed everything," he said.

"I would imagine a few weeks."

He uncrossed his arms and straightened to walk over to her, his boot heels clacking on the hardwood floor. He stopped when only an inch of space separated them, and she felt the brush of his breath as he exhaled on a sigh.

"As I see it we have two options," he said.

"They are?"

"I walk out of here and we continue the way we had been before last night, smiling politely when we see each other in town but otherwise pretending that there isn't a red-hot spark between us."

She nodded, nibbling on her bottom lip because it tingled when he stood this close.

"And option two?"

"We enjoy the time you have left in Texas together."

"I'd like that. However, tonight isn't good for me," she said. "I have to be over at the big house when Penny wakes up in the morning."

"I crashed your evening, and I'm glad that you allowed me to."

"I'm glad you did. I was feeling…unsure and I didn't like it. I've kind of stayed away from men for the last few years and I feel really awkward around you," she admitted. He seemed so confident, so sure, that she wished she was…well, stronger.

"You're perfect. Everyone says I'm better around horses than women."

"Who says that?"

"My brother, but he has been known to be an ass," Diego said, standing up and walking toward the door.

She followed him, not really wanting him to go but knowing she had responsibilities toward Penny and if he stayed she'd be distracted.

"Good night," he said, picking up his hat and settling it on his head.

"Good night." She reached out and touched his jaw before he turned and left.

Seven

"Mama said you're leaving," Penny said while she was taking her bath the next evening. Pippa had already washed the little girl's hair and was cleaning up the bathroom while Penny played in the water.

"I am, imp. You know my home isn't here in Texas."

"But I'm here," she said. "And Mama is, too."

She turned to look at Penny, whose red hair, so like Kinley's, clung to her heart-shaped face. There was sadness in her wide, blue-green eyes. The little girl was hurt that she was leaving.

"Nothing is going to change between us, Penny. I'm still going to be your Pippy and we'll talk every day on the video chat, like Benito does when his mommy is out of town," she said. "You have a daddy now and I think as you and your mama settle here in Cole's Hill, you are going to find you miss me less and less."

Water sluiced down Penny's little body as she leaned over to hug Pippa tight. Pippa wrapped her arms around her.

"I'll miss you."

"I'm going to miss you, too," Pippa said, feeling tears in her eyes. She'd been with this little girl since she'd been born. The bond they had was deep and important. "We'll always be the P girls."

"That's right," Penny said.

Pippa took the hooded towel from the heated rack and helped Penny dry off. Penny fastened the Velcro that made the towel into a sort of robe, put her hood on and ran into the bedroom to get dressed in the pajamas that Pippa had laid out earlier.

She pulled the plug on the bath water and finished cleaning up the bathroom, thinking of how much she'd liked the simple life. But a part of her knew that something had always been missing.

Kinley came in and they read Penny her bedtime story before tucking the little girl into bed.

"Glass of wine?" Kinley asked Pippa as she closed the door to Penny's room.

"Yes. I'm on edge waiting to hear back from London," Penny admitted when they were both sitting down in front of the gas fireplace.

"I'd be going nuts. You know how I am," Kinley said.

"I do. Penny asked me about leaving," Pippa said.

"Yeah, sorry I didn't give you a heads-up. It kind of came out and I decided I should probably tell her the truth," Kinley said. "But I should have had your back and told you first."

"It's okay. I hope that this doesn't change our relationship," Pippa said.

"I'm not going to let it. You know me better than just about anyone and you and Penny have a bond. You're like her best auntie," Kinley said. "You're not getting rid of us that easily."

"I'm glad to hear that," Pippa said. "I have really loved living with you both, but I think it's time for me to claim my life."

They talked about the different couples who had emerged from the charity auction Sunday night. And how sweet Ethan and Crissanne had been when he proposed. Pippa had had a good view of Mason, Crissanne's former boyfriend and Ethan's best friend, as it had happened. And he had seemed happy for the couple, despite the complicated circumstances that had brought them together.

"So what's going on with you and Diego?" Kinley asked in that blunt way of hers.

"Uh, we decided to date while I'm still here," she said. "I told him that I'm waiting to hear from the solicitor in England. I didn't want to lead him on."

"Good idea. So what does dating look like?"

"I'm not sure. He's busy with the ranch and I have Penny, so finding time to get together won't be easy," Pippa said, recalling how they'd been texting most of the day. But she didn't respond to texts while she was nannying, wanting to make sure Penny had her attention.

"Men are complicated," Kinley said.

"But worth the hassle," Nate said as he walked into the living room and gave Kinley a look so hot that even Pippa could feel the heat. She excused herself and walked the short distance to her cottage.

She let herself in and stood in the hallway with the lights off for a long minute. The house smelled of new wood flooring and lemon-scented cleaner, since Kinley had insisted that the housekeeping staff also clean her place. She'd decorated the rooms with some knick-knacks she'd collected in town and while she'd been in Las Vegas. There was a small laundry/mud room off the kitchen and a den that Pippa would have made into a library if she were staying.

There were bookshelves on all the walls and a nice window seat that overlooked the Rockin' C pastures. The shelves weren't full, as Pippa's book collection was mainly digital, but she'd recently joined a book club, so one shelf had ten books on it.

She had obsessively checked her email all night long, so she limited herself to one last look at the smartphone that Kinley had given her but kept in Kinley's name, hoping the solicitor had gotten back to her even though she knew that with the six-hour time difference that wasn't going to happen.

Tomorrow was Wednesday. Realistically she knew it was going to take a few days to verify everything, but honestly it felt like this was taking way longer than the last four years had.

Her phone pinged as she was washing her face and she fumbled for her face towel before running into the other room to see who it was.

It was a text from Diego.

A little thrill went through her.

Instead of meeting for coffee in town tomorrow, would you like a tour of Arbol Verde and a late breakfast with me?

Pippa's reply was instant.

I'd love that. I have to take Penny to school so I could be there around nine.

Perfect. Are you afraid of heights?

No. Why?

Just asking. What are you doing now?

Getting ready for bed.

Wish I was there with you.

Me, too. She thought it but didn't text it. She wanted to keep it light and casual. Those were her key words for Diego.

What are you doing?

Fantasizing about being in your bedroom. What does it look like? I didn't get a chance to see it when I was there earlier.

Light and casual.
Yeah, right.

She hesitated for one more second and then tapped out the message she'd been wanting to send since she'd seen it was his name showing up on her phone.

Come over and see for yourself...

There was no response at first, then the three dancing dots that indicated he was typing.

On my way.

Diego had intended... Well, he didn't know what he'd intended. With Pippa he was like a horny guy who'd never been laid before. He thought about her whenever she wasn't with him, wanting her in his bed. Not living on Nate Caruthers's property. Which made him slow down for a second as he was driving his Bronco hell-bent-for-leather down the old country road that connected his property to the Rockin' C.

He drove past the big house and the bunkhouse to the smaller residences behind them. He knew from past visits that the largest of the three belonged to Marcus Quentin, Kinley's dad, the former ranch foreman who'd retired a few years back. The next one was dark and looked empty and the last one was Pippa's. As his headlights illuminated the house, he saw that she was sitting on the porch swing waiting for him.

He turned off the truck engine and sat there for a

long minute in the cab of his truck parked in front of her cottage. If she'd changed her mind, he'd walk away.

And actually now that he saw her, that lust-driven rush that had made him hurry over to her was starting to calm. Once he was with her, he could take his time. It was only when they were apart that there was a problem.

Because he knew they didn't have much time before she'd be out of his life for good.

He put his head on the steering wheel.

What was he doing?

This was like Mauricio following Hadley when she was on a date with someone else, wasn't it? Of course, Diego wasn't going to start a fight with anyone, but the situation with Pippa was similarly an exercise in futility. He wanted more than Pippa was ever going to give… or at least that gnawing emptiness in the pit of his soul made him think he did.

He looked up and noticed how she kept rocking on the porch swing. Just sitting there waiting to see what he was going to do.

And he realized she was just as unsure about this as he was. The connection between the two of them shouldn't be this strong. They were supposed to be a bit of fun for each other, casually hooking up and then going back to their real lives.

Except that wasn't what was happening.

Not for either one of them, unless he missed his guess.

He got out of his truck and pocketed his keys as he walked up the stone path that led to her front porch.

"Hello, Pippa," he said.

"Diego," she said.

He couldn't help noticing she wore a cotton dress that ended at her knees and had a tie front that was undone, drawing his eyes to the hint of cleavage underneath it. She sat there on the swing as if she wasn't sure what to do now that he was here.

"So…still want me here?" he asked.

She nodded. "Yes."

He didn't say anything else, just climbed up the two steps that led to her porch and then went over to stand against the railing. She'd pulled her hair up into a ponytail and wasn't wearing any makeup, but he'd never seen her look more beautiful. It was as if each time he saw her he noticed once again how pretty she was.

"Tell me more about what is waiting for you when you go back to England," he said. It was the subject he was pretty sure was on both of their minds and he wanted to know the details…though he had no idea why. He wasn't going to leave Cole's Hill. His life and his soul were here. The land and his horses were so much a part of the man he was, he couldn't go with her. But he wanted to know what it was that she'd left behind.

She tipped her head back, looking away from him.

"The family business," she said. "My dad and I were never close, and when my mom died, the rift between us widened. He had control of my shares in the business and my other interests until I was twenty-five."

"Okay, so you're twenty-five and going back means

you get to be in charge?" he asked, trying to figure out what was at stake.

"Yes," she said. "When I left, he was pressuring me to marry a man who sided with him when it came to the family business and that wasn't the vision I had for it. Obviously, he wasn't going to force me to marry, but I realized he was never going to listen to me. And if I disappeared, it would tie up my shares. He wouldn't be able to vote them until they ascertained what had happened to me. My shares haven't been in play while I was gone and the company has only been able to continue operating as it had been when my shares were last voted. So I was able to slow down his agenda and give myself some breathing room."

He moved over and sat down on the swing next to her, stretching his arm out on the back. She shifted until she was sitting in the curve of his body.

She put her head on his shoulder and then looked at him with those gray eyes of hers, so sincere and full of vulnerability that he wanted to wrap her in a big bear hug and promise she wasn't going to be hurt again. But he knew that wasn't a vow he could keep. The man who'd hurt her was probably going to fight tooth and nail to keep from relinquishing his control over her fortune.

"What can I do?" he asked.

"Just help me forget what is waiting for me," she said. "I like being with you, Diego, because you are so far removed from that world and...don't laugh...but you make me feel as though you like me for me. All the things that aren't perfect don't seem to matter when I'm with you."

"You are perfect, so I don't know what you're talking about," he said, slipping his arm under her thighs and lifting her onto his lap.

Pippa was talking too much. She'd meant to keep most of the past to herself, but there was something about Diego and the quiet confidence in his eyes that made her feel like everything was safe with him.

Her cottage faced the open pasture and the big Texas night sky. The bunkhouse, barn and main ranch building were in the other direction as was the home shared by Ma and Pa Caruthers. It almost seemed as if they were the only two people on the land tonight.

He settled her on his lap and she wrapped her arm around his shoulders. Their eyes met. His were so big and dark with only the porch lights illuminating them. She suddenly didn't know if her trust was misplaced. There was something in his eyes—a hunger—that made him almost…almost a different guy than the one who'd been sweetly listening to her.

There was something almost untamed about him. As much as her mind might warn her to step back from him, there was another more primal part that wanted to claim him. But she'd never be able to tame him because she wasn't going to have enough time to do that.

She shifted so that she was straddling him, and pressed her lips to his. He spread his thighs underneath her hips, forcing her legs farther apart. She rocked back and forth, feeling his erection against her as their kiss grew more intense.

His breath was warm and sweet and smelled of peppermint and whiskey. She pulled back, putting her hands on either side of his face. "Did you pop a mint in for me?"

He flushed, and that charmed her. "Yeah."

"Thank you," she said. "I didn't do anything to prepare for your visit."

"You don't have to," he said. She felt his hands on the backs of her thighs, rubbing up and down and coming closer to her butt with each stroke. He was moving his hands in a counter-rhythm to her hips.

With his big, hot hands on her thighs and his thick erection underneath her, she let her head fall back as she rode him. She felt the brush of his breath against her neck a moment before his mouth was on it. He kissed her softly at first, but then as his hands urged her to move faster against him, he suckled her neck and shivers spread down her body as she continued rocking against him.

Diego wore a Western shirt that had snap closures; she tugged lightly and they all came undone. She pushed the shirt open before shifting slightly back on his thighs. He eased his legs farther apart and she undid the snap that held his jeans closed and lowered the zipper to see the ridge of his erection hard against the cotton of his boxer briefs.

He shifted again, freeing himself.

He handed her a condom and she smiled as she held it in one hand while circling his nipple with her fingernail, scraping the line where it met the smooth skin of his chest. Then she scraped her nail down his rock-hard stomach, lingering to trace his tattoo before moving lower.

She took the condom out of the package and rolled it onto his length.

He sat up straighter, pulling her more fully into his arms until she felt the tip of his erection against her center. He groaned deep in his throat.

He undid the laces on the front of her dress even farther until her breasts were visible. She hadn't put a bra on tonight, so when he dipped his fingers under the dress fabric, he brushed over her nipple, which made her shiver and rotate her shoulders to thrust her chest forward.

She moved again on his lap, and his hard-on nudged at her center. She loved the feel of his big hands as he put them under her skirt, caressing her thighs and then cupping her butt. He kissed her neck, biting at her collarbone as she shifted so that the tips of her breasts rubbed over his chest.

She shuddered, clutching at his shoulders, grinding her body harder against him.

He moved his fingers lower on her body, until she felt the tip of one tracing her folds and pushing up into her. She was moist and ready for him and leaned forward to take his mouth with hers. He continued to trace the opening of her body with his finger.

She captured his face, tipped his head back and kissed him hard. Her tongue thrusting into his mouth as he shifted, she felt him inside her. She rocked down hard on him as he plunged into her.

He used his thumb to find her center and stroked her as she rocked against him. His free hand cupped her butt and urged her to a faster rhythm, guiding her motions against him. He bent his head. His tongue stroked her nipple, and then he suckled her.

Everything in her body clenched. She clutched at his shoulders, rubbing harder and tightening around his fingers as her climax shattered her. She collapsed against his chest and he held her close. She put her head on his shoulder and they stayed like that without saying a word.

Pippa wanted to pretend it was because there was nothing to say, but she knew it was because there was too much.

Eight

There were a lot of cute boutiques in the historic area of Cole's Hill, but Penny and Benito wanted to go to Jump!, an indoor soft play area out on FM145. Pippa had volunteered to pick them up after pre-K and take them to play and then pick out their Halloween costumes.

Bianca had flown to New York to do a one-off fashion shoot for a famous American designer. Rumor around town was that she had been asked to do his spring show but had declined. Kinley was working longer hours than normal and had gone to Vegas with several of her brides-to-be. So Pippa was having both of the four-year-olds for a sleepover that evening. Diego had suggested they go for a ride at sunset and then have dinner around a campfire on his property.

And after securing the permission of all the parents,

she had accepted. They had fallen into a relationship that felt…well, like pretend, if Pippa was honest. They saw each other when their schedules allowed and had been sleeping over at each other's places at least three times a week.

She had a feeling in the pit of her stomach it wouldn't last…probably because she knew it wouldn't. But it had more to do with the funky peace they shared. It was like they were both on their very best behavior. So what was developing between them felt fake; at least on her side, she was offering a fake version of herself. She wasn't as sweet and nice as Diego seemed to think she was.

Normally she would have given the barista a bit of attitude when she skipped her pump of vanilla in her coffee, but because Diego had been with her this morning she'd just smiled and said that was okay, she was watching her calories.

And she knew that there was no way a successful rancher like Diego would be in town every morning at the coffee shop. That was prime time on a ranch. She knew because that was when Nate and the rest of the population on the Rockin' C were the busiest.

So Diego was faking it, too.

Then there was the other night, when he'd said he'd rather watch a repeat of the *Real Housewives* than the Spurs basketball game, which she knew was a lie. She smiled at the memory of her teasing him and asking him which housewife was his favorite. When he'd gone into the kitchen to get popcorn, she'd switched it over to the Spurs game. She frankly didn't understand a thing that was going on during the basketball game, but seeing the surprise and relief on his face had been worth it.

She realized that some things weren't fake between them—their passion, for one. But in general, she suspected they were being so careful of each other's feelings because they had a nebulous expiration date on their relationship. They both knew that it would end but not exactly when. And neither wanted to spoil their last moments together.

Whenever they would come.

It had been almost ten days and she'd still heard nothing from the solicitor except that he'd received her information and confirmed her identity. As far as her claim to her entire fortune, and the chair on House of Hamilton's board, he was still working on it. He'd paid her a small stipend via wire transfer to the bank in Cole's Hill. So she had some of her own money, even though she didn't need her fortune to live in Cole's Hill.

Room and board were covered by Kinley and she had an Etsy shop where she sold art pieces she made to practice her skills at design. Some of them were pretty good to her mind, others just so-so.

"Pippy, that was so much fun. I hope that I can find the perfect costume," Penny said as she and Benito came out of the soft play area and she was helping them both to put their shoes back on.

"It looked like fun," Pippa said to her. "Did you like it, Benito?"

"Yes, I jumped the highest," he said.

"He did. I tried to beat him, but I couldn't."

"Not everything has to be a competition," she said to the two toddlers.

"We know," they said at the same time.

"What costumes are we looking for today?" she asked as they stepped out of the play area and she took their hands. The costume superstore was across the parking lot, and since it was a sunny, warm day there was no reason for them not to walk to it.

"Cowgirl," Penny said, skipping next to her.

"I'm not surprised, but you know that Halloween is a chance to be something different than who you normally are. And you're a cowgirl now," Pippa said.

"Really?" Benito asked her.

"Yes. What are you going to be?" the little girl said.

"I was going to be a doctor like Daddy." Benito's biological father had been killed when he was six months old. Since Bianca and Derek had married, he called Derek Daddy and referred to his biological father as Papa. "But I might be an astronaut."

"That's a good idea," Pippa said.

When they got inside the store, Penny went straight for the cowgirl costumes, but she kept looking over at a pink princess one, as well. "What's the matter, imp?" Pippa asked.

"Could I be a cowgirl princess?"

"Yes. Or you could just be a princess," Pippa told her, finding the sizes in both costumes for Penny.

"Yay!" Penny said, turning to help Benito.

He decided on the astronaut and then they both wanted every piece of candy near the checkout, but

Pippa got them to compromise on a lollipop and a jar of bubbles instead.

"What about you?" Penny asked. "What are you going to be?"

She didn't know if she'd still be in Texas at Halloween. Surely everything would be sorted before then.

"I haven't decided yet."

"I hope all the good ones aren't gone," Penny said.

"I'm sure they won't be," Pippa replied.

Diego was waiting in the barn when Pippa and the kids arrived. Every time they made plans he was aware of the fact that they might be canceled due to Pippa's situation, and it was setting him on edge. Plus, being perfect—or as perfect as he could be—around Pippa was making him short-tempered with his brothers. Mainly just Mauricio, which suited the other man just fine, since he was out of sorts over Hadley being seen around town with another man.

So the Velasquez brothers were spending way too much time in town at the kickboxing studio that a former army captain and his brother had set up. Diego had a few bruises on his ribs and his knuckles ached, since he and Mo preferred bare-knuckled fighting, but it had been worth it.

He smiled easily at Pippa. She wore a pair of faded jeans that made her legs look even longer than he knew they were and a pale pink button-down shirt that made her blond hair and gray eyes stand out. Penny was dressed in a pair of jeans and boots and had a pink cowgirl hat on her head and Benito had boots, jeans and his black cowboy hat on.

He had his ranch hands set up dinner on one of the ridges that was an easy thirty-minute ride from the barn. He had saddled the gentlest horses he had for Benito and Penny. Pippa had told him that she'd ridden as a child and Nate had said that she was a good horsewoman, so he'd given her a spirited mare who he hoped would match her skill.

"*Tio*, I'm going to be an astronaut for Halloween," Benito said as he came skipping over to him.

Diego scooped his nephew up and hugged him close. He had been happy when Bianca had moved back home after Jose's death, so he could watch his nephew growing up.

"Sounds like it should be fun. I met the brother of one of the astronauts at the training center. Maybe I can arrange for you to go and visit him," Diego said, thinking that Manu would probably be able to arrange that.

"Can I go, too?" Penny asked.

"I think Diego will need to make sure that kids are allowed to go out there for a visit first," Pippa said.

"Yes, I will. But one thing I know we can do is go for a ride on the horses right now. Who's ready?"

"Me!" the children both yelled. Benito squirmed to get down out of his uncle's arms. Diego placed the little boy on his feet and he and Penny joined hands and ran toward the barn.

"Sorry, I was promising something I couldn't deliver, wasn't I?"

"You were," Pippa said. "It's probably not that big of

a deal, but Penny will go to school tomorrow and tell everyone you are taking them to the space station and it might start something."

"I guess you can tell I'm not around kids a lot," he said.

"I can and I like it. For once, I feel like I know more than you do," she said.

"That's not true," he responded. "You know tons more than I do about a lot of subjects."

"Not horses," she said.

"Nate said you were pretty good. Was he lying to me?"

She shook her head. "I can ride, but I feel weird sitting on a Western saddle. Kinley's been giving me some lessons on weekends when the little imp insists we all go for a ride together."

Diego pulled her to a stop just outside the barn. He could hear the kids talking to the grooms he'd had in waiting to help them with their tack.

"Won't you miss her?" he asked.

She bit her lower lip. "Yes. I'll miss her terribly, but this isn't my life. I know it, and so do Kinley and Nate. They include me in their weekends, but I know they are looking forward to being a family on their own."

Diego put his arm around her and squeezed her. "I can't imagine what that must be like."

But he could. He was dealing with that to a very small extent with Pippa right now. She was his for these few weeks. It had sounded like a great idea when he was horny as hell; when they were naked it always felt right. But now that he realized he could lose her at any minute, that when he planned an evening for the two of them he had to wait all day in suspense hoping she'd still show up, he knew it wasn't.

If it had been only physical attraction between them, things would be easier. Or if Pippa were a snob to people. But she was sweet to everyone, even the barista who never got anyone's order right. He'd lost it with her more than once, but not Pippa. She'd just smiled and put the other woman at ease.

It had made him realize how much he liked her. He was trying to be smart about this and not get in any deeper than he already was, but the only way that was going to happen was if he kept his distance from her and that wasn't in the cards.

He didn't want to waste a single second of the time they'd been given. So he was working longer hours around the times when she was available so he wouldn't have as many regrets when she was gone.

"What are you thinking?" she asked.

"Just how much I'm going to miss you when you leave," he said, then turned and walked into the barn and went to his horse.

He saddled his horse Iago and heard Pippa talking to the kids as they donned their protective helmets and were assisted onto the horses by the grooms. He guessed he hadn't spent long enough in the ring with Mauricio today, because he was out of sorts and he needed to adjust his attitude.

Hopefully the ride would do that.

Pippa knew she'd upset Diego, and she got it. Really, she did. She probably should just leave Cole's Hill

now and not prolong the inevitable. It was just that she
had nowhere to really go until the solicitor got back
to her. Even her passport was out-of-date. But hanging around here, starting something with Diego even
though they'd both said it was just temporary, hadn't
really been a smart idea.

"Texas is so different from Las Vegas," Pippa said
as they rode. The kids were a little ways ahead of them
and Diego never took his eyes off the pair.

"It's beautiful, isn't it? I can't imagine living anywhere but here," he said.

And that secret hope that she'd barely even realized
she'd been holding on to died. Diego was never going
to be a man she could bring with her to her new life.
Not that she needed a man by her side, but it would have
been nice not to return to England by herself. And Kinley obviously couldn't come with her.

"Stop your horse," Diego called out to the kids. "Do
you remember how?"

"Pull back on the reins," Benito said.

"I knew that, too," Penny chimed in.

The two of them expertly stopped their horses and
then held the reins loosely in their hands much the same
way Diego did. He guided Iago next to the two children
and Pippa watched them look over at him with rapt expressions on their faces. She fumbled for her cell phone
and snapped a photo of them as Diego was giving them
instructions.

She tucked her phone away before joining them,
knowing the photo would be one of her most cherished
because it would bring her back to the sun on her shoul-

ders and this moment when she realized that Diego meant more to her than she had wanted him to.

After thirty minutes, they got to the spot where they were going to have the campfire dinner. She saw that Diego had gone out of his way for them. He had four chairs set up around the campfire and had torches lit. One of his ranch hands was cooking the meal and there were two others waiting to take the horses back to the barn. She noticed he had a four-wheel ATV parked to the side. There were jackets for the kids and blankets in case the evening turned cold, but so far the weather was perfect, with only a slight breeze.

"I made cowboy chili for dinner," Diego said. "This recipe has been in our family for almost two hundred years. In the old days they'd make a batch of this and it was all the hands would have to eat for a week."

Benito and Penny both went closer to him as he told them the history of the first Velasquez ancestor who'd come over to Texas by order of the King of Spain and started to carve out a life for himself and his family. Diego kept Pippa and the children entertained as they ate the chili, which he'd made mild enough for the kids to eat. When they were done, he brought out the makings of s'mores for dessert, which she'd never had growing up but had learned to love since being in Texas.

She realized as they ate dinner how much she would miss Diego and Texas. The stories here were big legends that fired her imagination, but more than that she was going to miss Diego. And it was clear to her that he wouldn't suddenly leave his ranch and come with her to England. He couldn't. His history was here. His horses and his equine breeding program, which had just received another award according to a couple grooms she'd overheard discussing it, were all here.

He belonged here. As much as she didn't.

"Cowboys and cowgirls used to use the stars to find their way back home," Diego was saying. The kids had their heads tipped up to the sky. They were far enough from town that there was no real light pollution except for the glow of the torches and the fire.

"I'll show you how when we're done eating," Diego said.

"This summer, Daddy is going to take me to a cattle drive," Penny said.

"Really?" Diego asked. "On the Rockin' C?"

"No. Fort something. Do you remember, Pippy?"

"Fort Worth," she said. "Apparently they still drive cattle down the street there twice a day."

"They do. It's one of the oldest traditions in the state. There used to be a cattle market there and everyone would drive their herds up for the sale," Diego said. As he continued talking to the kids about life on the cattle trail, Pippa just sat there and listened to him.

She wondered why he wasn't married. Diego was really good with the kids. They'd moved to sit closer to him, and he had them both cuddled on his lap as he talked. Their eyes met over the kids' heads and her heart beat a little faster. He winked at her and the earlier turmoil she'd felt between them disappeared at least for a few moments.

She closed her eyes and some of the resentment she had been carrying with her since she'd left her old life dissipated. She'd never have been here if not for those events that had driven her to run away.

"In fact, the Five Families of Cole's Hill used to pool their resources and they would journey up to the cattle markets together. Back then there were all kinds of dangers from snakes to outlaws to treacherous river crossings. That bond was what made Cole's Hill what it is today," Diego said.

They finished their food and Pippa cleaned up both kids' faces and hands. Then they piled into the ATV and Diego drove them halfway back to his ranch house, stopping in an especially dark area. "Close your eyes for a few minutes and then I'll show you the star that will point you to home."

Pippa glanced in the back seat of the open-air vehicle to where the kids were buckled into their car seats. When she turned back around, Diego was so close to her, their breaths mingled. And he kissed her. It was hard, passionate and deep but over before it began. "Couldn't resist your lips," he whispered.

"Open your eyes, kiddos, tip your head back and look toward the front of the vehicle. Do you see the star to the left of the moon?"

Both children weren't sure how to tell left from right, so Pippa moved to the back seat and sat between the two of them to help. She glanced up, pretty sure that Diego meant Venus when he talked about the star that would lead them home. A good Texas legend, she thought, just like the man himself.

She carefully pointed to the "star" so Penny and Benito could find it.

"Now you will always be able to find your way back home," she said.

"We all will," Diego added.

She clamored back over the seat and he drove them back to the ranch house.

"Want to come back to Pippa's for our sleepover?" Benito asked.

"Um…"

"Please," Benito pleaded.

"It would be nice if you joined us," Pippa said.

"Then I will," he said. "I have to be back at the ranch first thing in the morning."

"That's fine," she said.

Pippa got Penny into her car and Diego followed her with Benito. As she drove away, she couldn't help thinking that home wasn't what she'd once believed it would be. For one thing, she hadn't imagined she'd live anywhere but London, but now her idea of home was changing and morphing into something new. And that was dangerous.

Nine

Diego followed Pippa in his ranch truck with Benito buckled into his car seat beside him. His nephew talked excitedly all the way back to Pippa's cottage.

By the time they got there, the kids were exhausted from their outing. Diego helped Pippa get the kids bathed and into bed and then hung back waiting for her to check her email.

"Nothing firm yet. But I did just get a brief email. The solicitor said he should have news no later than Friday," she said.

It was Wednesday.

So that meant he had two more nights with her. His gut said he needed to take her as many times as he could. Imprint on her so that when she was back in the UK she wouldn't be able to forget him or their time together.

He took her hand. "Can you hear the kids if we're downstairs?"

"Yes. I have a monitor app on the smartphone that Kinley gave me," she said. "Why?"

"I want you," he said, under his breath.

She flushed. "Me, too."

He led her down the stairs after she made sure both kids were sleeping in her big bed, then into the kitchen, where he lifted her up onto the counter and tunneled his fingers into her hair and kissed her deeply.

He had told himself this was so she wouldn't forget him, but he knew this was for him. He wanted her as many times as he could have her and in as many different ways. For himself. For those long winter nights he knew were coming. Long nights when he'd be all alone and hungry and hard for a woman who had never thought of him as anything other than her temporary man.

She pushed her hands up under his shirt and then reached into the back of his jeans, cupping his ass and drawing him farther in between her legs. He shifted around, rubbing the tip of his erection against her. Running his hands up and down her back, he pulled her forward toward him, but there was too much clothing in the way.

His jeans, her jeans. He lifted her off the counter and knelt to help her take off her boots. She put one foot on his thigh. He grabbed the toe with one hand and the heel with the other and helped her take off the first boot. Then he made quick work of the other.

She was wearing socks with hearts and flowers

on them. He pulled them off and tossed them toward her boots. Her feet were small and delicate in his big hands. Her pedicure was a racy red color that matched the lipstick he recalled her wearing to the bachelor auction.

His cock jumped as he remembered the way she'd looked that night, and he groaned at the pain. He straightened and reached for the button at his waistband and undid it, lowering the zipper so that his erection had room. She reached down and touched the tip of it, stroking with her fingers in the opening of his jeans.

He took her hand in his and placed it on the counter next to her. He was so close to the edge that if she touched him again, he'd spill himself right there and this would be the shortest encounter in history. And he needed more than that.

He undid her pants, pushing them down her legs along with her panties. As she scissored her legs and the jeans and underwear fell to the floor, he reached into his back pocket where he'd put a condom earlier this evening.

She smiled and took it from him.

"I like a guy who's prepared," she said.

"Just call me a Boy Scout," he said. He was always prepared for sex. But he was also trying to be prepared for when she left. He shook his head, tore open the packet and shoved his underwear down to put the condom on.

She placed her hand on his hip and he realized he was going too fast. The control he'd always taken for granted had deserted him. That email from her lawyer had just served to remind him of how little time he actually had left with her. And that was doing things to his emotions that he didn't want to deal with.

But she was his for now. That was about as much as he wanted to think about tonight. He pulled her toward him.

"Wrap your legs around me," he said. She did as he asked, and he shifted his hips, feeling the tip of his erection nudging at her entrance.

But she wasn't ready, and he cursed. He brought his mouth down on hers and his hands to her shirt, undoing the buttons while his tongue teased and played with hers. She sucked his deeper into her mouth as her hands cupped his backside and she drew him closer. She arched against him as his fingers found the cami bra she had on, and he fumbled around, trying to find a fastening before realizing there wasn't one. He pushed the bottom of the bra up until her breasts were free and then he rubbed his finger around her nipple, feeling it bead under his finger.

She parted her legs farther and he plucked at the nipple as he once again thrust against her. This time he slid easily inside. She arched her back and he looked down at her breasts angled toward him, lowering his head to catch the nipple of one in his mouth and sucking on it hard and deep.

She funneled her fingers through his hair and rocked harder and harder against him until he heard that tiny gasp and knew she was close to her climax. He lifted his head from her breast and took her mouth in an urgent kiss, swallowing her cries as he drove into her again and again until he came long and hard. She tightened around him, her body squeezing him so perfectly, and he kept thrusting until he felt her shiver in the throes of orgasm.

He held her against his chest as their breathing slowed and his heartbeat started to calm. She wrapped her arms and legs around his body and held him tightly to her.

And he hoped he wasn't the only one who was going to have a hard time saying goodbye.

Diego knew he couldn't spend the night, but he didn't want to leave. So instead he convinced Pippa to take the baby monitor with her to her back porch, where there was a fire pit. He lit a fire and then sat down on one of the big Adirondack chairs, pulling her onto his lap.

"Did you always know that you were going to take over the stud farm?" she asked, leaning her head against his shoulder.

He knew his arms were going to feel empty when she was gone and hugged her tightly to him without saying a word.

"Yes," he said at last. Sparks from the fire danced up into the night sky as a log shifted. He stared at it and pondered their situation.

If he were a different man, he'd just give up everything and follow her, but he wasn't. He'd always just known that he was meant to stay at Arbol Verde. He'd never had a moment of doubt. He'd gone to Texas

A&M and studied animal husbandry, coming home on the weekends because he'd missed the land and his horses.

He was trying to find a way to keep seeing Pippa when she returned to the UK, not that she'd even suggested the possibility. But Diego knew that he wasn't going to transition well to living without her. A part of him wondered how he could have such strong feelings for a woman he'd known for such a short time.

But she wasn't just a woman. She was Pippa.

She was classy and funny, feisty and sexy. But she was still a mystery to him no matter how much they talked and he knew that letting her go was going to be hard.

"Tell me about it," she said, a note of humor in her voice.

What was there to say? "You know how some people grow up and can't break free from their hometown?"

She nodded. "Yes, but I wasn't one of them. I wanted out from under my father's thumb something fierce."

"I didn't have that. My dad and I have always been on the same page when it comes to the stud operation. My earliest memories are of following him around the barn. I think I learned to ride as soon as I could sit in the saddle. There was never a moment when I felt like I didn't belong to the land," he said.

She nodded. "I wish I had that sense of belonging. I've felt lost over the last few years, but at least finding Kinley and helping her to raise Penny grounded me somewhat. I mean, I knew it was temporary, but at the same time I couldn't have wished to be anywhere else. It was the closest I'd come to having a home since my mom died."

"I'm sorry you lost your mother," he said. He didn't ever let himself think what life would be like without his mama. She was a force of nature. With her long career in television, she'd always been outspoken and encouraged her kids to be the same.

"Thanks. I didn't realize what a barrier she was between my father and me until she was gone. Most of the year I was at boarding school, but once she was gone, my father and I hardly saw each other. I had never realized how hollow that relationship was. I thought… Well, it doesn't matter because I was wrong," she said.

She turned to face the fire, leaning forward, and Diego realized that talking about her father made her put a barrier around herself. He doubted she was even aware of it, but she'd just changed. There was a coldness that hadn't been there a moment before.

He wanted to pull her back against him, but he was already holding on too hard and knew that he wouldn't do it. "Tell me about your family business."

"We design high-end jewelry," she said. "I have been taking business courses through an online university while I've been living with Kinley and I did a few extension classes in art."

"Have you made any designs to take back with you?" he asked.

"Yes. I've made a lot of them, but ours is a legacy brand. Part of the falling-out I had with my father was that I wanted us to move with the times, become more modern," she said.

"Will the rest of the board support you?" he asked. "You said he votes your shares, so I assume that all of the board members are family, is that right?"

She pushed herself off his lap, walked a few steps away and stared up at the night sky. He wondered what she was looking for.

She glanced back at him, her long blond hair sliding over her shoulder. "Yes. Most of them are family, but they are second and third cousins... I'm the main shareholder."

"So your father has been controlling the company because of that?" he asked, trying to understand what she was going to be up against when she returned to England.

"Yes. He and my mother were third cousins, so he has a small stake of his own in the company, but voting mother's shares, which are now mine, gives him a majority vote. I think he will fight against me being reinstated."

Diego hoped not. He could see the struggle in Pippa's face as she talked about the company and her father. It would be better if the old man just graciously accepted her return and stepped aside.

"Do you think there is a chance he's mellowed? Perhaps your being missing for all this time has made him realize what he'd lost," Diego said.

"That's a nice thought," she said. "But I doubt very much that's the case."

He wanted to give her space. To be cool and pretend that she hadn't already made him care more than he wanted to. But he got up and went to her, pulled her back into his arms and held her until the fire died and they both went inside. He wanted to stay and claim every second he had with her before she had to leave. But the kids were upstairs. After saying goodbye, he drove home, away from her, wondering what the future held for her and how he was going to manage his part in it.

Penny and Benito were up early and Pippa, who hadn't really slept at all, struggled not to be cranky with them. She was very happy when Kinley, who'd come back from Vegas overnight, had volunteered to take them to school. She passed the children off to her friend, who looked like she wanted to ask questions, but Pippa just shook her head and waved them all off.

She went back to the computer. Still no email about her request to assume her position on the House of Hamilton board and be put in full control of her fortune. She was frustrated and more than a little angry with herself because she knew that a part of her wasn't upset about the lack of progress on that front. The longer it took to hear back from the solicitor, the more time she'd have with Diego.

And what did that say about her?

Hadn't she seen what happened when a man she cared about tried to take control of her life? Wasn't she right now in this mess because her father had taken more than he'd been given?

She showered and got dressed and then took her notebook and pencils out onto the porch. She remembered

last night, sitting in Diego's arms. He made her feel…
well, too much, she admitted. Safe, secure, lust, longing,
a desire for something that she couldn't name.

She channeled all of that into her notebook. The
dancing sparks from the fire were her guide and she
created a sketch for a necklace that would have a series of rubies set in fine gold chain dancing up from a
large stone.

She fiddled with it, realizing that the morning was
gone by the time she finished. She felt better. After
braiding her hair, she texted Kinley to see if her friend
was available for lunch at the Five Families Country
Club.

She wasn't, as she had a full-fledged bridezilla on
her hands.

Pippa had never been the type of woman who was
comfortable sitting in a restaurant by herself, so she
thought about staying home. But there was no food in
her fridge. So she got in the car but instead of turning
toward town when she exited the Rockin' C property
she turned toward Arbol Verde.

She shook her head as she realized this might have
been her intent all along. When had she started lying
to herself?

But she had.

She wanted to pretend that Diego meant nothing.
That he was a friend with benefits, because it had been
clear from the beginning that they had a bond that could
almost be called friendship. But there was also something else.

Something she kept shoving further and further

to the bottom of her emotional well and pretending didn't exist.

She turned under the sweeping wrought-iron banner that proclaimed the name of the ranch and drove slowly up to the main house. She saw Diego's truck and his sports car parked in the drive. Off to one side was a horse trailer.

She sat in her car with the engine on and realized that she probably should have called or texted instead of just showing up. As she started to back out of the circle drive, Diego walked around the side of the horse trailer and their eyes met.

He took his black Stetson off and lifted one hand and waved at her. She shut the engine off, got out of the car and began walking toward him as he put his hat back on and approached her.

"Hiya," she said. "I… I was on my way to lunch and wanted to see if you had time to go with me."

He leaned over and kissed her, in just the briefest touch of their lips, and stepped back. He smelled of sun, the fall air and his spicy cologne. She closed her eyes and realized she was exactly where she wanted to be. There hadn't been too many times that she'd been able to say that, but today she could.

"I'd need to shower and change if we're going into town and I have to finish giving some instructions to my staff. Or we could eat lunch here. I could have my housekeeper make us something."

"I don't mind waiting. I have to pick Penny up at two, so I need to leave by about one fifteen."

"Then let's eat here," he said. "Do you want to come to the barn with me? Or wait in the house?"

"The barn," she said. She hadn't come to his place to sit in his house with the housekeeper.

"Good. I have two new horses that I think we're going to be able to use at the riding center Mauricio and I are working on. We have secured the property and should have that finalized by the end of the week," he said. "I can't wait to get started on the building. A guy we went to high school with has a company that has been doing this sort of facility in North Texas, so we're hoping to get him to do the design."

"That sounds very exciting," she said.

"Are you okay?" he asked as they walked to the barn. He took out his phone and she noticed he was typing out a message to his housekeeper.

"Yeah. I'm waiting for the weekend, too. I should have some news by then."

"That will be a relief," he said. "It's not even my news, but I'm on edge. I hope I didn't push too hard last night, but I feel like I have to make the most of every moment we're together."

"You didn't," she said. "I feel the same way, which is why I'm here today."

"I'm glad you are," he said.

He led her into the barn, which smelled of hay and leather. The sounds of the horses were soothing. While he went to discuss something with one of his ranch hands, he left her in his office. She sat there taking in all the photos on the wall of a younger Diego with his father and admitted she was jealous of the life he had.

Of the family that had surrounded him with love and let him grow into the man he was today. Until her twenty-first birthday she'd just sort of coasted along following her father's script for her life, never realizing that she was invisible to him. That she only showed up on his radar to help him further his own agenda.

Ten

Lunch with Diego was nice, but she kept checking her phone the entire time hoping to hear from the solicitor. Sure, he'd said he'd get back to her by tomorrow, but she had run out of patience. Finally, Diego called her on it.

"What are you checking for?"

"Waiting for that email. I know it's getting later in London. I just don't want to miss hearing from the solicitor."

"I don't think there's any chance of that," he said.

"Sorry. I guess I shouldn't have come here," she said. But she'd thought they were friends and she needed someone who had her back right now. Because she felt too vulnerable and unsure of herself.

"Why did you?"

She shrugged. What was she going to say? The truth?

That was complicated, and really, she wasn't even sure what was going to happen between them. She felt this bond. What could she say; when she felt nervous, her first thought was to find Diego. Just being with him calmed her down.

But that wasn't really fair to Diego. It made her feel like she was using him.

"I... You make me feel safe," she said at last. "So if I have bad news while I'm with you, I think I'll deal with it better."

He sighed and pushed his chair back before standing up and turning away from her. They were seated at a large table on his stone patio that overlooked the horse paddock and the rolling hills. He put his hands on his hips as he stared out at the land and she wondered what he saw when he did that. She knew when she stalked the House of Hamilton website she felt a sense of possession and expectation because she belonged as part of the company, not as an outsider.

Right now, she felt like an outsider.

Fair enough.

"I wish you wouldn't say things like that," he said.

"Why not? It's the truth," she said, carefully folding her napkin and getting up from the table. She went to stand next to him, looking out over the fields. "We said no lies."

"I thought that would be safer somehow, but it isn't."

"Safer how?"

"That maybe being brutally honest would make it easier to think of a time when you wouldn't be by my side, but that isn't the case at all. I hate that you are checking your email and waiting for the all clear to move so far from me. It's not like I have a claim on you, Pippa. I know that. Yet at the same time the thought of your leaving dominates my every waking moment and even some of my sleeping ones."

She put her hand in the middle of his back and then laid her head on his shoulder blade. Closing her eyes, she felt his heat and breathed in that scent that was so distinctive to Diego. She wrapped her other arm around his waist and held him.

She wished… She didn't know what she wished. That maybe he was just that bit of fun she'd found on her birthday night at the bachelor auction. But he had become so much more.

He put his hand over hers. "What do you expect the lawyer to say?"

"I don't know," she answered, because she didn't want to admit that she was hoping her father loved her enough to just step aside. But she had a feeling she was going to have to fight to get the right to vote her shares and she knew and expected that she'd have to prove herself. "I think it's going to be hard, but until I hear something it's so much worse. You know how when you're a kid and you hear a noise outside and you're sure it's a monster? That's how I feel right now. Everything seems like there is a monster under the bed. And I know I can fight it, but I'm not sure what kind of fight it's going to be," she said, pulling her arm from Diego and moving to stand next to him.

As much as she took comfort from being near him, she couldn't let herself start to rely on him. She needed to stand on her own. She'd known that all along, but she was still drawn here.

She was a mess. She hadn't felt like this before—never—and it was freaking her out.

"I'm used to having a plan. Every day for the last four years I've been waiting for this moment, but I had no idea what would happen when it came…and waiting even longer like this is just so much worse than you can imagine."

He turned to face her, hands on his lean hips, his hat back on his head so that his eyes were in shadow. "I get it. My brother-in-law Jose was in an airplane crash and for three days we waited to hear about survivors. We knew he'd been cheating—um, that's not for anyone else's ears—but as a family we weren't sure how to feel. I wanted Bianca to have a chance to confront him. But she never got it. So I understand how time can feel like it's moving so slowly and the wait is lasting too long."

She'd had no idea that Bianca's first husband had been unfaithful. The former supermodel was drop-dead gorgeous and one of the sweetest people Pippa had ever met.

"I won't say anything," she reassured him. "I guess you're right that you do understand where I'm coming from."

"I'm here for you, honey," he said, his voice sweet and gentle. And when he used that term of endearment, she felt things that she didn't want to admit to.

"Thank you. That means more than you can know," she said. Her phone pinged, and she looked at it and then back at him.

"Go on. See if it's the email you've been waiting for," he said.

There was a note in his voice that she didn't recognize, but she turned to her phone, picking it up and unlocking it. She'd set an alert for the solicitor's email, so she knew it was from him.

Diego stood there looking out at the pasture and paddock where his prized mares all roamed together. The breeding stock of Arbol Verde were his true assets. He sold some of the mares overseas, especially to clients in the United Arab Emirates. But today, for the first time in his life, the land didn't give him the pleasure it always had and he didn't want to try to process why.

"Okay. I need to talk to him on a secure video phone," she said. She had that edge in her voice that made Diego want to scoop her up and carry her far away so she didn't have to deal with this, but this was exactly where she needed to be.

"You can use my den," he said.

"Thank you."

He led the way into the house, which was cooler than outside but not cold. Given that it was early October, some fallish weather had arrived. This morning when he'd taken his stallion out for a morning run it had been almost cold.

His boot heels echoed on the Spanish tile and he heard the sound of Mona, his housekeeper, working in the kitchen. She was making enchiladas for the ranch hands for dinner and then she had her book club in town this evening.

So he'd be alone.

Unless he could convince Pippa that they should spend the evening together. But that felt like the worst kind of mirage. Pretending that she was his regular, steady girl instead of acknowledging that she was leaving.

"Here it is. Do you want to use my computer for the video chat?" he asked. "You'll probably have a better signal, since it's hardwired to the LAN instead of a Wi-Fi connection."

"Okay," she said. "Thank you."

She tucked a strand of hair behind her ear. Maybe it was his imagination, but her demeanor seemed to have changed since she'd received the email. She stood taller. Her motions were more controlled and the passion and…joie de vivre he always associated with her were tamped down.

He walked over to his desk, which was made of Spanish oak and had been one of the treasures his ancestors had brought with them from Cádiz when they'd come over to this new land. He rubbed his hand along the edge, feeling the past in the wood grain as he always did. Then he pushed his Swedish-designed ergonomic chair back and reached down to log on to his computer. The screen background was one of the photos that they used on the stud farm website, featuring him riding on their prizewinning stallion King Of The Night.

"There you go. I'll be back in the barn if you need me," he said.

He tried to ignore how close she was as he turned to leave. The scent of her flowery perfume wrapped around him and he felt a pang realizing this was her first step toward goodbye. He moved past her and she put her hand on his arm. Her fingers were light against his bicep.

He looked down at her.

"Thank you, Diego," she said again.

"You're welcome, honey."

He walked away before he did something stupid like pull her into his arms and make love to her on his desk, trying to reinforce the bond that had been growing between them since the bachelor auction. He'd never been one of those people who believed in love at first sight and he still wasn't sure he did, but that was what he felt for Pippa, he thought as he stalked out of the house toward the barn.

When he entered the barn, he heard his brother Mauricio talking to Brenda, one of his best trainers.

"Just let him know I stopped by. I didn't want to disturb him, so I left some paperwork on his desk back there," Mauricio said.

"I got it, Mo. I promise I'll tell him that it's there," Brenda said.

"I'm here," Diego said.

"Thank God. This one is acting like I've never been given a message before," Brenda said, full of sass the way she always was. Probably because she had known him and his brothers since they were boys. She'd hired on to the ranch when she'd been eighteen and had watched them all grow up.

"It's not that I don't trust you, Brenda," Mo said with a smile.

"Of course not," she said, turning to walk away. "I have lessons this afternoon, so I need to go and get the horses prepared."

"See you later," Diego said as she walked by him and out of the barn.

"I didn't want to bother you, but the contract came through for the training center property and I know we want to get moving on that project," Mauricio said.

"You're not," Diego said, heading toward his office at the back of the barn.

"Wasn't that Pippa's car in the drive?"

"It was."

He sat down at his desk and drew the folder that Mauricio had left there toward him. He opened it and just stared at the writing on the contract like he'd never read a word before. His mind was swirling with the fact that Pippa was in his den and probably being given the keys to her old life. Paving the very path she needed to leave Texas and return to her old life.

"D?"

"Yeah?"

"Pippa."

Mauricio wasn't going to let this be. And Diego wasn't sure what he was going to say. How was he going to make it seem like it was no big deal that she was leaving when a part of him felt like he would die without her? Dammit, he was acting like a sap. He was stronger than this. He was going to be cool with Mo. And when Pippa left, he was going to get drunk and get over her.

"So?"

"So what? She came by for lunch. I think she's leaving tomorrow."

"Damn. That's—"

"Reality."

"I was going to say that sucks. I'll be back later," Mauricio said after Diego had signed all of the papers and handed them back. "I just have to get this over to the broker."

"You don't have to."

"We're brothers, D. Of course I do."

Pippa had never felt more nervous than when Diego walked out of the den and she took a seat in front of his computer. She double-checked the number in the email from the solicitor and then typed it in. He was expecting her video call.

As soon as the camera pop-up window opened on the screen, she took a good look at herself. She used to wear a bit more makeup and look more polished, but objectively she thought she looked okay. She smoothed her hair and then made sure that the necklace her mother had given her when she turned ten was visible in the opening at the front of her shirt.

She took a deep breath before hitting the connect button.

The solicitor Simon Rooney answered the call on the first ring.

"Philippa, we are so happy you were able to call this afternoon. I have your father in the other room along with Giles Montgomery," Simon said. Giles was House of Hamilton's COO, she knew from her reading up on the company.

"I'm just happy that you were able to verify my identity so quickly," she said.

"I am, too. Before I bring the others in, I wanted to let you know that your father will not sign off on the transfer of shares until he's seen you in person. Unfortunately, he's willing to take legal action to support his position, which would tie things up in the courts whether he has a case or not. You had mentioned in your first email that you were hopeful of voting your shares at the board meeting in November. We need you back in the UK as soon as possible for that to happen."

"I'm ready to leave," she said, not quite sure that was the absolute truth because she had so many friends here. She would miss them all...especially Diego. But this was what she wanted. "Also, I have a private jet from my friends the Caruthers at my disposal, so as soon as my renewed passport arrives I'm ready."

"Good. I've sent all of your documentation to the address you gave. It should arrive before six p.m. your time."

"Thank you, Mr. Rooney," she said.

"You're very welcome. Now, I'm going to bring your father in first. I'm not sure how much you have been following the House of Hamilton."

"Very closely," she admitted. "Or as closely as I can, being a world away. I've read about the rumored infighting between Father and the board."

"It's more than a rumor, I'm afraid. So Giles won't speak to you while your father is in the room. I'm afraid your reappearance comes at a very crucial time for the company. But I'll let your father and Giles explain their positions to you," Simon said.

"Thank you. Mr. Rooney—"

"Call me Simon," he said.

"Very well. Do you work for me or the company or my father?" she asked.

"I work for you," he said. "I hope once you've seen everything I've done for your trust over the last four years you will be happy with my work. Why do you ask?"

"I just wanted to know who was on my side," she said.

"I am."

"Okay, I'm ready to see my father first."

Simon nodded and disappeared from the screen. She heard the sound of a door opening and the rumble of voices.

Her palms started sweating and she realized she was breathing too shallowly. She closed her eyes and remembered the way that Diego had held her in his arms last night when they'd sat in front of the fire. Remembered how safe and confident she'd felt in that moment. Then she opened her eyes to see her father sitting where Simon had been.

He looked older, she thought. Of course, he was four years older, but he seemed to have aged a lot more than that. His face, which had always been thin, now seemed gaunt, and his blue eyes were duller than she remembered. His previously salt-and-pepper hair was now all gray.

When he saw her on his screen, he stared at her face. Probably processing everything, she thought, the same way she was.

"Father."

"Pippa," he said, his voice just as low and rumbly as it always had been. For a moment she was torn between the memories of the man who'd tried to force her to marry and the man who'd read her bedtime stories when she'd been very young.

"It's good to see you again," she said, her old manners coming to the fore.

"I find that very hard to believe given that you've been hiding from me for four years," he said.

"You gave me no choice," she said. "I didn't feel like I had any options."

He inclined his head. "I've only ever had the best interests of you and your mother at heart. I thought she would have wanted you married to a good man who would give you the life you'd always known."

Pippa felt the sting of tears at the mention of her mother. "I don't think Mum would have wanted me to marry a man who didn't love me and who was a stranger."

"We can agree to disagree on that. So you're coming back. What does that mean?"

"I will be voting my shares and taking my place on the board of directors at House of Hamilton. I think we are just waiting for your signature on the paperwork," she said.

"We are. I wanted to make sure it was you. I've had

men looking for you for all these years. A few times we've had some false leads."

"Now you know it's really me."

"I do know. I will sign the papers once you return to London," he said, standing up, and she hugged herself around her chest, rubbing the goose bumps on her arms.

"Father?"

"Yes?" he asked.

"Nothing," she said. What was she going to say? Admit that she was glad to see him? Ask him if he was happy she was alive? There was no answer that would satisfy her.

He walked away from the screen and Giles Montgomery got on the call next. The COO said he was excited for her to take a temporary role in the company, and once she proved herself, to take a more permanent one.

"Pippa, I'm so glad that you're coming back. I am interested in starting discussions with you to catch you up on where we are today."

"Thank you," she said. "I'm interested in taking an active role and not just being a figurehead."

"We'd like that, too. We've been at a standstill while you were missing and we are all eager to start moving the company forward again."

"I am, too, and have a few ideas that I'd like to bring forward," Pippa said.

"When you land in London, we can start our discussions, but for now I thought you might want to know more about the directors and where we stand as a company. I've asked Simon to forward you a packet with all of this information."

"Thank you," she said. "I was planning to return to the UK at the end of October."

"We need you back before that," Giles said. "There's a labor dispute with our service staff, and now that you're back, if we had an emergency board meeting, we could resolve the issue regarding pensions."

The call ended almost two hours after it had started. Her back aching, she stood up and stretched. She walked out of the den and down the hall to the family room, where she found Diego sitting in a large leather armchair watching the doorway.

"Is it settled?"

She nodded. "I'm going to leave tomorrow."

Eleven

Diego sat there watching her as she stood on the threshold. Her arms were wrapped around her waist and she was looking…shaken.

"My father…he was all business," she said. "I guess I should have expected it. I think I've spent too much time in Cole's Hill around the Carutherses. I sort of expected the bond of family to be stronger than it ever was."

Diego stood up and walked over to her, pulling her into his arms. She stood there stiffly for a few moments and then hugged him back, burying her nose in the center of his chest. He rubbed his hands up and down her back and tried to tell himself he wasn't turned on by her, but the fact was any time he held her or thought about her he reacted this way. But that wasn't what this moment was about, so he shifted his hips so that she wouldn't notice.

"So you're leaving tomorrow, then?"

"Yes," she said, pushing away from him. He let her go. "If I can use the Caruthers jet like Nate has offered. I just have to double-check that. My passport documents are being delivered to the Rockin' C today." She rubbed her hands up and down her arms. "I have so much to do."

She really did, and not a lot of time to get it done. Diego mentally went over his schedule for the next week and assigned most of the tasks to different people who worked for him. If he did some careful maneuvering, he might be able to take a week off.

"I know this is spur-of-the-moment," he said, "but do you want me to come with you to London?"

She tipped her head to the side. Her gray eyes met his and her lips parted. "Can you do that?"

"It will take a little bit of juggling in my schedule, but yes, I can do that."

"Oh, Diego, yes, please. I'd love to have you come with me."

"Then I will. I need to make some calls and go and talk to my hands," he said. "Do you need me to do anything else?"

"Not right now," she said. "Are you sure you want to do this?"

No, he wasn't, but he didn't want to say goodbye to her now and like this. She had other things on her mind and he cared about her. More than he wanted to think he could. But the truth was, no woman had ever dominated his thoughts and feelings the way she was…well, aside from his sister or his mom.

He might not be the smartest of men when it came to the opposite sex. But something his father had said to him when he was a teenager and dealing with his first breakup had stuck with him. His dad had told him to never let a good woman slip away until he was sure they weren't meant to be together.

"I'm positive. Do you need to head back to the Rockin' C right now?"

"I… Why?"

"I have to talk to my staff and then pack. Frankly, I have no idea what to bring to London," he said.

"How about you go and talk to your staff and I'll lay out some clothes for you before you go? It will be cold and rainy and it's not unheard of for it to snow in October."

"Snow? What have I gotten myself into?"

"It's not too late to change your mind," she said.

He walked over to her and caressed her cheek because being this close to her and not touching her was nearly impossible. He ran his finger down around the back of her neck, bringing his mouth to hers and kissing her.

"Yes, it is," he said when he broke the kiss. "I gave you my word. And to a Velasquez a promise is a promise."

She nodded.

"That means a lot to me. I mean, I can do this on my own. I'm a total 'hashtag girlboss,'" she said, making air quotes, "but it's nice to know I don't have to."

"I know where you're coming from even though I'm not a 'hashtag' anything," he said with a wink. "Just make a list of things I should pack, and then if you don't mind I'll come over to your place tonight. That way I'll be ready to go when you are."

"That sounds great," she said.

She turned and walked down the hall to his bedroom, and he watched her go for a minute thinking of the things he should be doing but knowing there was only one thing he wanted.

Pippa.

In his bed for the last time.

The depth of the need he felt for her surprised him and that was the last thing he wanted to dwell on. He wanted this to be physical. He was running out of moments like this.

Moments when she was his.

"I thought you had things to do," she said.

"I do," he replied. "At the top of that list is you."

"Me?"

"Unless you don't want me."

She shook her head as she leaned against the door that lead to his walk-in closet. "Don't be foolish. I will always want you."

He hoped that was true, but he knew she was leaving and going back to her real life. Soon the rancher from Cole's Hill would be a memory. He had no idea what her future held, but he was pretty damned sure it didn't involve a long-distance affair with him.

And that made him angry and sad at the same time. He had no idea how to ask her to stay. He knew he had no right to. She had to focus on returning to her old life and claiming what she'd walked away from, but it was what he wanted.

"Diego?"

He shook his head. He couldn't talk. Not right now. At this moment he needed his woman in his arms.

He pulled her into an embrace, and her breath caught as he lifted her off her feet and carried her into his bedroom, setting her down at the edge of the bed. The fabric of her dress was gauzy and soft under his fingers but not as supple as her skin.

The navy color of her dress made for a striking contrast with her blond hair and creamy skin. He found the zipper at the side of the dress and slowly drew it down the side of her body, watching as it parted and each inch of her skin was revealed.

She lifted her arms up, twining them around his neck as he pushed one of his hands into the opening, caressing her and then skimming his fingers along her back until he could reach the clasp of her bra. He undid it with one hand.

He felt her fingers on his chest, slowly pulling apart the buttons of his shirt. He heard the pop of each one as she freed him and then pushed the shirt open and down his arms. The buttons at the wrists held the fabric in place and she carefully undid each of them. He let his shirt fall to the floor.

Leaning forward, he felt the brush of her hair against his torso and the warmth of her lips as she nibbled at his pecs and then found the scar and tattoo, tracing it with her tongue. He couldn't help the growl that escaped him as he felt the sharpness of her teeth against his muscles as she nipped at him.

He could only watch her as she slowly moved down his body. His jeans were getting tighter and tighter by the moment. He watched her tongue his nipple and his hips jerked forward as her hand moved over the button fly of his jeans.

He shifted against her, lifting and holding her with one arm under her hips. She put her hands on either side of his face and their eyes met. He wanted to think he saw the same affection and desperation in her gaze as he felt deep in his soul.

Her mouth came down on his hard, their tongues tangled and he realized he was desperately hungry for her. That there was no way he was going to be able to fill that hunger in just a week.

He pulled his mouth from hers, letting her slide down the front of his body. Once she was standing in front of him again, he pulled her arms out of her dress and pushed it down her torso. It caught at her hips, which were pressed to his. He ran his finger along the edge of her matching navy-colored bra where it met the creamy globe of her breast.

She trembled against him as her hips came into contact with the tip of his erection. He pulled her bra away from her skin and down her arms, tossing it toward his shirt on the floor.

Then he pulled her to him, letting their naked chests rub against each other. He loved the pebbly hardness of her nipples against his chest. He rubbed his hands up and down her back and lowered his head to the crook of her neck, where the scent of her perfume was stronger.

He felt her hands rubbing down his shoulders, her nails scraping down his back, and then she forced her hand between their bodies, tracing each of the muscles that ribbed his chest as she let her fingers move lower toward the fastening of his jeans.

His heart was beating so fast that he felt his pulse in his erection. He was seconds away from losing control and coming in his jeans, but he had to hold back. He wanted this time to last.

She stroked his shaft, running her hands over the ridge of it through his jeans. Everything inside him quieted and all he could think about was her naked on his bed. He needed to be inside her.

Now.

He pushed her backward and she fell onto the bed. He undid the top buttons of his jeans as he put one thigh between her parted legs. He patted her through the fabric of her underwear. She moaned his name and her legs parted even farther as he brushed the backs of his knuckles over her mound.

The lace fabric was warm and wet. He slipped one finger under the material and didn't pause for even a second as their eyes met.

She watched him through half-closed lids and sucked her lower lip into her mouth as her hips arched and thrust against him. It was only the fact that he wanted her to come at least once before he entered her that made it possible for him to keep himself in check. That and the tightness of his jeans.

She shifted against him and he pushed his finger into her, teasing her with feathering touches.

"Diego…" she said, her voice breathless and airy.

"Hmm?"

"This is nice, but I want…"

"This?" he asked, pushing his finger deep inside her.

"Oh…oh, yessssss," she said. Her hips rocked against his finger for a few strokes. He wanted to get her to the place where she was once again caught on the edge and needing more.

"Diego, please."

He used his thumb to trace around her clit. She rocked harder against his hand, her hips bucking frantically against him. She arched her back, which drew his eyes to her full breasts and hard nipples. He shifted over her on the bed and caught one in his lips, suckling her deeply as he continued to finger her. He kept his thumb on her clit as he worked his fingers deep inside her body until she threw her head back and called his name.

He felt the tightening of her body against his fingers. She kept rocking against him for a few more minutes and then collapsed into his arms.

He kept his fingers inside her body and slowly started building her toward the pinnacle again. He tipped her head toward his so he could taste her mouth. Her lips opened over his. He told himself to take it slow, to make this last. He didn't want this to end, needing to prolong their ecstasy as long as possible. Because once they left the bedroom, she would begin the final process of moving away from him, even if he was going to accompany her to London for a week.

But Pippa didn't want slow. Her nails dug into his shoulders and she shifted so that when she arched her back the hard points of her nipples brushed against his chest.

He held her with his forearm along her spine and bit lightly at the column of her neck as he used his other hand to cup her backside.

Her eyes closed and she exhaled hard as he fondled her. She moaned a sweet sound that he leaned up to capture in his mouth. She tipped her head, allowing him access. She held his shoulders and moved on him, rubbing her center over his erection.

He unbuttoned his pants, freeing himself. He then reached for the box of condoms he kept in the nightstand drawer. He fumbled for the box, finally getting one out, and shifted back to remove it from the foil wrapper and put it on. When he was done, he came back to her and put his hands on either side of her hips as he shifted his erection so that he was poised at the entrance of her body.

He scraped his fingernail over her nipple and she shuddered. He pushed her back a little bit so he could see her. Her breasts were bare, nipples distended and begging for his mouth. He lowered his head and suckled.

He kept trying to make this last, taking it slow as he slid his body up over her so that they were pressed together. He lowered his forehead to hers and their eyes met, their breaths mingling, and he shifted his hips and plunged into her. He stopped once he was buried hilt-deep inside her and held his breath.

He wanted to remember the feel of her underneath him and wrapped around him forever.

He wanted her to remember him, as well. Long after he'd returned to Cole's Hill and his lonely bedroom and she was back at the helm of her family business.

He needed to know that she wouldn't be able to forget him.

So he claimed her, claimed Pippa as his, even if it was only in his soul that he could acknowledge it.

He thrust into her sweet, tight body. Her eyes were closed, her hips moving subtly against him, and when he blew on her nipple, he saw gooseflesh spread down her body.

He loved the way she reacted to his mouth on her. He sucked on the skin at the base of her neck as he thrust all the way home, sheathing his entire length in her body. He knew he was leaving a mark with his mouth and that pleased him. He wanted her to remember this moment and what they had done when she was alone later.

He kept kissing and rubbing, pinching her nipples until her hands clenched in his hair and she rocked her hips harder against his length. He lifted his hips, thrusting up against her.

"Come with me," he said.

She nodded. Her eyes widened with each inch he gave her. She clutched at his hips as he continued thrusting. Her eyes were half-closed, her head tipped back.

He leaned down and caught one of her nipples in his teeth, scraping very gently. She started to tighten around him. Her hips moved faster, demanding more, but he kept the pace slow, steady, building the pleasure between them.

He suckled her nipple and rotated his hips to catch her pleasure point with each thrust. He felt her hands clenching in his hair as she threw her head back, hair brushing over his arm where he held her.

He varied his thrusts, finding a rhythm that would draw out the tension at the base of his spine. Something that would make his time in her body, wrapped in her silky limbs, last forever.

"Hold on to me tightly."

She did as he asked, and he rolled them over so that she was on top of him. He pushed her legs up against her body so that he could thrust deeper. So that she was open and vulnerable to him.

"Come now, Pippa," he said.

She nodded, and he felt her body tighten. Then she scraped her nails down his back and clutched his buttocks, drawing him in. Blood roared in his ears as he felt everything in his world center to this one woman.

He called her name as he came. She tightened around him and he looked into her eyes as he kept thrusting. He saw her eyes widen and felt the minute contractions of her body around his as she was consumed by her orgasm.

He rotated his hips against her until she stopped rocking. Then he rolled to his side holding her in his arms until the sweat dried on both of their bodies. Neither of them said a word and after a short time had passed he got up and carried her to the shower.

He made love to her again in the shower and then forced himself to leave the house to talk to his staff. Otherwise he knew he would beg her to stay.

Twelve

"I wish I could go with you," Kinley said as she stood next to Pippa's closet.

"Me, too," she said. "I had no idea I'd accumulated all this stuff."

"Don't worry about that. Just pack what you need. I will get this all boxed up and sent to you."

Kinley came over and hugged her tightly. "I thought I was prepared to let you go, but I'm not. I mean, I still haven't decided what to do about Nate and having another baby. And you're the only one I can bitch about him to because you know I love him and am just being a spaz because I'm scared."

Pippa hugged her friend back. "I feel the same way. I haven't even had a chance to tell you about Diego or how cold my dad was on the call… We should have a standing date on video chat."

Kinley stepped back and sat down on the edge of Pippa's bed. "I love that. Let's do it on Saturday. That way Penny can chat with you, too. She's mad at you, by the way. Told me that I could tell you bye-bye from her."

Pippa's heart broke a little hearing that. "I wish there was some other way, but I can't stay."

"I know. We both know it. Even Penny. She made you this," Kinley said, going over to her big Louis Vuitton Neverfull bag and retrieving a small stack of papers that was bound with yarn. She handed it to Pippa.

"It's a book about the P girls," she said, looking down at the cover, which had a hand-drawn picture of two stick-figure girls, one with red hair and one with blond hair. She hugged the book to her and blinked to keep from crying.

"Look at it later," Kinley said. "We've been working on it since you told me you were leaving."

"Thank you, Kin. You're closer to me than a sister and I can't help wondering what a mess my life would have been if it wasn't for you," Pippa said.

"It was no big thing," Kinley said. "We found each other."

"We did," Pippa said, going to her dresser and picking up the box she'd placed there earlier. "This is for you."

"You didn't have to get me anything, but thank you."

Kinley opened the box. It contained two matching wire necklaces with pendant charms that Pippa had

made over the summer during her class at the Cole's
Hill Art Center. She'd known that she would be leav-
ing in the fall and had wanted to create mementos for
Kinley and Penny. "The smaller one is for the imp."

"We are going to miss you so much. These are so
perfect," Kinley said.

There was a knock on the door before she could say
anything else. "I'll go get it. You finish packing."

Pippa sat down on the bed after Kinley left and
wrapped her arms around her waist. Who would have
thought leaving her pretend life would be this hard? But
then again it wasn't pretend. Everything about her time
with Kinley and Penny had been real. They'd been so
young and scared when they'd found each other.

She was proud of how far they'd each come. But she
knew that as hard as it was to say goodbye she couldn't
stay here.

Someone knocked on the wall near the entrance to
her bedroom and she looked up to see Diego standing
there. He held a small bag in one hand and his Stetson
in the other.

"Is that all you packed?"

"Nah," he said. "I left my suitcase downstairs. Kinley
said to remind you that the jet would be ready whenever you are. I suggested that you might want to leave
tonight."

She hadn't thought about that. She'd been sort of
pushing off the moment when she'd have to get on the
plane and head to England. "Yeah, that makes more
sense. I guess I'm dreading seeing my father and not
really sure what's waiting for me."

"Well, I'm just along for the ride, so whatever you decide is fine with me."

He might have been along for the ride, but only temporarily. She knew he was a crutch she was going to have to let go of. But she was glad she'd have a week with him. Diego couldn't stay longer than that. He'd told her earlier that he had a sire coming in two weeks and it was too important to trust to any of his staff.

"Let me finish this up and then I'll be ready to go. Will you let Kinley and Nate know that we'll leave tonight? I should be ready to go in an hour."

"Sounds good to me. I'll drive us and leave my truck at the airport so when I come back… I'll be able to get home."

The weight of that lay between them as their eyes met. Then he turned and walked down the stairs. She realized how much she was giving up to reclaim her heritage. It made her mad that she'd ever had to leave it, because she realized that a part of her wanted this life she could call her own here in Cole's Hill. But another part of her wasn't willing to let her father win. The man who couldn't tell her he missed her and had looked at her like she'd irritated him.

She knew Diego understood, which made it that much harder as she walked out of the house next to him to say goodbye to everyone. The entire Caruthers clan had shown up. Little Benito gave her a sweet hug and at the last moment Penny came running outside and threw herself in Pippa's arms.

"Take care, imp."

"You, too, Pippy."

She put Penny down and got into Diego's truck, turning her head toward the rolling pastures so she could pretend she wasn't crying and that a part of her soul wasn't suddenly barren and sad.

She was nervous. He could tell by the way she kept looking out the window, but he had no words to comfort her. He knew her father had been as cold as ice on the call. But Diego had no idea what to expect when they landed in London. The private plane that the Caruthers family owned had been a boon. A chance for them to be alone as they returned to her uncertain future.

Even though he was accompanying her they both knew his stay in the UK could only be temporary. He had Arbol Verde, which he couldn't walk away from. And even if he was willing to contemplate that, he wasn't a citizen, for one thing, and he wasn't sure he wanted to live in a cold, foggy city. Though knowing that he'd have Pippa by his side was almost enough to tempt him to try.

He swirled around the mint he'd popped into his mouth at takeoff and looked over at her. She sighed again. She wore a faux-fur jacket around her shoulders. They were the only passengers on the plane. The pilot and copilot were up front, but it was only the two of them in the back.

"Are you wearing panties?" he asked.

She shifted in her seat and looked over at him. "I am. Why?"

"Go take them and your blouse off. Come back with just your fur coat on."

"Diego—"

"Do it, baby. It will take your mind off whatever is waiting for you when we land," he said.

She licked her lips. "I... Okay."

She got up slowly. He'd expected her to go to the bathroom at the back of the plane, but instead she lifted one of her legs encased in a knee-high stiletto boot. "Can you get that zipper?"

He nodded, stretching his legs out as he started to get hard. He lowered the zipper and then drew her foot out of the boot, setting it on the empty chair next to his. Then he helped her with the other one. When she pulled her slim-fitting skirt slowly up her legs, he saw that she was wearing garterless thigh-high stockings. She held her skirt up at her waist.

"Will you give me a hand, Diego?" she asked coyly.

He put his hands on either side of the waistband of her small bikini-style underpants, letting the backs of his fingers brush over her pubic area before slowly drawing the cloth down her thighs, making sure to spread his fingers out so he could caress each inch of her skin. He pushed the tiny ivory-colored panties down to her feet and she stepped out of them. He picked them up and put them in his pocket.

She arched one eyebrow at him and he just smiled at her.

She slipped the coat off her arms and set it on the padded chair she'd been sitting on and then slowly pulled the tails of her fitted shirt out of the waistband of her skirt. She undid the buttons one by one. The curves of her breasts pushed up by her demi bra became visible. When she had the buttons of her shirt undone, she slipped it off and turned around, bending over to put her blouse in her carry-on bag.

But honestly all he could see was the heart-shaped curve of her ass. He reached out, tracing the seam running down the center of her skirt. She pushed her hips back toward him and he groaned again. She stood up and turned, still wearing the bra, which shoved her breasts up and brought his gaze to them. He saw the tiniest hint of her nipple peeking out of the top of one cup as she reached between her breasts and undid the clasp. She took the bra off and held it out to him. "Do you want this, too? It'd be a shame to break up the set."

He took it and shoved it in his laptop bag and she stood there, her shoulders back, breasts bare, proud and confident. This was the Pippa he wanted to see. Not the one who'd been so worried a few moments earlier.

"Are you sure about the fur coat?" she asked.

"I am. I think you'll like the feel of it against your nipples," he said.

He took it from her chair and stood up, holding it out for her. She turned away from him and reached back to slip her arms into the sleeves. Once she had it on, he pulled her back against him, wrapping his arms around her and cupping each of her breasts in his hands. He kissed her neck as he plucked at her nipples, feeling them harden under his touch.

Then he drew the satin-lined coat closed and rubbed the fabric over her engorged nipples. She gasped, shifting her hips back and rubbing her butt against his erection.

He bit lightly at the spot where her neck met her shoulder and then slipped one hand inside the opening of her coat to tease her nipple while he continued to suckle her neck.

She moaned and shifted in his arms as he rubbed the ridge of his erection against her backside, fitting himself nicely against her. He reached lower, drawing up the fabric of her skirt with his free hand until he felt the tops of her thighs where the elastic at the top of her hose met her smooth skin. He traced one finger around the edge of the fabric and then drew his hand higher, rubbing the seam where her thigh and hip met.

Then he brushed over her mound with his fingers. She moaned, putting her hand over his, and he quickly changed their positions, putting her hand under his and using her fingers to part her slick folds.

"Open up for me," he whispered into her ear, and she shivered against him as she nodded.

He touched her exposed clit lightly with his finger, just tapped it as gently as he could. With each touch she let out a soft moan. He continued to increase the pressure of his touch, rubbing his finger around her sensitive bud and then tapping it again and again until she was writhing in his arms. She clawed at his wrist with her free hand, arching her back and turning her head to find his mouth. Their tongues mingled and she sucked hard on his as he plunged one finger deep inside her. He felt her tighten around it as she rocked her hips against his hand and cried out with the force of her orgasm.

He lifted her off her feet and sat down in his large chair, holding her on his lap. She curled her head into his chest as he kept his finger between her legs, thrusting in and out until she calmed in his arms.

Curled in Diego's arms wearing only her skirt and a fur coat, she never would have guessed she'd feel so safe. And dare she say it, so accepted.

He made her feel so warm and whole. No one else who'd known her given name, known of her life and fortune in London, had made her feel like none of it mattered, that she was enough. No one before Diego.

She reached between their bodies and pushed his zipper farther down until she could fit her hand into his pants. He was still rock hard, and as she awkwardly maneuvered herself until she could straddle him, she felt a drop of moisture on the tip of his erection. She captured it with her finger and brought it to her lips, licking it off. He groaned and shifted around. "Can you reach my wallet?"

He lifted his hips off the seat.

She felt her way around to his back pocket and found his wallet, struggling to pull it out and almost falling off his lap, which made her yelp and him laugh.

She handed it to him. He opened it and took out the condom she'd seen him put in there earlier. "What if you can't find any in England?" she joked.

"I think we'll manage," he said with a wink.

She thought they would, too. At least while it lasted between them.

At least for one more week.

As he put the condom on with one hand, she looked down at him, totally clothed except for his naked erection. She loved the idea of how respectable they might look to anyone who saw them when they were out together in public, but that secretly she was on the edge.

She could lie to herself and pretend that this thing with Diego was an affair, but she knew it was much more. He brought out parts of her that she'd never explored or thought about exploring.

Putting her hands on his shoulders, she shifted around until she could feel him at the entrance of her body and she shifted forward. "My favorite kind of ride," she said, putting her hands on either side of his face. She reached between them and took his erection in her hand, bringing him closer to her. Spreading her legs wider so that she was totally open to him.

Their eyes met as she slid all the way down on him, embedding him deep within her body. She let her head fall back and felt his breath on her breast a moment before his mouth closed over her nipple. She shivered and wrapped her arms around his shoulders, drawing him closer to her as she started to move on him.

He bent down to capture the tip of her breast between his lips. He sucked her deep in his mouth, his teeth lightly scraping against her sensitive flesh. His hand played at her other breast, arousing her, making her arch against him in need.

He lifted his head; the tips of her breasts were damp from his mouth and very tight. He rubbed his chest over them before sliding even deeper into her body.

She eased her hands down his back, rubbing his spine as he pushed himself up into her. She stared deep into his eyes, making her feel like their souls were meeting.

She was hoping he'd forgive her because she hadn't wanted to go back to London on her own.

"Pippa. Now."

His voice set off a chain reaction and she arched against him again, head falling back as her climax ripped through her body. He kept driving up into her and his hands tangled in her hair, bringing their mouths together as she came harder than before. She felt him thrusting into her and rode him hard until he grunted and she felt him jerk as he came.

She collapsed on top of him and he held her with his arms inside her fur coat, his hand rubbing up and down her back. She drifted off to sleep in his arms.

He held her closely knowing this was the last moment that they had before she would have to be Philippa Hamilton-Hoff, billionaire heiress and head of a legacy company that had been floundering in the last four years. He wondered if he'd made a big mistake by saying he'd come with her to London, but he knew that there had been no other choice for him.

He wasn't ready to let her go.

Not yet.

Thirteen

Diego put on his shearling coat as they exited the immigration area at the private airport where the Caruthers jet had landed. It was overcast and a light rain fell. The pilot and copilot were going to stay in the UK for a week and fly him back on Saturday. Diego was grateful for that, though he could have flown commercial and wouldn't have minded.

"I'm so nervous. Simon said he was sending a car for us and I'm not sure if my dad will be at the town house that I inherited in Belgravia," Pippa said.

He put his hand on the small of her back and walked beside her until she came to an abrupt halt. A severe-looking man stood before her, blocking her path.

"Father."

"Philippa."

Diego looked at the older man dressed in a suit with an overcoat. There was someone next to him who held an umbrella over his head to keep him from getting wet.

"Hello, sir. I'm Diego Velasquez."

"Mr. Velasquez, are you my daughter's… What are you to my daughter?" he asked.

"Her friend," Diego said.

"I wasn't expecting to see you today," Pippa said to her father.

"I asked Simon to keep me posted. I needed to catch you up on where our family stands as far as the decisions that Giles Montgomery has been making," her father said. "Perhaps we can discuss it over breakfast?"

Diego noticed that her face went very still and hard. "I can't, Father. I have a meeting with Giles this afternoon and Diego and I were hoping to get settled at the town house before then."

He nodded. "So you've already made up your mind? Giles has turned you against me."

"Father, that's not what happened. I've had four years to think about what you would do when I saw you again and—" she broke off, realizing she was getting very emotional. Had she lost her British stiff upper lip after years of living in the United States?

Diego rubbed her back and her father reached over and squeezed her hand.

"Me, too."

Just those two words. Clipped and not very emotional. But there was a look in his eyes that told her she might be missing something.

She looked at Diego and he subtly nodded. She turned back to her father.

"Okay. Let's have breakfast and you can tell me what you've been doing."

Her father looked relieved and nodded. "I'll give you both time to settle in and perhaps we can meet at the Costa near your town house in two hours. Will that do?"

"Yes."

Pippa's father turned and walked to the waiting Bentley and Pippa looked over at him. The misty rain had coated her hair and she looked cold. But for the first time he saw a sign of stubbornness in her expression.

"I can't tell if he was trying to manipulate me or if he feels something for me. But if he thinks he can manipulate me, it's not going to be easy."

"I believe that," Diego said as they were approached by a man in a black suit.

"Ms. Hamilton-Hoff?"

"Yes."

"I'm your driver, Dylan. And I'm here to take you to your town house, and of course wherever you want to go," he said. "Is that your luggage?"

He pointed to the three suitcases stacked near the curb.

"Yes, it is."

"Let's get you both in the car and then I'll see to it," he said.

Diego followed Pippa to the car and got in the back seat next to her. She didn't say anything and for once he had no idea what to do. She was giving off don't-touch-me vibes and he was smart enough to just sit next to her quietly.

"Sorry about that. I think my dad is going to be difficult about everything," she said.

"It's okay," he said. He felt bad that her father hadn't tried to hug her or anything like that. But maybe that was just some sort of British stiff upper lip that he wasn't used to. He only knew that both his father and mother had driven out to Arbol Verde to hug him and tell him to be safe before he'd left for this trip. And it was only a week. If he'd been gone for four years, he knew that his parents would start off with a lot more than conversation about the family business when they were reunited.

"He looked like he couldn't care less that I was back. I mean, I thought maybe it was because of the video chat and him being restrained because he was in Simon's office the last time…but no, he really doesn't like me," Pippa said.

Diego reached his arm along the back seat and pulled her into the curve of his body. "Everyone shows emotion in a different way."

She pulled back and glared at him. "Really? Do you think there was a shred of emotion in him?"

"No," he said. "But I don't know him. You do. You said that after your mother died he kept you in boarding schools. Maybe his way of dealing with emotion is to lock it away… I don't know."

"I don't, either," she said. "I know that was bitchy. Sorry. I'm tired and everything here is harder than I thought it would be."

And they hadn't even left the airport yet. He wondered if he'd made a mistake in coming with her now. He knew that his purpose was to help her, but it felt like the next few days were going to be hard and he didn't have anything to bring to the table. It wasn't like her family owned a horse ranch or were breeders. They were jewelers to the queen. That was a completely different world than the one he lived in.

And as the driver got behind the wheel and started to take them to her house, he realized how different this world was. He had to mentally adjust to driving on the opposite side of the road; for the first few minutes, he kept feeling like the driver wasn't paying attention. But as they got on the M25, it really struck him that he definitely wasn't in Cole's Hill anymore. There were no trucks, just luxury sedans and hatchbacks. When they exited the highway and headed toward Pippa's town house, he couldn't help but notice how pristine the Georgian rowhouses were. And there wasn't a lot of space like he was used to. He was out of his element and he knew that caring for Pippa wasn't going to be enough.

When they entered her town house, he began to get a real sense of how wealthy Pippa was. It was filled with antiques, the kind of place his mom would love. She had decorated her condo in Houston very similarly.

Pippa immediately showed him to their room and told him he could sleep.

"Where are you going?"

"I have to meet my father, and then I have the thing with Giles, but I should be back for dinner."

"Okay. I'll go with you," he said.

"I think you'd find that boring," she said.

And she didn't want him there.

"Okay. What time for dinner?"

"Seven," she said.

It was just 10:00 a.m. now.

"Thanks," she said, giving him a kiss that brushed his cheek before she left to meet her father and her attorney.

Diego watched her go, sitting in a house that wasn't his. It was about 4:00 a.m. back in Cole's Hill, so Diego texted his brother to call him when he was awake. While he was here, he needed to stay busy because otherwise he would feel like he'd followed Pippa for reasons he didn't want to admit.

He wanted her in his life. He cared about her. But she wasn't in any position for that kind of relationship, he realized. She was focused on claiming her heritage and he had to hope he was strong enough to support her while she did it.

Mauricio called him when he woke up. Talking to his brother made him feel better.

"D, I heard that there's a riding stable not too far from where you're staying. In Surrey, I think. It's the kind of operation we've been talking about setting up here."

"I'll go and check it out. Send me the details."

"I will. So how's jolly old England?"

"Cold," he said. And lonely. But he wasn't about to say that to his brother.

"Good thing you have Pippa with you to warm you up."

"Good thing," he said, ending the call after that. He had a plan. He called the riding stable in Surrey and set up an appointment for the next day. Then he got a text from Bartolome Figueras, a friend of his who was a jet-setting polo player, who wanted his opinion on a horse he was going to buy. When he texted the photo, Diego realized they were both in the UK and made plans to meet with him later in the week. Now he had something to do for the rest of the week other than sit around and wait for his heiress.

Six days of being in London and she was still trying to catch up to everything. She'd gotten home late every night and spent a few minutes trying to listen to Diego tell her about his day before she'd fallen asleep. Sometimes he made love to her in the middle of the night, but mostly she was too tired. When her alarm went off every morning, they both groaned, and she dashed out of bed and to the House of Hamilton's offices on Bond Street, where a uniformed doorman with a top hat always greeted her by name when she arrived at their showroom before going up to the office housed on the fifth floor.

She wasn't even close to getting to design jewelry or talk about new revenue streams. The power struggle between her father and the board had taken its toll on the company and she was caught in the middle. Now that she was back she had to make some hard decisions and she was ready to make them. From a standpoint of emotional revenge it would be easy, but from a business standpoint it was harder.

Some of her father's ideas were actually quite good, but all of the infighting had made the board dismiss them out of hand. On top of that, her father's arrogant ways made it harder for her to side with him.

She needed someone to talk to, but when she tried to get Diego to come meet her for lunch, he'd told her he was on his way to meet some breeders in Hampshire. She felt a little annoyed but then reminded herself he'd come with her because he'd wanted to and, really, she couldn't expect him to just sit around while she wasn't there. But a part of her—the tired and unsure part— was annoyed that he hadn't.

"My meeting is at ten and according to the GPS I should be able to get back to London by two. Do you want to meet then?" Diego asked her on the phone.

"I can't. I have a meeting that starts at two fifteen," she said.

"We could talk while I'm driving. Except that this thing keeps trying to take me down narrow single-lane roads. I think there is something wrong with the mapping app on my phone. I'm going to have Alejandro look at my phone. He's a genius with apps."

Pippa didn't really have time to chat like this. "I think that's just the way the roads are out that way. I'll talk to you later. Don't forget we have dinner tonight with the board. It's black tie. If you don't have—"

"I'm not a country bumpkin, Pippa. I can figure out black tie. Are you coming home first or should I meet you at the venue?" he asked.

There was a tone in his voice that made him sound like a stranger. It wasn't something that she'd ever felt with Diego before. Even when they'd been meeting at the coffee shop and exchanging small talk, he'd never seemed so aloof. "I'm going to try to make it home."

"Okay. I'll be ready when you get there," he said.

"Diego?"

"Yes?"

"Thank you for coming with me," she said. She knew this week wasn't turning out the way either of them had anticipated and he was due to head back to Cole's Hill on Saturday. Two days from now.

"You're welcome. I'm sorry that everything that comes along with your inheritance is harder than you anticipated."

She was, too. She had expected this to be hard, but not this hard. In fact, she was surprised that her father wasn't even the biggest obstacle she had to surmount in taking control of the company. But she also realized that for years now, she'd had a fantasy about her return: that she'd just waltz back in, present her jewelry designs and make her suggestion for a wedding line, and they'd all applaud her. Things would be smooth, as though she'd never run away or had a power struggle with her father.

But coming back to the House of Hamilton wasn't like that at all. Not even close.

"I guess that's reality, isn't it?" she asked.

"It is," he said, then she heard a horn honk and Diego curse savagely.

"I should let you go," she said. "Be careful."

"You, too," he said.

The call ended, and she put the phone back in the

cradle on her desk and glanced up to see Giles standing in the doorway.

"Do you have time for a quick coffee?" he asked.

"Sure," she said. But Giles was part of the problem. As she had coffee with him, she realized that he and her father were playing her. They both assumed that she was going to back one of them to keep control of the company.

"I know you mentioned partnering with Jacs Veerling for a limited-edition wedding collection and I wanted to let you know that once we have everything sorted at the board meeting we'd like you to start discussions with her."

"I'm glad you like the idea. I've already started discussions, Giles. I know that we're going to want to move quickly to bring some new products onto the market in the second quarter next year. My father and you both have strong ideas for the company."

"We're both men who know what we want."

"You are," she said, realizing that she needed to figure out what she wanted. She'd been sincere when she'd told him she wanted to take an active role in the company, but as far as she could tell, Giles thought she'd side with him and let him move the company in the direction he wanted. She needed to find out where the rest of the board stood because every day when she walked into the House of Hamilton showroom she was reminded of her heritage and felt a responsibility to keep that luxury and quality going for another generation.

She finished her meeting with him and knew she had to go talk to the other board members because the only solution she could come up with was one where neither man retained any control over the day-to-day running of the business.

She made a few calls and then left the office, going to the meetings she'd set up. She'd been surprised to learn that many members of the board hadn't realized she was back to take her place at the helm. She spent the rest of the afternoon and early evening convincing them that she was ready to do just that.

She reflected on how she had her work cut out for her as she took a taxi back to the Belgravia home she'd been sharing with Diego. She let herself into the house and could hear voices down the hall.

She walked toward the sound and saw that Diego was entertaining two very beautiful women and a man. He stood up when he saw her.

"Pippa, I'm so glad you're here," he said. "Please come and meet my friends."

But she didn't want to meet his friends. She needed to talk to him about what she'd learned today and they had to be across town in less than forty minutes.

"I have to get changed," she said, turning on her heel and walking out of the room.

What had she expected? But she knew she'd antic-ipated more from Diego. She entered their bedroom and knew she'd behaved horribly to his guests and she wasn't being a very good…what? She wasn't his girl-friend. He was leaving on Saturday and she was going to be here working hard to save her heritage.

There was an ache deep inside her that she pushed aside. It was about to be over between her and Diego.

She knew she would mourn, but she was going to be very busy making sure that House of Hamilton had the future she knew it deserved.

Diego had been surprised when he'd run into Bartolome Figueras at the stables of the breeder he'd visited earlier that day. The Argentinian polo player turned model now spent his days working closely with breeders for his award-winning ponies. They'd met last year when Bart had come to Arbol Verde to look at Diego's mares for breeding. So earlier in the week, when Bart had texted him about the horse, Diego had invited him to stop by for drinks before dinner, hoping that he could talk shop but also introduce him to Pippa.

For the first evening since he'd been here, he hadn't just felt like her boy toy—he'd felt like he had a purpose of his own in London. But then she'd stormed in and been so rude to his guests.

Bart arched his eyebrow as Pippa left the room. The two women with him, his sister Zaira and her friend Luisana, looked at each other. "I'd say she's not too happy we are here," Luisana ventured.

"She's under a lot of stress," Diego said.

"I read a bit about it in *Hello!*" Zaira said. "I have often thought of running away and hiding from my overbearing brother, but alas, he holds the purse strings, so I have to stay."

Luisana laughed and Bart just shook his head. "We will go and leave you with your lady. But I would like to bring my sire to Arbol Verde, Diego."

"I'm looking forward to it," Diego said. He showed his guests out and then went upstairs to find Pippa.

She had changed into a lovely navy velvet gown that was fitted on the top and then flared out from the waist to her knee. She'd twisted her hair up into a chignon and had a string of pearls around her neck.

"I'm sorry I was rude. I've had a really long day," she said.

"It's all right. Bart was in the UK and I have an opportunity to do business with him, so I thought it might be nice for you to see that I'm more than just…what is it you think I am?" he asked.

He could excuse her tiredness, but this felt like more than fatigue. He had felt a distance growing between them from the moment she'd had her first meeting the day they landed.

"What do you mean?"

"I mean that you ignore me most of the time, and then when you need me, you expect me to drop everything—"

"Don't do that. I was just surprised that you had guests. I acted like a toddler and I'm sorry. Just leave it at that."

He would, except he was leaving in two days and he knew that this was something that had to be discussed in person.

"I can't."

"I know," she said, sitting down on the bed. And he could tell that she had already made her decision. "Coming back into this world has been harder than I thought it would be. Even though I'm not good at showing my appreciation, having you with me has given me the strength to stand up for myself and to try to see more clearly what it is that I can bring to the table."

He wasn't convinced. He sat down next to her, but he felt like they were oceans away from each other. Felt the gulf between her world and his very clearly. It wasn't a monetary one but more about lifestyle. And he'd never thought about that before this evening.

"I'm glad to hear that. I have felt very out of place here, but today going to meet with the breeder helped. I'm sorry that you've had a bad day."

She sighed and stood up, and he looked up at her. She had her back to him and he noticed the deep vee of her dress and how creamy her skin was. He wanted her as he always did, but he sensed she was trying to say something.

Possibly goodbye.

"It's more than a bad day. I had no idea of the amount of work that I am going to be required to do. I think I thought I could have you and the company and everything would sort itself out. But that's not fair to you. You have a life and a business of your own," she said.

"I do. But I'm… I think we both knew this was never going to be more than this week," he said at last. He'd hoped for more, but the truth had always been staring them both in the face. He couldn't live here, and her place was in London.

He needed to be back in Cole's Hill, despite how great it had been to meet Bart today and talk about future business. His core breeding program was for the US market, and as much as he thought it would be nice to expand to Europe and maybe the polo market, he knew that he was fooling himself. He had been trying to come up with a reason to stay. A reason to come back to London so he could see her more often.

And she obviously had no time for a man or a relationship.

"I think you're trying to figure out how to tell me this is it," he said. "That the good time you wanted from the bachelor you bid on and won back in Cole's Hill is over."

"Oh, Diego, I don't know if that's true," she said.

But he heard it in her tone. She did know.

"I do. It's been fun, Pippa, and I wish...well, I wish we were different so that this could have worked, but I think it's time for me to go."

She nodded, standing there awkwardly, her arms wrapped around her waist. She waited for him. He hoped to see some sign that she wanted him to stay, but he didn't find one.

He walked to the armoire and took out his suitcase. Chewing on her lower lip, she watched him for a minute.

"Goodbye, then."

She walked out the door and he watched her leave. Just stood there, way calmer than he felt on the inside, and let her go.

He packed his bags while she was gone and left a note and the bracelet he'd picked up for her earlier in the week when he'd still had hope that he could figure out a way to make this last. And then he left.

Fourteen

That night in October, Pippa had known that Diego would be gone when she got back from her dinner, but it had still hurt when she'd walked into the empty house and found him gone. She hadn't opened the note he'd left her on the nightstand but had worn the bracelet he'd left. It was a tiny House of Hamilton hinged bangle in rose gold with two diamonds on either side. But that wasn't what made it valuable to her. He'd had it engraved.

Courage is being scared to death and saddling up anyway.

Just a little bit of Diego's courage on her wrist. She'd taken back her company from Giles and her father and it had been too late to get any new product ready for the Christmas season this year, but they had a solid plan in place for the coming seasons.

December was lonely, and Pippa admitted she missed Kinley and Penny, who had been so much a part of her holidays until this year. Despite talking with Kinley on video chat once a week like she was currently doing, she still felt lonely and missed Texas.

"Are you even paying attention?" Kinley asked.

"No. I'm not," she admitted. She'd been looking at her bangle and wondering when the ache of losing Diego would go away.

"Well, at least you're honest about it," Kinley said. "I have news."

"Is it that you're pregnant?"

"No. Don't even say that too loud. Nate said he would give me some space and he's been so sweet," Kinley said, looking over her shoulder. "I stopped taking the pill."

"Good. You know I'm your friend and I support you, but you and Nate need more kids. The imp is turning into a diva. She needs a sibling to bring her in line," Pippa said.

"She does. Plus, Bianca is expecting, so Nate and Penny are both in a tizzy."

"I'm sure Nate appreciates you saying he's in a tizzy," Pippa said. It was nice hearing about everyone in Cole's Hill, but she wanted to know about Diego and wasn't sure she should ask.

"He's out riding with Penny, so it's safe," Kinley said. "In fact, I asked him to take her because I have to give you some tough love today."

"What about?"

"Diego."

"There's nothing to be tough about, Kin. I told you we both decided it wouldn't work out," Pippa said. "I have been very busy getting the board in order over here and renewing contacts and working with Jacs. We're both happy with this decision."

Kinley leaned forward on her elbows. "You are a rotten liar. I know you miss him, and unless you're going to be stubborn about this, you'll admit it."

Pippa sank back against the cushions of the armchair she was sitting in and looked out at the street. There was a light snow falling and she could see her neighbor's kids outside playing in the snow. Of course she missed him. She had never expected him to be so important to her. Never guessed that she could fall for a man that quickly or completely.

She had tried dating since he'd been gone, but no one could hold a candle to Diego. It was him she wanted.

She touched the bangle on her wrist.

"I miss him. But we both made the decision, Kin. I can't just show back up in his life. Besides I have to be here and he has to be in Cole's Hill."

Kinley shook her head. "Girl, those are details. I fly to Vegas for two weeks each month and Nate and I are making it work."

"You have a kid together," Pippa pointed out.

"That has nothing to do with it and you know it. If you love him, then the other stuff will be easy to sort out. You do love him, right?"

Yes. But she wasn't ready to say those words out loud. And she didn't want to say them to Kinley. "What if he doesn't want me anymore? What if he's moved on?"

"You must think I'm some kind of crappy friend," Kinley said. "Would I bring him up if he'd moved on?"

Pippa shook her head. "No, of course you wouldn't. How is he?"

"Well, he was drinking at the Bull Pen last night and Derek had to break up a fight between him and Mo. Those two are both brokenhearted…the entire town says so. Mo at least deserves it—everyone knows he wouldn't commit to Hadley. But no one can figure out what happened to you. They figured that being an heiress, you can live anywhere."

She sighed. "It's not that simple. Running House of Hamilton takes a lot of time and energy and I don't want to walk away from it."

"I think Diego would be willing to work something out with you. You know he's started a breeding program with Bart something-or-another. That hottie Argentinian. Even Nate had to admit he was good-looking."

"Exactly how did you get Nate to admit that?" she asked.

"We were both drinking with Diego," Kinley said. "That's not the point. If you love him, you need to come and claim him. He is miserable and so are you. And I think he feels like he can't ask you to come back. Plus, I miss you. Even if you were only here once a month or every other month, it would be nice."

Pippa hung up with Kinley a few minutes later, but her mind was on Diego and how he'd come here and supported her. And when she'd told him she needed space, he'd given it her. If she wanted him back in her life, she was going to have to go to him. Support him and show him that she was there for him.

She knew that Kinley was right. She loved Diego and it was time to go back and claim her rancher.

She'd need some help to do it and she knew just whom she could turn to for it.

Diego woke up with a hangover, which wasn't surprising, since he and Mauricio had decided to shut down the Bull Pen again. And Manu had been there celebrating the high school football team winning the state playoffs. Things had gotten more than a little out of hand.

But it had distracted him from the fact that it was only three days until Christmas and the only thing he wanted was a certain British woman who had made it very clear she needed nothing more from him.

For the first few weeks he'd been back in Texas he'd expected her to contact him. The bangle had been a sentimental gift and he'd thought…well, that she'd—what? Suddenly realize she loved him and come running back to him?

Wake up, loser.

He knew she had a life in London. He'd kept up-to-date with her takeover of House of Hamilton by reading the *Financial Times* and watching the profiles cable business networks had done on her. She'd come back into her own and was setting the tone for the company, repositioning it for a new generation of high-end customers.

He'd been impressed and proud of her.

Because no matter how long he was away from her or how far apart they lived, he knew he was never going to get over her.

It hadn't taken him very long to realize that. He'd gotten on with his own business and he had Mauricio developing the riding center on the outskirts of town. Bart had come to visit and stayed for a few weeks in November and they were going to start a new breeding program, building on the stamina of his horses and the agility of Bart's. They were both excited about the prospect.

Honestly, his business had never been better. Every night during the week he fell into bed exhausted. Even so, he got only a good thirty minutes of sleep before he woke in a fever for Pippa. Taking her that last time in his bedroom had been one dumbass idea because every time he lay on his bed he remembered holding her in his arms there and it made him miss her more keenly than before.

He got out of bed and walked naked to the bathroom. He showered but didn't shave, and got dressed in a shirt and jeans. That was all he'd need. Technically it was winter, but December in Cole's Hill wasn't always that chilly. The highs were in the 70s this week.

His sister was waiting in the breakfast room when he came downstairs. Benito was sitting quietly next to her.

"Bianca, what are you doing here?"

"I'm worried about you," she said. "I sent Alejandro to check on Mo. You know they're twins and sometimes that bond helps. But you. What's going on?"

"Well, I'm planning to eat breakfast and then probably check on my mares. We have two that might foal early, which of course isn't good news."

He helped himself to the breakfast burrito that his housekeeper had left on the counter and a cup of coffee before sitting down next to Benito. He gave his nephew a kiss on the top of the head and Beni hugged him before hopping down from his chair.

"Can I watch TV now?" he asked.

"Yes. Let me get you set up," Bianca said, standing and taking him into the other room.

Diego took a huge bite of his burrito, wondering if he should just ghost while Bianca was in the other room. He stood up, pushed his chair back and was halfway to the back door.

"Don't even think about it. I'm pregnant, have already been sick once this morning, and if I have to chase you down, it's not going to be pretty," Bianca said.

"Uh, sorry, sis. I just don't want to have this conversation," he said.

"Me neither," she admitted. "You're my big brother and one of the best men I know, so I hate to see you like this."

"It's nothing," he said. "I'll get over it soon. I just need time."

She shook her head. "I don't think time will heal this."

"I do."

He wasn't going to talk about his broken heart and the way he kept waiting for something to happen between himself and Pippa. Something that wasn't going to happen.

"Fine. Are you sure you're okay?" she asked.

"Yes," he said, sitting back down. "Thank you for caring."

"Of course I care, you big dummy. Listen, I have a friend flying into Houston later this afternoon and Derek is on call, so he can't go get her. And like I said, I've been sick this morning… Would you mind picking her up?"

"Is this a setup?" he asked. Because there was something in his sister's tone that made him very suspicious. "I'm not ready for that, Bianca."

"I know," she said, putting her hand on his wrist. "Believe me, I know. It's not a setup. I just need someone to pick her up."

"Okay," he said. "I'll do it."

"Thanks. I'll text you the details of where to meet her. But I think bag claim would be a good spot."

"Will she know where to find me?" he asked. He still wasn't sure that his sister wasn't up to something, but he wasn't going to keep questioning her. He wondered if while he was there, he should book himself a ticket out of town for the holidays just to get away from everything that reminded him of Pippa.

"Yes, I told her to look for you," Bianca said. "Wear your black Stetson so she can spot you."

His sister stayed for a few hours. They talked about Christmas day and how odd it was now that she had to split her time with the Velasquez family and the Caruthers. He thought he did a good job of coming off as normal, but as soon as Bianca left he felt that gaping emptiness again and knew he wasn't adjusting as quickly as he should be.

He didn't want to keep missing Pippa for the rest of his days.

But the thought of spending Christmas without her made him sad. He promised himself that starting January 1 he was moving on. He had to. He didn't like the man he was becoming: drinking, fighting, wanting something that was beyond his reach. He wasn't that man.

It had taken her longer to get through immigration and border control at the Houston airport than she'd expected. She'd barely had enough time to dash into the ladies' room to fix her makeup and tidy up her braid. She still looked nervous and tired when she looked back at herself in the mirror.

She almost—*almost*—wanted to run back to the departure lounge and head back to London. But she wouldn't.

Not unless Diego told her he wanted nothing to do with her. And she was perfectly prepared for him to do just that.

She was just going to… She had no idea what. But Bianca had promised to pick her up, since Kinley was in Vegas with Nate and Penny today. Bad timing on her part, Pippa thought. She'd rehearse what she was going to say to Diego on the drive from Houston to Cole's Hill.

She texted Bianca and got back a text saying to meet in the baggage claim area. She towed her suitcase behind her in that direction and then froze as she saw a familiar long, tall Texan with that distinctive black Stetson on his head, standing off to the side of the luggage carousel.

Bianca had tricked her. But Pippa didn't blame her. She guessed that it would be better to do this here in Houston. But not in the baggage claim area with all these people around.

She was trying to think of a plan to use the priority lounge to change into something more presentable when he looked up and their eyes met. Suddenly it didn't matter where they were or what they were wearing.

He was surprised to see her. That was the first thing she noticed. And then she realized he'd let his beard grow in. She liked it.

He straightened from the wall and walked toward her, and she left her suitcase and ran to him. She threw herself into his arms and he caught her. She put her hands on his jaw, framing his face, and kissed him for all she was worth.

"I missed you so much."

"I missed you, too," he said.

He kissed her and then put her on her feet. "Let's get out of here and we can talk."

She nodded. But she didn't let go of his hand. Seeing him had reinforced what Kinley had said to her. There had to be a way to make this work.

He got her suitcase and they walked out into the afternoon Houston sun. The sun felt good on her skin.

She had missed more than Diego, she realized.

He led the way to his truck and put the tailgate down, lifting her up onto it after he'd tossed her suitcase in the back. He leaned on it next to her.

"So…you're back for Christmas?"

"Yes and no," she said. "I'm really back for you,

Diego. I realized I should never have let you leave. I love you. I want to figure out a way to make our lives work for us."

He didn't say anything, and she realized he might not love her.

Why hadn't she thought of that before?

But it didn't change anything. She still loved him.

He rolled his hip along the edge of the tailgate and stepped between her legs, putting his hands on her hips.

"I love you, too, Pippa," he said. "God, I've missed you."

She pulled him close, wrapping her arms and legs around him and kissing him hard and deep.

"So how's this going to work?" he asked.

She shook her head. "I have a few ideas, but really I wasn't sure what to expect when I got here."

"Fair enough. Let's go home so I can make love to you and welcome you properly back to Texas. And then we can figure out how to make this work."

"I can't wait."

He drove her home and they made love as soon as they were on his property. He pulled the truck off the road and took her hard and deep. They stared into each other's eyes and professed their love.

When they got to his house, they made love again in the bathtub and then sat in his big bed and talked about the future.

"How long can you stay this time?" he asked.

"I'm off until January 7," she said.

"Good. I can fly back with you, if you'd like me to," he said. "Do you remember Bart—the polo player?"

She groaned. "How could I forget. I was a grade-A bitch to him."

"You weren't, and everyone understood what you were going through. He and I have been working together here in Texas, but he has purchased a large country house with a stable that he wants to use to develop polo ponies in the UK. I am one of his investors now."

"That's great. So you would be staying with him?"

"During the week I would," Diego said. "Then we can spend the weekends together. I can't be away from Arbol Verde for more than three weeks at a time."

"That will work for me. I can come here and work from Texas for a few weeks. We can sort of play it by ear until we figure out what works for us."

"I like that. Together I feel like we can do anything," Diego said.

They knew it would be hard to make their relationship work, and at first Pippa was going to have to spend more time in the UK than in Texas, but they came up with a plan that they thought would work for them.

"The important thing is that we are both in each other's lives," she said.

"Amen to that."

* * * * *

THE BOYFRIEND
ARRANGEMENT

ANDREA LAURENCE

One

"You have got to be kidding me!"

Sebastian West scanned his proximity card for the third time and yet the front door of BioTech—the biomedical technology company he co-founded—refused to open. Seeing his employees moving around inside, he pounded his fist on the glass, but all of them ignored him.

"I own this company!" he shouted as his secretary walked by without making eye contact. "Don't make me fire you, Virginia."

At that, she came to a stop and circled back to the door.

"Finally," he sighed.

But she didn't open the door as he'd expected. Instead she just shook her head. "I'm under strict orders from Dr. Solomon not to open the door for you, sir."

"Oh, come on," he groaned.

She couldn't be moved. "You'll have to take it up with him, sir." Then she turned on her heel and disappeared.

"Finn!" he shouted at the top of his lungs, pounding on the glass with angry fists. "Let me in, you son of a bitch."

A moment later Sebastian's former college roommate and business partner, Finn Solomon, appeared at the door with a frown on his face. "You're supposed to be on vacation," he said through the glass.

"That's what the doctor said, yeah, but since when do I take vacations? Or listen to doctors?" The answer was never. He certainly never listened to Finn. And as for vacation, he hadn't taken one in the decade since they'd started this company. You couldn't be off lying on a beach and also breaking barriers in medical technology. The two were incompatible.

"That's the whole point, Sebastian. Do you not recall that you had a heart attack two days ago? You're not supposed to be in the office for a minimum of two weeks."

"A mild heart attack. They didn't keep me in the hospital for more than a few hours. And they're not even sure I really had one. I'm taking the stupid pills they gave me, what more do you want?"

"I want you to go home. I'm not letting you in. I've had your badge deactivated. I've also sent out a memo that anyone who lets you in the building will be terminated."

So much for piggybacking through the door behind someone else. He did have a laptop, though, if he could get Virginia to bring it out to him. That wouldn't technically be breaking the rules if he worked from home, right?

"I've also had your email and remote access accounts temporarily suspended, so you can't even work from home." Finn was always remarkably good at reading his mind. He'd been able to do it since they were in college. It was great for working together. Not so great for this scenario. "You are on mandatory medical leave, Sebastian, and as a doctor, I'm sorry, but I'm going to enforce it. I can handle things for two weeks, but I can't run this company with you dead. So get some R and R. Take a trip. Get a massage. Get a hand job. I really don't care. But I don't want to see you here."

Sebastian was at a loss. He and Finn had started this company after school, pouring their hearts and souls into technology that could make people's lives better. He was the MIT engineer and Finn was the doctor, a winning team that had developed advanced technologies like prosthetic hands and electric wheelchairs controlled by a patient's brain waves. That seemed a noble enough cause to dedicate his life to. But apparently a decade of trading sleep and vegetables for caffeine and sugar had caught up with him.

Of course he didn't want to die; he was only thirty-eight. But he was close to a breakthrough on a robotic exoskeleton that could make paraplegics like his brother walk again.

"What about the new prototype for the exo-legs?"

Finn just crossed his huge forearms over his chest. "Those people have gone a long time without walking. They can wait two more weeks while you recover. If you keel over at your desk one afternoon, they'll never get it. As it is, I'm having a defibrillator installed on the wall outside your office."

Sebastian sighed, knowing he'd lost this fight. Finn was just as stubborn as he was. Normally that was a good match—they never knew when to take no for an answer. But that wouldn't benefit him in this situation. He knew the doctor's orders, yet he'd never once imagined that Finn would enforce them this strictly. He'd just thought he'd work ten-hour days instead of the usual eighteen.

"Can I at least come in and—?"

"*No*," Finn interrupted. "Go home. Go shopping. Just go away." With a smug expression Finn waved at him through the glass and then turned his back on his business partner.

Sebastian stood there for a moment, thinking maybe Finn would come back and tell him he was just kidding. When it was clear that Finn was deadly serious, he wandered back to the elevator and returned to the lobby of the building. He stepped out onto the busy Manhattan sidewalk with no real clue as to where he was going to go. He'd planned to take it easy for a few days and head back to work today. Now he had two full weeks of nothingness ahead of him.

He had the resources to do almost anything on earth that he wanted. Fly to Paris on a private jet. Take a luxury cruise through the Caribbean. Sing karaoke in Tokyo. He just didn't want to do any of those things.

Money was an alien thing to Sebastian. Unlike Finn, he'd never had it growing up. His parents had worked hard but as blue collar laborers they'd just never seemed to get ahead. And after his brother Kenny's ATV accident, they'd gone from poor to near destitute under the weight of the medical bills.

Scholarships and loans had gotten Sebastian through college, after which he'd focused on building his company with Finn. The company eventually brought money—lots of it—but he'd been really too busy to notice. Or to spend any. He'd never dreamed of traveling or owning expensive sports cars. Honestly, he was bad at being rich. He probably didn't even have twenty bucks in his wallet.

Stopping at a street corner, he pulled his wallet out of his back pocket and noticed the leather had nearly disintegrated over the years. He'd probably had this one since grad school. Maybe he should consider getting a new one. He had nothing better to do at the moment.

Up ahead, he spied Neiman Marcus. Surely they sold wallets. He made his way across the street and over to the department store. Sebastian stopped long enough to hold the door for a group of attractive women exiting with enough bags to put a kid through a semester or two of college. They looked vaguely familiar, especially the last one with the dark hair and steely blue eyes.

Her gaze flicked over him for a moment and he felt it like a punch to his gut. His pulse pounded in his throat as he tried to unsuccessfully swallow the lump that had formed there. He didn't know why he would have such a visceral reaction to the woman. He wanted to say something but he couldn't place the woman and decided to keep his mouth shut. Half a second later she looked away, breaking the connection, and continued on down the street with her friends.

Sebastian watched them for a moment with a touch

of regret, then forced himself into the store. He made a beeline for the men's department and quickly selected a wallet. He wasn't particularly choosy with that sort of thing. He just wanted black leather and a slim profile with enough room for a couple cards and some cash. Easy.

As he found a register open for checkout, he noticed a strikingly attractive brunette ahead of him. Sebastian realized she was one of the women he'd just seen leave the store a few minutes before. The one with the blue-gray eyes. He wished he remembered who she was so he could say something to her. They'd probably met at one event or another around town—Finn forced him to go to the occasional party or charity gala—he couldn't be sure, though. Most of his brain was allocated to robotics and engineering.

Not all of it, though. He was red-blooded male enough to notice her tall, lean figure, long, chestnut hair, big blue eyes and bloodred lips. It was impossible not to notice how flawlessly she was put together. She smelled like the meadow behind his childhood home after a warm summer rain. Deep down inside him something clenched tightly at the thought.

What was it about her? He told himself it was probably nothing to do with her, exactly. The doctor had told him to refrain from strenuous physical activity—*Yes, that includes sexual relations, Mr. West*—for at least a week. It had been a while since he'd indulged with a lady, but maybe since it was forbidden, his mind was focusing on what it couldn't have.

Why was he so terrible at remembering names?

As Sebastian got closer to the counter, he realized the woman was returning everything in her bag. That

was odd. If the register was correct, she'd just purchased and immediately returned about fifteen hundred
dollars' worth of clothes. He watched as she slipped
out of her leather coat and shoved it into the empty department store bag, covering it with the packing tissue
so you couldn't see inside.

His chronic boredom was temporarily interrupted
as she piqued his curiosity with her actions. "Excuse
m—" he started to say.

She turned suddenly and slammed right into his
chest, forcing him to reach out and catch her in his
arms before she stumbled backward on her sky-high
heels and fell to the ground. He pulled her tight against
him, molding her breasts to his chest until she righted
herself. He found he really didn't want to let go when
the time came. He was suddenly drunk on her scent
and the feel of her soft curves pressing into his hard
angles. How long had it been since he'd been this close
to a woman? One he wasn't fitting a prosthetic to? He
had no clue.

But eventually he did let go.

The woman took an unsteady step back, pulling
herself together with a crimson flush blooming across
her cheeks. "I am so sorry about that," she said. "I'm
always in such a hurry that I don't pay attention to
where I'm going."

There was a faint light of recognition in her blue-
gray eyes as she looked up at him, so he knew he was
right about meeting her somewhere before. "No, don't
apologize," he said with a wry smile. "That's the most
exciting thing to happen to me all week."

Her brow furrowed in disbelief.

Perhaps, he mused, he didn't look as boring as he was.

"Are you okay?" she asked.

He laughed off her concern. She was tall for a woman, especially in those stilettos, but he didn't really think she could inflict damage to him. "I'm fine. I'm just glad I was able to catch you."

She smirked and looked down self-consciously. "I suppose it could've been worse."

"You actually look really familiar to me, but I'm horrible with names. I'm Sebastian West," he said, offering her his hand in greeting.

She accepted it tentatively. The touch of her smooth skin gliding along his sent an unexpected spark through his nervous system. He was usually focused on work, and other pursuits, like sexual gratification and dating in general, typically took the back burner. But with one simple touch, physical desire was moved to the forefront.

Unlike their brief collision, this touch lingered skin-to-skin, letting him enjoy the flickers of electricity across his palm. The connection between them was palpable. So much so that when she pulled her hand away, she rubbed it gently on her burgundy sweater as if to dull the sensation.

"You do look familiar," she agreed. "I'm Harper Drake. We must've met around town. Perhaps you know my brother Oliver? Orion Computers?"

That sounded familiar enough. "He's probably pals with my friend Finn Solomon. Finn knows everyone."

Harper narrowed her eyes for a moment, looking thoughtful. "That name sounds familiar, too. Wait…

are you involved in some kind of medical supply business?"

Sebastian's brows rose in surprise. That wasn't exactly how he'd categorize what he did, but the fact that she remembered that much stunned him. And, to be honest, it pleased him just a little bit.

"You could say that." He grinned.

Harper beamed. She was pleased to finally place this guy in her mind. When she'd caught a glimpse of him earlier, he'd grabbed her attention. He'd looked so familiar when he'd held the door for her that she was certain she'd known him from somewhere. Unfortunately, Violet being so hell-bent on running up the street to pick up Aidan's wedding present had meant she couldn't stop.

Once she'd split from her best friends, Lucy Drake, Violet Niarchos and Emma Flynn, she'd stealthily circled back to Neiman Marcus to return everything she'd just bought. She couldn't have that weighing down her credit card for long. She hadn't expected to run into the familiar man again. Certainly not literally.

Real smooth, Harper.

"Okay, well then, I think it must've been one of the hospital benefits this past winter."

He nodded. "I do think I went to one of those. Finn tries to get me out every now and then."

Sebastian West didn't have a face she could forget, even if she lost context. He had a strong jaw, a nearly jet-black goatee, eyes just as dark, and a crooked smile that stirred something inside her. No, she'd remember him for sure. If she had a type, he'd be it.

It was a shame he wasn't one of the rich CEO guys

her brother associated with all the time. She didn't mean to be shallow, but meeting a guy with his act together financially would certainly benefit her current situation. It would also make her feel a little better about how things would be handled once it all changed on her birthday.

The last seven years had been one long, hard lesson learned for Harper. One in the value of money the spoiled little rich girl she'd once been had never really experienced before. She would be the first to admit that her father had basically given her everything she'd wanted. After her mother died, he'd spoiled her. And continued to spoil her until he'd no longer had the resources.

Harper had never imagined that the well would run dry. When it had, she'd made a lot of necessary adjustments in her life. At least secretly. It was embarrassing enough that she'd blown all the money she'd inherited when she'd turned eighteen—especially since she was an accountant—she didn't need anyone else knowing about what she'd done.

After falling from the top of the world to her current spot near the bottom, she'd earned a whole new appreciation for money and for the people who were good at managing it. And soon, when she had money again, she intended to be very careful about how she handled it. That included triple-checking every guy she dated. Not that she intended to date Sebastian…

"Well, I'm glad we bumped into each other today," Sebastian said with a sly grin.

Harper chuckled. As her gaze broke away from Sebastian's for a moment, she saw Quentin—her ex, of all people—walking toward them. Grabbing Sebastian's arm, she turned them both toward a display of men's shoes, hoping maybe Quentin hadn't seen her. "I'm sorry," she muttered under her breath. "I'm trying to—"

"Harper?"

Damn it.

Harper turned to face the ex-boyfriend she'd done her best to avoid for the last two years. She stepped away from Sebastian, leaning in to give her ex a polite but stiff hug. "Hello, Quentin," she said in a flat, disinterested tone she knew he wouldn't pick up on. He never did.

"How have you been?"

Lonely. Anxiety-riddled. "I'm great. Never better. How about you?"

"Amazing. I actually just got engaged."

Engaged? Quentin was engaged. The one who didn't want to commit. If Harper hadn't already been feeling crappy about being the last single friend in her social circle, this moment would've been the straw that broke the camel's back. She pasted a fake smile on her face and nodded. "That's great. I'm happy for you."

Quentin didn't notice her lack of sincerity. "Thank you. Her name is Josie. She's amazing. I can't wait for you to meet her. I think you two would really get along."

Harper had to bite her tongue to keep from asking why his ex would have any interest in hanging out with his fiancée. "I'm sure we would."

"So, Harper…" Quentin said as he leaned in to her. His arrogant smile made her shoulders tense and the scent of his stinky, expensive cologne brought to mind nights with him she wished she could forget. "Will I be seeing you at Violet's wedding? It's the event of the year, I hear. I can't believe she's flying all the guests to Dublin for it. And renting out a castle! It's wild. Maybe I should've dated her instead of you." He chuckled and she curled her hands into fists at her sides.

"I am going," she said with a bright smile she hoped didn't betray her anxiety over the upcoming trip. "I'm one of her bridesmaids."

"Are you going alone?" Quentin cocked his head in a sympathetically curious way that made her hackles rise.

Why would he assume she was going alone? They'd been apart for two years. He'd moved on. Surely she could've found someone to replace him by now. She hadn't, but she could've. "No. I'm not going alone. I'm bringing my boyfriend."

The minute the words passed her lips she regretted them. Why had she said that? Why? He mentions a fiancée and she loses her damn mind. She didn't have a boyfriend. She hadn't even committed to a houseplant. How was she supposed to produce a boyfriend in a couple days before the trip?

Quentin's eyes narrowed in disbelief. "Oh, really? I hadn't heard you were dating anyone lately."

Harper was surprised that he'd been paying attention. "I've learned to keep my private life private," she snapped. After their messy, public breakup, it had been another lesson hard learned. She hadn't even considered dating for six months after they'd ended due to the trauma of the whole thing.

"Well, who's the lucky guy? Do I know him? I look forward to meeting him at the wedding."

A name. She needed a name. Harper's mind went

completely blank. Looking around the department store, her gaze fell on Sebastian as he perused a nearby display of dress loafers.

"You can meet him now. Sebastian, honey, could you come over here for a minute? I'd like you to meet someone."

Sebastian arched his brow inquisitively at Harper as she mouthed the word "please" silently to him. He wandered over to where she was standing. "Yes, *dear*?"

"Sebastian, this is my ex, Quentin Stuart. I've mentioned him, haven't I? Anyway, I was just telling him about the two of us going to Ireland for Violet and Aidan's wedding."

Quentin stuck out his hand to Sebastian. "Nice to meet you, Sebastian…?"

"West. Sebastian West." He shook Quentin's hand and quickly pulled his away.

"Sebastian West as in BioTech?"

"Actually, yes."

Harper didn't recognize the name of the company, but then again she didn't know much about Sebastian because they weren't really dating. She remembered a brief discussion at a party about him working in medical supplies and how he didn't get out very much. She'd figured he'd sold wheelchairs and hospital beds or something. Maybe she'd been wrong. Quentin wasn't the type to waste brain power on remembering things that didn't impress him.

"Wow, Harper. Quite the catch you've got in this one." An uncomfortable expression flickered across his face and quickly disappeared. "Well, I've got to run. I was on my way to meet Josie and I'm already late. I'll see you two lovebirds on the plane to Dublin. I look forward to speaking with you some more, Sebastian."

Harper watched Quentin walk out of the store. Once he was gone, her face dropped into her hands. She just knew she was bright red with embarrassment. "I am so sorry," she muttered through her fingers.

Sebastian surprised her by laughing. "Want to tell me what that was all about?"

She peeked through her hands at him. "Um… Quentin is my ex. It was a messy breakup, but we still hang in the same social circles from time to time. When he asked about my date for the wedding we have coming up, I panicked. I told him you were my boyfriend. It's a long story. I shouldn't have dragged you into that, but he put me on the spot and you were standing right there." She gestured toward the display and shook her head. "I'm an ass."

"I doubt that," Sebastian said, a twinkle of laughter still in his dark brown eyes.

"No, I am. I've made the whole thing ten times worse because now I'm going to show up at the wedding without you and he's going to know I lied. And I just know he's going to show up with his beautiful, new fiancée and I'm going to feel even more like crap than I already do."

Harper knew she should've just owned that she was single. How bad would that have been? To just state proudly that she'd been dating and not interested in settling down or settling on the wrong guy. She was almost thirty, but that was hardly the end of the world. In fact, *her* thirtieth birthday couldn't come soon enough. It brought a twenty-eight-million-dollar payout with it that she was desperate to get her hands on.

"Don't worry about what he thinks," Sebastian said. "He seems like a schmuck."

"I'm no good at the boyfriend thing. I have questionable taste in men," Harper admitted. "It's probably better that I just make up boyfriends instead of finding another real one."

Sebastian nodded awkwardly. "I'm glad to help. Well, I hope the wedding goes well for you."

"Thanks." She watched him leave. But with every step he took, the more panicked she became. She had no easy way of contacting this guy once he walked out the door. She didn't want to let him get away quite yet for reasons she wasn't ready to think about. "Sebastian?" she nearly shouted before he got out of earshot.

He stopped and turned back to her. "Yes?"

"How would you like to go on an all-expenses-paid trip to Ireland?"

Two

Sebastian didn't know what to say. He'd never had a woman offer him a vacation, much less a woman he hardly knew. Actually he didn't have women offer him much of anything. It was impossible when he never left the lab. The only woman he was ever around on a daily basis was his assistant, Virginia, who was in her late fifties and married.

"Um, run that by me again?"

Harper closed the gap between them with an apologetic smile on her face and a sultry sway of her hips. So many of her features were almost masculine in a way, with piercing eyes, sharp cheekbones and an aquiline nose, but there was nothing masculine about her. Her dark brows were arched delicately over eyes that were like the stormy seas off Maine where he was born.

He imagined a similar maelstrom was stirring inside

her to make an offer like that to a complete stranger. Surely she could find a romantic interest if she wanted one. But he was willing to say yes to almost anything she offered when she looked at him that way.

"My friends are getting married in Ireland next weekend. They're flying everyone there, plus putting all the guests up in a castle that's been converted into a hotel. It wouldn't cost you anything to go but some leave from work. I'm not sure what your boss is like, since this is short notice, but I was hoping you would be interested."

"In going to Ireland?"

She nodded. "With me. As my boyfriend. I just introduced you to Quentin as my boyfriend and said you were going, so he's going to expect you to be there."

His brow furrowed. Her boyfriend. For a week. In Ireland. What could go wrong? Absolutely everything. Pretending to be her lover could be complicated. But what could go right? His gaze raked over her tall, lean figure with appreciation. Everything could go very right, too.

Wait—*crap*—he wasn't supposed to be "active." Just his damn luck. "Just to be clear—are you wanting or expecting you and me to…um…"

"No!" Harper was quick to answer with wide eyes. "I mean, not for real. We'd have to pretend to be a couple around everyone else—kiss, be affectionate, you know. But when we're alone, I promise it's strictly hands off. I'm not that hard up. I just can't go to this thing alone. Not after seeing Quentin and finding out he's engaged. I just can't."

Sebastian blinked his eyes a few times and tried to mask some of his disappointment. He wasn't sure if he could stand being around her, touching her in public and then just flipping the switch when they were alone. The doctor wanted him to, but he wasn't the best at following doctor's orders.

This day had done well to throw him off his game. First, getting locked out at work with mandatory vacation and now this. A beautiful woman wanted him to travel with her to Ireland for free and pretend to be her lover. That just wasn't business as usual for him. He wasn't entirely sure what to say to her. It seemed foolish to say yes and downright stupid to say no.

"I'll pay you two thousand dollars to go. It's all the money I have in my savings account," Harper added, sweetening the pot as she seemed to sense his hesitation.

She was serious. Her insecurity struck him as odd considering how confident and put together she seemed. He wasn't sure why this was so important to her. There must be more to the situation with her ex than she was telling. "Aren't your friends going to wonder where I came from? You've never spoken about me before and suddenly I'm your wedding date?"

Harper waved away his concern. "I'll take care of that. My friends have been so wrapped up in their own lives lately they'd probably not notice if I did have a boyfriend. They certainly haven't mentioned that I don't have one."

"And why is that?" Sebastian couldn't stop himself from asking. But if he was going to pretend to be her boyfriend, he needed to know if there was something about her that repelled men. From where he was standing, he didn't see a thing wrong with her. She was beautiful, well-spoken, poised and polished. Aside from the slight hint of desperation in her voice, she seemed like quite the catch. There had to be something wrong with her.

She shrugged and sort of fidgeted before responding, showing the first sign of vulnerability, which he was glad to see. "Like I said, I don't have the best taste in men. Things haven't worked out with anyone I've been attracted to since Quentin and I broke up."

"You can't find a decent man to go to dinner with you, but you trust me enough to travel across the ocean with you, share a bedroom and make out in front of your friends?" There was a flaw in her logic here. "I could be crazy. Or a criminal. Or married. I could attack you in your sleep or steal your jewelry. The possibilities are endless."

Harper scoffed at his trepidations. "Honestly, I take that risk on every date I go on in this town. Have you seen the guys on Tinder lately? No…you probably haven't." She chuckled. "I know you have a job, you smell nice, you're handsome and you went along with my lie just now, so you're easygoing. You're already a head and shoulders over every date I've had in the last six months. If you don't want to go, or can't, just say so. But don't turn it down because you're concerned about my blatant disregard for my own welfare or poor sense of judgment. My friends are already well aware of that flaw in my character."

"No, I can go. As of this morning my schedule is amazingly wide open for the next two weeks." That was an understatement. But was this what he should spend his time doing? He didn't exactly have a more tempting offer.

"Do you find me physically repulsive?"

Sebastian swallowed hard. "Not at all. To the contrary, you're the most beautiful woman I've laid eyes on in a very long time."

Harper's eyes widened a touch at his answer, but she quickly recovered with a sly smile curling her lips. It must have boosted her confidence because she moved a step closer to him, closing the gap until they were nearly touching. "Do you think you'd have trouble pretending to be my lover? Or have a problem kissing me?"

Every muscle in Sebastian's body tightened as she spoke. The warmth of her body and the scent of her so close caused an instant physical reaction that would answer any of her questions if she bothered to notice. He balled his hands into fists at his sides to keep from reaching for her. He'd craved the sensation of touching her again since the moment he'd let her go after the collision.

He shook his head stiffly. "No. I think I can manage that."

Harper's gaze never left his. "Okay, great. Are you opposed to a free trip to Europe? You have a passport, right?"

"I have a passport, yes." It had no stamps in it, but he had one. Finn did most of the travel around the world, schmoozing on behalf of their company. Sebastian kept his nose in his paperwork and schematics, but Finn had made him get a passport anyway.

"Okay. Then I see no reason why you shouldn't say yes."

Neither did he. Why was he making this so hard?

It really was a simple thing. He had no reason not to go. All he had to do was walk around Ireland with this stunning woman on his arm. He had no intention of taking her money, but a trip would be a nice distraction without any work on his plate for the next few weeks. What else was he going to do? Finn was right that he could help more people healthy than dead, but taking a break was hard for him. Being a couple thousand miles from his work would make it easier.

"When do you leave for the wedding?"

"Monday afternoon."

"It's Friday morning. Three days? Are you serious? Won't your friend think it odd that you're suddenly adding a guest to her wedding on such short notice?"

"Not really. I RSVP'd for two. I just needed to find my plus one."

"You're cutting it awfully close. Desperate?"

"I prefer to think of it as optimistic."

"Three days…" he repeated. Something about this whole situation struck him as insane, but there was a fine line between insanity and genius.

"So does your silent resignation mean you're at least considering coming with me?" Harper grinned wide, her whole expression lighting up with excitement.

It was hard for him to turn her down when she looked at him like that. He wanted her to keep looking at him that way for as long as possible. "Well, yes, I am. I'm just not sure I'll make a very good boyfriend, fake or otherwise. I'm kinda out of practice."

"I'm not worried about that." Harper leaned into him and wrapped her arms around his neck in an unexpectedly intimate way. His whole body stiffened as she pressed against him. "You know what they say."

Sebastian took a deep breath and tried to wish away the sudden rush of desire that coursed through his veins as she stood close. It seemed wrong to react like this to a woman he'd just met, despite how easily she was able to coax it out of him. "What's th-that?" He stuttered in his response, something he hadn't done since elementary school. She had managed to get under his skin so quickly.

"Practice makes perfect."

He nodded. "I've heard that."

Harper frowned, lowered her arms and looked down to where his hands were tensely curled at his sides. She took them in her own and moved each one to rest at the curve of her hips. "Relax, Sebastian. I'm not going to bite. We've got to be a lot more comfortable touching each other if we're going to convince anyone we're really together."

He splayed his fingers across her denim-clad hips and pressed the tips into the ample flesh there. With her so close, he wanted to lean down and kiss her. Her full, pouting lips and wide, innocent eyes seemed to plead for it. Indulging seemed like the natural thing to do. She felt good against him. Perhaps too good for the middle of Neiman Marcus. There was definitely not going to be a problem faking attraction with Harper. The problem would be pretending that the attraction wasn't real when no one was watching.

"I'll go," he blurted out, almost surprising himself.

Harper stiffened in his arms, looking up at him with a smile that was hesitant to believe him. "Are you serious?"

Sebastian nodded. "Yes, I'm serious. I'll go to Ireland with you as your fake boyfriend."

With a squeal of excitement, Harper hugged him tight. Before he could prepare himself, she pressed her mouth to his. He was certain it was supposed to be a quick, thank-you peck, but once their lips touched, there was no pulling away.

Sebastian wasn't imagining the palpable sexual energy between them. The way Harper curved against his body and opened her mouth to him was proof of that. He wanted to take it further, to see how powerful their connection really was, but this was neither the time nor the place, so he pulled away while he still could.

Harper lingered close, a rosy flush highlighting her cheeks. "Listen, I've got to go. Would you care to walk me to my apartment? I don't live far."

"I can't." He wanted to—quite badly—but he got the feeling it was an invitation better declined at the moment if they were going to spend the next week together. Things could get weird before they even left.

Harper pulled away just enough to let a chill of air rush in where the heat of her body had been. "Why not?"

He picked up the wallet he'd set down on a display when he'd spoken with Quentin. "I still have to buy this."

A light of amusement lit her eyes. "You're so literal. I can wait while you check out."

It would be so easy to say yes. He took a deep breath and thought up another valid reason. "I also have some things to take care of if I'm going with you on Monday."

Harper pouted for a moment before she nodded and covered her disappointment with a smile. "Okay. Well, I'm going out with my girlfriends tomorrow, but how about we get together on Sunday night? We can get to know each other a little better before we get on the plane."

"At your apartment?"

"A bar is probably a better idea. Being you're a stranger and all, right?"

He breathed a sigh of relief. He could avoid temptation in a bar. Once they got to Ireland, he wasn't so sure. "That sounds good."

"Give me your phone."

Sebastian handed over his cell phone and Harper put her information into his contacts.

"Text me so I have your information, too. We'll get together Sunday."

With a smile and a wave, Harper handed over his phone and disappeared from the store. Sebastian watched her walk away and, with every step she took, was more and more convinced that he was making a big mistake.

"I know that we're leaving Monday and I should probably be packing or getting ready, but I really needed one last girls' night before we go." Violet eased back into the sofa cushions with a large glass of wine in her hand. "Why didn't any of you tell me how stressful weddings could be?"

"Well, Oliver and I eloped, so it wasn't stressful at all," Lucy said. "Besides, in the end it's just a party. Now, nine-month-old twins…that's stressful."

Harper chuckled at her new sister-in-law's observation. The twins—Alice and Christian—were little darlings, but the minute they started walking, she got the feeling they would be tiny tornadoes of destruction. Especially Alice. She was a little spitfire, like her namesake, their great-great-aunt Alice.

"No one said you had to fly all your friends and family halfway around the world to get married," Harper pointed out, taking a sip of her wine. "You could've had a ridiculously expensive and over-the-top affair here in Manhattan like Emma did."

Emma came into the room with a frown pulling down the corners of her flawlessly painted rose lips. "My wedding was not over the top. It was small and tasteful."

Harper arched an eyebrow and laughed. "You may have only had thirty people there, but I'd hardly classify it as small and tasteful."

"I had a beautiful reception."

"You had an ice vodka luge," Harper challenged.

Emma twisted her lips and sighed. "That was Jonah's thing. He insisted." She settled beside Violet on the couch. "And it would've been ten times bigger if my mother'd had her way. You saw what she did with my baby shower. But seriously, don't stress too badly about the wedding, Vi. It's in Ireland. In a castle! It will be beautiful, I promise."

"It will," Lucy chimed in. "You've got an amazing wedding planner who has it under control. The best in the city. All you need to do is show up and marry the love of your life. That's easy."

Violet smiled. "You're right. Aidan has told me the same thing a dozen times. I just can't stop stressing out about every little detail. In a week from today I'll be Mrs. Aidan Murphy! Have I forgotten something?"

"If you have, it doesn't really matter. As long as both of you show up, say I do and sign your license with a qualified officiant, you'll be married at the end of the day. Everything else is just details," Emma said.

Violet nodded. "You're right. I know you're right. I just need to say it until I believe it. What about you guys? Are you packed and ready to leave yet?"

The women around the coffee table nodded. "Everything is ready. Just a few more things to throw in the luggage before we go. We're leaving the twins with Oliver's dad," Lucy said. "That's the biggest stressor for me. I haven't been away from them since they were born, but there's no way I'm flying overseas with twins at that age.

"Knox is older than the twins, so I'm hoping he does okay on the flight. It will be his first," Violet explained. "I couldn't leave him behind, though. It seems wrong to marry his father without having him there."

"Of course. I'm sure he'll do great. Georgette is staying with my parents, but they'll have her nanny with them, so I'm not worried." Emma turned to Harper. "What about you? Are you ready to go? At least you don't have men and kids to wrangle before the trip. I almost forget what it's like to just have to worry about myself."

"Yep," Harper said. She took a deep breath and prepared herself to tell the story she'd come up with after talking to Sebastian. Her intention was to tell them as little as possible, but she knew she had to fill the girls in on her new beau before the trip. They were the only ones who would really care. If she sold the story to them, everyone else would take it at face value.

Including Quentin. Hopefully. If he didn't buy it, there was no point in continuing the ruse. This whole ridiculous scheme was designed with the sole purpose of making him believe she had someone in her life. That she wasn't pathetically single and still pining for him. Because she was anything but pining. She was glad to have Quentin out of her life. He was just too egomaniacal to see her single status as anything other than a reflection of her wishing they were still together.

Selling it to her friends wouldn't be so easy, though.

"I've got the dress, the passport and…uh…the boyfriend all ready to go." She said the words quickly and then waited for the inevitable response.

Emma, Violet and Lucy all paused as anticipated and turned to look at her. The questions came too fast and furiously for her to respond to any of them.

"What?"

"Your boyfriend?"

"Am I missing something, here?"

Harper winced and nodded when they finally quieted down. "Yeah, um, his name is Sebastian." She got up to refill her wine and stall the conversation a moment. She was going to need some alcohol to get through this conversation. When she came back into the room from the kitchen, the girls were sitting frozen in place with expectant looks on their faces. "He's the guy I've been seeing for a few months."

"Months?" Violet wailed. "You've been seeing a guy for *months* and didn't think to mention it to us?"

"You guys have all been busy with your own lives. Babies, weddings…" Harper explained. "And, to be honest, I didn't want to jinx it. It wasn't that serious at first and I got tired of mentioning guys to you all and then we didn't get past the third date. Things were going well, so I wasn't ready to talk about him yet. Just in case."

"And now you're ready to talk? 'Cause you're sure as hell going to give us every detail," Lucy sassed.

Harper shrugged. Not really, but the time had come to spill some information if she was going to pull this off. "I guess I have to if I want to bring him on the trip."

"I noticed you RSVP'd for two, but you left off the guest's name," Violet said. "I was wondering what that meant."

"Yeah, I was hopeful that things would work out for him to come," Harper continued to lie, noting that after pretending she had money for a decade, pretending to have a boyfriend wasn't as hard as she'd thought it would be. "But if it fell apart between us, I thought I might bring a friend. Or no one. But things are great and so Sebastian is coming. I'll give you his information to add to the travel manifest."

"I'm eager to meet him," Emma said. "And intrigued. You haven't really had much luck dating since you and Quentin broke up. Where did you two meet? He's not one of your Tinder finds, is he?"

"Oh, no. Those were a mess. I actually met Sebastian at one of the hospital fund-raisers this winter. The one raising money for the orthopedics center, I think." That, at least, wasn't a lie. They had met there. They just hadn't started dating. "He works with medical equipment. He can tell you more about all that. Anyway, we hit it off and he asked me to dinner. Things have just sort of progressed from there."

"Wait," Violet said, sitting at attention on the sofa. "We were all at that fund-raiser. Do we know him? Sebastian who?"

"Sebastian West." Harper was suddenly nervous that maybe they did know him. She and Sebastian hadn't gotten together to talk yet, so she ran the risk of getting caught not knowing something obvious about him if any of the girls knew who he was. Quentin had recognized his name and company, so it was a possibility.

Thankfully none of them perked up at hearing his full name. "I doubt any of you know him. He spends more time working than socializing. He's super smart. I'm excited for you all to meet him." She grinned wide and hoped she was selling her story.

"We're all excited," Violet echoed as her eyes narrowed at Harper in suspicion. "I can't wait for Monday."

Harper took a large sip of her wine and nodded with feigned enthusiasm. "Me neither."

Three

Sunday evening Sebastian arrived at the bar a full fifteen minutes before he was supposed to meet Harper. He wasn't particularly anxious about their meeting, but he couldn't stand just sitting around his apartment any longer. He'd sat there for the last two days trying to fill the hours. Without work, he found he had far too many minutes on his hands.

He'd spent as long as he could packing and preparing for the trip. He'd taken his clothes and his tuxedo to the cleaner. He'd carefully collected his toiletries and underthings, but that had taken only a few hours out of his newfound free time.

Sebastian had tried reading a book. He'd watched some television. Both had bored him after a short while. By Sunday afternoon he'd had nothing to do but pace around his apartment and wish away the hours. He wasn't sure how he'd get through the next two weeks if he hadn't met Harper and had this trip to Ireland fall into his lap. He might just go insane. How was that supposed to improve his health? Mentally weak but physically strong? What good was that?

When his watch showed it was almost time to meet Harper, he'd rushed out the door. He'd taken a table in a quiet corner, ordered himself a gin and tonic with lime—ignoring doctor's orders—and awaited her arrival with his notebook open to read over some notes. He carried it almost everywhere he went, writing down ideas and schematics when they popped into his head. He'd learned the hard way that he could lose the spark of inspiration if he didn't immediately capture it.

This way he was still waiting, but at least he was out of the house and potentially doing something productive in the meantime. Thankfully, Harper showed up a few minutes later. She was looking attractive and fashionable once again with layered lace tops and a long sweater over skinny jeans. Today her dark hair was pulled up into a bun, highlighting the line of her neck and her dangly earrings.

Sebastian was once again struck by the fact that this woman should be able to find a boyfriend easily. He didn't understand why he was even there pretending to be one. Then again, the same thing could probably be said of him. Life was complicated sometimes.

"Thanks for coming. And thanks for doing all of this," she said as she settled into her chair across from him.

"No problem. Would you like a drink?"

"Just water for me," she said with a polite smile. It surprised him. A glass of wine or a martini seemed far more her speed. He didn't question it, however, and waved down the bartender for her water.

"Are you packed and ready to go?" she asked.

"Mostly. What about you?"

"The same. I feel like I'm not ready, although I can't imagine what I haven't packed yet."

"Don't forget the slinky lingerie," Sebastian said. The sudden image of Harper wearing some kind of silk-and-lace chemise came to his mind and made him immediately regret his words. He didn't need that vision haunting him over their next week together.

"What?" Harper's eyes were suddenly wide with concern.

"It was a joke," Sebastian soothed. And that's what he'd intended it to be, even if a part of him wouldn't mind if she threw a nice piece or two in there.

"Oh," she said, visibly relaxing. Apparently the idea of being his girlfriend for real was not nearly as appealing to her as it was in his own mind. "Yeah, no, I'm packing the ugliest pajamas I've got."

"Flannel footie pajamas with a zip front?" he asked.

"Yep. I'll be dressed as a giant pug dog."

Interesting. "Trapdoor for convenience?"

"No, just a front zipper, but they do have a tail and a hood with puppy ears and a nose I can pull up."

"Excellent. Since pugs aren't my thing, I'm sure the sight of you in that dog outfit will squelch any misplaced attraction that might arise between us."

"Perhaps I should buy you one, too. I saw one that was basically a poop emoji costume."

"Not Spider-Man or Deadpool? You went straight for the poop emoji?"

"Yeah, sorry."

They both laughed for a few moments and the tension dissipated between them. Sebastian was relieved. He didn't want either of them to be uncomfortable. It would make the week ten times longer than it would be already.

"So tell me everything I should know about you," Harper began. "I'm your girlfriend, after all, so I need to know all the important things."

Sebastian tried not to wince at the thought of talking about himself. He hated doing that. He tried to think of what he would share with someone if he were really dating them, but he found he didn't know the answer to that, either. "I'm from Maine. A small coastal town called Rockport, specifically. I went to MIT. Technically, I'm a mechanical engineer, but I've branched out quite a bit after college."

"I thought you worked for a medical supply company."

Sebastian frowned. That was probably his fault. He liked to keep the details of his work vague. "Not exactly. BioTech is a medical research and development company. My partner Finn and I develop new medical technology."

"Your partner? You mean you don't just work there?"

"Eh, no. We started the company together out of college. I own it."

Harper frowned, wrinkles creasing her forehead. "Are you serious? I offered you every penny I had in savings to go on this trip and you're the CEO of a company? You probably make more in an afternoon than I do in a paycheck."

Sebastian held up his finger in protest. "You offered

me the money. I never said I would actually take it. And I'm not going to, of course."

"So you're rich. Why didn't you say something? Like when Quentin asked about your company?"

At that, Sebastian shrugged. "I'm not the kind to flaunt it. Finn is the face of the company. I'm the mad scientist behind the scenes. I'm happy with the anonymity. I've seen how being well-known and wealthy has complicated his love life and I'm not interested in that."

"In a love life?" Harper asked with an arched brow.

"In a *complicated* love life. Or, hell, maybe a regular one. I work too much for any type of relationship to succeed."

"But you're going to drop everything and go with me on a trip to Ireland on short notice?"

Sebastian sat back in his chair and sighed. It would be easy to tell her that he'd had a heart attack and was on mandatory vacation, but he didn't want to. He didn't like people knowing his business, especially when it changed how they perceived him. Whether it was knowing he was rich, or sick, or used to be poor… it didn't matter. He liked private things to stay private. "When you're the boss, you can do what you want," he responded instead.

She shook her head. "I can't believe you didn't say anything until just now. What if I hadn't asked? Would you have waited until someone recognized you on the plane and I looked like a fool for not knowing my boyfriend is a millionaire?"

"Of course not! I would've told you. And you're one to point fingers, Harper. You're keeping plenty of secrets yourself."

She straightened in her chair and narrowed her gaze at him. "What is that supposed to mean?"

"I saw you walk out of Neiman Marcus with your friends. Then you ditched them and came back ten minutes later to return everything you'd bought. What is that about? It's not buyer's remorse, I'm pretty certain."

Harper's lips twisted in thought as she considered her answer. "I'm trying to save money."

Sebastian looked at her with a pointed expression on his face. There was more to it than just frugality, of that he was sure. He'd done his research since they'd met. Her family owned Orion Computers. She lived in a really nice apartment on the Upper East Side. But she only had two grand in her savings account? That didn't add up in his mind.

His silence prompted her to keep talking. "I'm having a bit of a cash flow shortage. I'm embarrassed about it, so I haven't told anyone, even my friends and family. Until I get things straightened out, I'm trying to be smart about my money, but I have to keep up appearances."

"Like blowing a fortune on designer clothes and then immediately returning them?"

"Yes."

"Don't they notice you never wear them after you buy them?"

She shook her head. "You need a map to get through my closet. Things disappear in there, never to resurface."

Sebastian nodded thoughtfully. "Sounds like a complicated charade to keep up. Pretending to have a boyfriend should be a piece of cake."

"Well, thankfully it's a short-term thing. I should be

back on my feet soon and then no one needs to know I lied about it. And as for you and me...well, I'm sure we will have a sad, but not unexpected, breakup not long after we get back from the trip. Not so soon as to be suspicious, but we can't wait too long or people might start inviting us to things as a couple here in town."

"Sounds tragic. I'm already sad."

Harper looked at him with a smile. "I'm enjoying your sarcastic sense of humor. We might actually be able to pull this off."

"I think so, too. Of course, over time I think you're going to become too clingy for me and we're going to want different things from our relationship."

She groaned. "Ugh. You sound like Quentin. Don't do that or we'll have to just break up now."

Sebastian laughed. "So since we're going to be around that guy, should I know what happened between you two?"

Harper winced at the thought. "That is a story that would require something stronger than water to talk about."

"A cocktail then? My treat," Sebastian added. He waved over the bartender. It wasn't until then that it occurred to him she might be drinking water out of necessity, not desire.

"That's sweet of you. A Cosmo, please."

Once the man returned with the dark pink beverage, Harper took a sip and sighed. "We were together for three years and we've been broken up for two. We met at a party and we really seemed to hit it off. Things went well between us, but I noticed that it didn't seem to be going anywhere. We'd stalled out at the point where most people take the next step."

"He didn't want anything serious?"

"I thought we were already serious, but I suppose that was my mistake. I was thinking we were on track to get engaged, moving in together...do all the things that other couples around me were doing. But he was always working. Or said he was. He's an attorney and kept insisting he had to put in the long hours if he was going to make partner. I thought it was because he wanted to build a solid future for us, but the truth was that he was perfectly content where we were."

"He was seeing other women."

"Bingo. While I was officially his girlfriend in the public eye, I found out there were three of us he was keeping on the hook. He used long hours at work as his excuse to run around town with different women, and I didn't even question it. I don't know if he couldn't decide and thought that he'd eventually know which one he wanted, or if he just liked keeping that many balls up in the air at once. But eventually I found out about the others and broke it off. When I confronted him, all he said was that he just wasn't ready for a commitment."

Sebastian frowned. "He told you the other day that he's engaged now, didn't he?"

Harper's posture deflated slightly in her chair and he found he hated that. He wanted to punch Quentin in the face for taking such a beautiful, confident woman and leaving her broken.

"Yes," she said softly. "He's bringing her on the trip. You see why I can't go alone? I just can't face him and his fiancée in the state I am in. I'm almost thirty. I'm happy with my life on most days, but I have to admit that I'm not at all where I expected to be at this point.

I'm sure everyone else looks at me and thinks I'm the sad, single one in the group."

Sebastian understood. He knew what it was like to be judged by people. While Harper had worked hard to keep up appearances, he'd simply buried his head in his research and tried to block out the rest of the world. It had served him pretty well. Eventually, though, he'd known his avoidance mechanisms would fall apart. His had fallen apart when he'd hit the floor in cardiac arrest. Hers might all come crashing down when her delicately structured pyramid of falsehoods took a hit. He hoped he wouldn't be the reason it fell.

"I will strive to be the imaginary boyfriend you've always dreamed of having someday."

"You go up first," Sebastian said as they stood on the tarmac together. "I prefer to sit in the aisle seat if you don't mind."

Harper nodded and climbed the steps ahead of him to board the private plane. The minute she stepped on and turned the corner, she realized the Boeing Business Jet that Violet's father, Loukas Niarchos, had chartered for the flight wasn't going to be like any plane she'd been on before. Instead of a first-class cabin, she found herself walking through a lounge with a bar, seating areas with couches and swivel chairs, flat-panel televisions and a variety of tables. To the left there was a doorway leading to an executive office where she could see Loukas already chatting on the phone, his laptop open.

A flight attendant greeted them with a smile and directed them through the lounge into the next room to the right. There they found what could be either a conference room or a dining table that sat twenty for a meal. Each chair was plush camel-colored leather with a seat belt if it was necessary. Harper got the feeling the kind of people who chartered flights on this plane wouldn't tolerate turbulence.

"This is like being on Air Force One," Sebastian muttered into her ear as they walked through a narrow hallway past a fully appointed bedroom suite, two full-size bathrooms with showers, and a galley kitchen currently manned by two more smiling flight attendants. "Is this how you're used to traveling?"

Harper shook her head. "No. I'm used to boring old first class unless I'm traveling with family on the Orion corporate jet. That's nice, but it only seats eight. And there's no bedroom. Or office. Or cocktail lounge. My family is normal rich, not filthy rich."

Sebastian chuckled and nudged her forward. "Good. I don't think I could handle a filthy-rich girlfriend. I'm glad this is a first for us both."

At that point, the plane finally opened up into a traditional seating area. Appointed like a large, first-class cabin, there were six seats in each row. They were in sets of two, divided by two wide aisles. Each seat had its own television screen, blanket, pillow, and controls that allowed its occupant to lay fully flat for sleeping on the overnight flight. A flute of champagne and a chocolate-covered strawberry stenciled with the letters *V&A* in edible gold awaited each guest at their seat as well as a handwritten card in calligraphy with each person's name.

Violet was certainly out to throw a memorable wedding, if nothing else.

They'd been assigned row thirteen of sixteen, seats

A and B, so she made her way down the right aisle through the crowd of familiar faces. They were nearly the last to board, so the area was bustling with activity as guests settled in. Quentin hadn't been kidding when he'd said this wedding was the event of the year. People salivated over the idea of receiving a coveted invitation, but the guest list had been kept down to less than a hundred by virtue of the plane and the wedding venue.

Even then, Harper still knew almost everyone on the plane. A few friends and family of Violet's fiancé, Aidan, were unfamiliar to her, but there were far more of Violet's circle than anyone. She smiled and waved politely as she pressed on, even when she saw Quentin in the back row on the far left. He was sitting beside an attractive brunette who seemed a little young for him, but Harper was trying not to let her bitterness color her opinion.

"Here we go," she said as she stopped at their row. Emma and Jonah were seated across the aisle from them in the center section, and Harper could see Emma was already heavily appraising Sebastian from her seat. She tried not to focus on that, instead stowing her bag and her coat in the overhead bin to clear the aisle for others to board.

"Introductions!" Emma said before Harper could even slide into the row to sit.

She pasted on a bright smile and turned their way. "Sebastian, these are my good friends Jonah and Emma Flynn. I work for Jonah's gaming software company, FlynnSoft. You guys, this is my boyfriend, Sebastian West."

Jonah stuck out his hand and the two men exchanged a firm handshake. "Good to meet you both," Sebastian said. "Harper has told me how much she enjoys her job at FlynnSoft. I'm sure that reflects well on you, Jonah."

She tried not to look impressed and instead turned toward her seat. It wasn't until that moment that she noticed a small, white envelope on the window seat. She picked the envelope up and settled in so Sebastian could take his place at her side. She looked around, wondering who might've put it on her seat, but no one seemed to be looking or paying any attention to her. There weren't envelopes like this one on the other seats. Just one for her, with her name written on the front in nondescript block letters.

While Sebastian put his bag in the overhead bin, Harper opened the envelope and pulled out the single page inside. It was handwritten, and relatively short, but it delivered a huge impact.

I know your little secret. If you don't want everyone to find out the truth and risk your big inheritance, you'll do exactly what I say. Once we arrive in Ireland, you'll go to the bank and withdraw a hundred thousand dollars. Then you'll leave it in an envelope at the front desk of the hotel for "B. Mayler" by dinnertime tomorrow. Miss the deadline and I'm going to make a big problem for you, Harper.

She read the words a dozen times, trying to make sense of it all, but there was no way to make sense of what she was seeing. Her heart was pounding in her ears, deafening her to anything but the sound of her internal panic. The fantastic plane and everyone on it faded into the background.

This was blackmail. She was being blackmailed.

How was that even possible?

Harper had been so careful about her secret. Aside from sharing some of it with Sebastian yesterday, no one, not her closest friends or family, knew the truth. Not even her brother or father knew about her financial difficulties. She'd kept it quiet for over eight years, working hard to make ends meet until the next payment came and she didn't have to fake it any longer. Sebastian had been the first to question her curious behavior, and it hadn't seemed to hurt to share a little information with him considering her birthday was right around the corner.

But someone had found out her secret, and that was a big problem.

Her grandfather on her mother's side of the family had set up a thirty-million-dollar trust fund for both her and her brother when they were born. It included a two-million-dollar payment on their eighteenth birthdays followed by a twenty-eight-million-dollar payment on their thirtieth birthdays. Harper's thirtieth was only a few weeks away now. She could see the light at the end of the tunnel. She should be coasting to the finish line, but her foolish youthful behavior had put everything at risk.

After her father ran into financial troubles with his gold-digging second wife, her grandfather had added a new provision to the grandchildren's trusts—if it was discovered that they had been financially irresponsible with their first payments, there would be no second payment. Ever-responsible Oliver had had no problem managing his money and had made his own fortune many times over. He hardly needed the second payment by the time his thirtieth birthday came around. But not Harper. By the time the provision was added, her frivolous lifestyle had already helped her blow through most of the first two million.

When she found out about the addendum, she'd realized she had to keep her situation a secret. Her grandfather couldn't find out or she'd risk the money she desperately needed. That second payment would put an end to her charade. She wouldn't have to eat ramen noodles for weeks to pay her massive building fee at the beginning of the year. She wouldn't have to return everything she bought and scour the thrift stores for designer finds to keep up her facade of a spoiled heiress. Harper wouldn't blow this new money—she wasn't a naive child any longer—but it would be nice not to have to pretend she had more than two grand in her savings account.

Thankfully that two thousand dollars she'd earmarked for Sebastian could stay put. It was all she had aside from her FlynnSoft 401K with its stiff withdrawal penalties. Where was she going to come up with a hundred thousand dollars by tomorrow? In a month, easy. But now…it was an impossible task.

"Are you okay?"

Harper quickly folded the letter closed and shoved it back into the envelope. She looked over at Sebastian, who had settled into his seat and buckled up. "I'm fine," she said. "Just reading over something."

"You look like the plane is about to crash," he noted. "You're white as a sheet. Since they haven't even closed the cabin door yet, I was concerned."

"Flying isn't my favorite thing," she lied, and slipped the note into her purse. "Even on a fancy jet like this.

My doctor gave me some pills and I hope to wake up in Ireland before I know it."

"Sleep? And miss a minute of this luxurious travel?" Sebastian picked up his crystal champagne flute. "Shall we toast before you slip into a drug-induced coma?"

Harper picked up her drink and fought to keep her hand from trembling with nerves. "What should we drink to?"

"To a safe, fun and *romantic* trip," he suggested with a knowing smile.

"I'll drink to that." She gently clinked her glass to his and downed the entire flute in one nervous gulp. Sebastian arched a curious eyebrow at her, but she ignored him. She needed some alcohol, stat, before that note sent her into hysterics.

Turning away from him, she fastened her seat belt, sat back and closed her eyes.

"You'll be fine," he soothed. "You're surrounded by friends and family. I'm here to hold your hand through the whole flight if you need me to. You don't have a thing to worry about."

Normally he would be right, and if her nerves were over flying, it might be helpful. But she couldn't feel safe and relax knowing that one of the people on this plane—one of her very own friends and family—was her blackmailer.

This was going to be a long trip.

Four

"What a great room!"

Harper followed Sebastian into their room at the hotel, grateful to finally be there. The flight itself had been uneventful once they'd taken off. She'd taken the pills with another glass of champagne—probably not the best idea—and woken when the wheels touched down in Dublin. Even if she'd had the money to pay her blackmailer, she hadn't had the chance to stop at a bank and get it. Two chartered luxury buses had picked them up at the airport and transported everyone on the nearly three-hour drive through the Irish countryside to their final destination of Markree Castle. The castle and its sprawling grounds had been renovated into a hotel and the entire location had been rented to house their group and host the wedding and reception.

Sebastian had looked out the window on the bus,

contentedly taking in the lush green landscape as it went by, but Harper hadn't been able to enjoy it. Every person who'd passed by her was run through a mental checklist of potential guilt or innocence. She supposed that was the most unnerving part of it all. This wasn't just some random internet criminal who'd dug up some dirt and tried to make a dime off her. It was someone she knew. Someone she trusted. She couldn't quite wrap her head around that.

Like she didn't already have enough to worry about on this trip. She eyeballed Sebastian as he sat on the bed and gave it a test bounce. It wasn't a large bed—a double perhaps—which would mean close quarters at night. Harper hadn't thought much about that when she'd concocted this plan. A lot of hotels in Europe had twin beds and that was what she'd expected. Just her luck that they'd end up with a room obviously appointed for lovers. Lovers who wanted to be close all the time.

She'd have to thank Violet for hooking her up, she thought drily.

The room was small but well done. There were towels twisted into swans in the bathroom, rose-scented bubble bath on the edge of the claw-foot tub, candles, lace curtains, red foil-wrapped heart chocolates on their pillows, a velvet love seat by the fireplace… Were this any other trip with any other man, Harper would be thrilled with the romantic vibe. It might help set the mood for their romantic ruse, but at the moment, pretending to have a boyfriend seemed pretty unimportant. Now she wished her only problem was being single.

As it was, it felt like the universe was just screwing with her.

"What's wrong with you?"

Harper turned toward Sebastian with a frown. "What do you mean?"

He watched her, stroking his dark goatee with thought. "I mean, you've been acting funny since we got on the plane to come here. I thought it was nerves, but it's been hours since we landed and you seem as distant as ever. We're in Ireland. Everyone thinks we're an adorable couple. You should be happy. What's going on?"

It was just her luck that her fake boyfriend would be so in tune with her emotions. Quentin wouldn't have noticed, but he was rarely concerned with anything but himself. She opened her mouth to tell him that she was fine, but his movement stopped her.

Getting up from the bed, he crossed the room and stood directly in front of her. He was close enough to reach out and touch. It took everything she had not to fall into his arms and let his strong embrace protect her from the outside world. But that felt a little too forward for their current situation.

Instead he stood close, without touching, looking deeply into her eyes. "And don't tell me it's nothing," he added. "My mother carried the weight of the world on her shoulders but would always insist that everything was fine. It was something then and it's something now. I know it when I see it."

Harper wanted to tell him. She needed to tell someone. Maybe he would know what to do, because she sure as hell didn't know how to handle this situation. She'd never been blackmailed before. Pulling away from him, she grabbed her purse off the entryway table and withdrew the small envelope from inside it. She handed it to Sebastian without a single word of explanation.

Sebastian's gaze flickered quickly over the note. By the time he was finished, his mouth had fallen into a deep frown of displeasure. Combined with his dark hair and eyes, something about his usual easygoing demeanor seemed to shift to almost wicked. Like she'd angered Bruce Banner. She almost expected his eyes to glow red with fury when he looked up at her. Instead she found them unexpectedly soft with concern. He was irate, but not with her.

"Where did this come from?" he asked, holding the note up.

"It was on my seat when we got on the plane. That's all I know." Harper wrapped her sweater tighter around her, as though it would help. She wished she had something more to go on, but she didn't. It was on generic white stationery and written with a block print text that anyone could do. There was nothing to give any kind of hint about who had left it there.

"Why didn't you say something to me?" he asked.

"When? When we were trapped on a plane for eight hours with eighty other people—one of whom was probably the blackmailer? They were likely watching me, waiting for my reaction to finding their little love note. So I didn't give them the satisfaction of panicking. I took my pills and went to sleep like it was nothing. But it's not nothing. I'm worried sick about this whole thing. Thankfully you're the only one to notice."

Sebastian looked over the note again before handing it back to her. His mouth tightened with irritation, highlighting the sharp, square lines of his jaw and the dark goatee that framed it. "So you suspect it's one of the wedding guests? Not the flight crew?"

Harper shrugged and tore her gaze from the tempting curve of his bottom lip. She wanted more than anything to focus on that. To lose herself in Sebastian's kiss and forget about the mess she was in. She got the feeling he wouldn't mind indulging her with a little distraction. But this wasn't the time. Blackmail was serious business.

"I'd never seen any of the crew before. We were one of the last couples to board, so almost any of the guests could've put it on my seat. As you've read, I'm supposed to leave the money at the front desk, so it has to be someone that's still here in Sligo with us. I'm sure the flight crew is back in Dublin."

She sank onto the bed, clutching the note in her hand. Where she hadn't allowed herself to really react on the flight, now, in the privacy of their hotel suite, she felt herself starting to emotionally unravel. "What am I going to do, Sebastian?" she asked with eyes squeezed tightly shut to trap the tears. She hated to cry.

She felt the bed sag beside her and Sebastian's comforting warmth against her side. "The way I see it, you've got three options. One, you pay the blackmail. That will keep your secret under wraps, but you're giving the blackmailer the upper hand. I don't know what you're being blackmailed for, but at any time they could demand more money to stay quiet. You'll never really be free of the blackmailer's hold on your life. But that's a risk that might be worth taking. Only you can answer that question."

She knew paying the blackmailer wasn't the best

choice, but it was the one she'd take if given the chance. Unfortunately that wasn't an option for her. "I couldn't pay it even if I wanted to. I told you before that I was in a tight spot financially. It's possible that given some time I could go to a bank and get a loan with my apartment for collateral. But they want it tonight. By dinnertime. That's just impossible, especially considering we're in the middle of a remote estate in the Irish countryside. Even in Dublin, I couldn't have pulled it off."

"Okay," Sebastian said after listening to her logic. "The second option would be to call the police. Blackmail is illegal. They could take prints off the card, perhaps leave a dummy package at the desk for the culprit to pick up and then arrest them. You'll run the risk of the secret being exposed in the process, but they'll get their punishment."

Harper shook her head. She didn't want cops involved. Not in this situation. It would be bad enough for her to lose her inheritance and for everyone to find out what she'd done. She didn't need her story being in the newspapers, too.

"What's option three?" she asked.

"Option three is to expose the secret yourself and take their power away."

She could do that, but it would be a twenty-eight-million-dollar decision. Just the thought made her stomach start to ache with dread. She was stuck between a rock and a hard place. "I... I can't. It will ruin everything I've worked so hard to achieve."

Harper felt Sebastian's arm wrap around her shoulders. She couldn't resist leaning into him and resting her head against his chest. It was soothing to listen to the beating of his heart and enjoy the warmth of his embrace. It had been a long time since she'd had someone in her life to hold her like this. To listen to her when she had worries on her mind. She knew she had been lonely, but she didn't realize how deeply she'd felt it until this moment.

"Harper," Sebastian said after a long silence with her in his arms. "I have to ask this. Whether or not you answer is up to you, but it's hard for me to help you when I don't know. What could you have done to be blackmailed for?"

She knew the question would come eventually. Harper dreaded having to explain her youthful stupidity to anyone, but for some reason it was worse to tell Sebastian. He was successful, like her brother. He never would've made the mistakes she'd made. But she needed to tell someone. To have one person on this trip she could trust. He was the only one she could eliminate as a suspect since he couldn't possibly have left the note on her seat.

Harper sighed heavily and buried her face into his chest to avoid speaking for a little while longer. She pressed her nose to his collar and breathed in the spicy scent of his cologne and his skin. It was easy to stay there and pretend that everything would be okay for a little while longer.

"I'm a spoiled little rich girl," she said at last.

"Tell me something I don't know," Sebastian responded unexpectedly.

Harper sat up sharply and frowned at him.

"I'm kidding," he said. "Please continue. I'm just trying to keep things light."

Harper slumped over and sighed. "My brother and I originally had trust funds set up for thirty million dollars each. When my mother died, my grandfather decided that, without her guidance, it might be better to break it into two payments. A small, two-million-dollar payment when we turned eighteen, followed by the rest when we turned thirty."

"Makes sense. An eighteen-year-old is more likely to blow all the money and have nothing to show for it."

"Exactly. And, basically, that's what I did. My father had given me everything I could ever want. When I went off to college, I continued to live that way, just on my own money for a change. When I started to run low, my father pitched in. But then he ran into his own financial problems and I was on my own."

"I don't hear anything that's blackmail worthy. Did you spend all the money on drugs or something?"

"Of course not! I spent it on shoes. Clothes. Trips. Makeup. Designer handbags. Expensive meals. Nonsense, really, but what I'd always been used to. And, no, nothing was criminal. Embarrassing, but not criminal. I went to Yale for a finance degree and yet I was a fool with my own money. No…the problem came after my father got a divorce. My grandfather was worried that our dad had set a bad example and added an additional requirement to the trust to keep us in line—if we blew the first payment, we wouldn't get the second."

"Does he know what you did?" Sebastian asked.

"No. Most of the money was long gone before he even added the stipulation, but I'd transferred the funds into my private accounts so no one had any insight into my finances. But someone has found out. And if I can't magically come up with a hundred grand, it's going to cost me a cool twenty-eight million instead."

* * *

Sebastian's blood was boiling. He was pretty sure his doctor wouldn't be too pleased that his relaxing vacation time had been overshadowed by drama of the worst kind. He could hear his pulse pounding in his ears as he marched down the stone hallway of the castle.

Harper was still in their room, spinning in circles and attempting to unpack her luggage. He'd stepped out to give her some privacy and to get a little air. The truth was that he didn't want her to know how angry he was over her whole situation. After her confession, she might mistakenly think he was angry with her and he was anything but.

Instead he was feeling remarkably protective of Harper. It was almost as though she really was his girlfriend. With her curled up in his arms, it was hard for him to remember this was all a sham. It certainly felt real. Maybe too real for the first day of the charade.

Before he'd left the room, he'd promised to keep her secret, with one caveat. If he found out who her blackmailer was before she did, he couldn't promise her that he wouldn't cause some trouble for the jerk. She might not know that Sebastian had grown up on the wrong side of the tracks, but he had and, at a moment's notice, the scrappy kid who'd used his fists to defend himself could come out. Whomever was putting Harper through this hell deserved a black eye. Or two.

Even as Sebastian headed down the staircase to the main lobby, he could feel his hands curl into tight fists. He was strung tight, clutching his notebook under his arm and ready to fight at the slightest provocation. He hadn't been sure where he was going when he'd left the room, but he found himself loitering around the front desk. Perhaps the culprit would be there, waiting on a payment to be dropped off.

He was in no mindset to work, so he set aside his notebook, grabbed a copy of the local paper and settled into a large wingback chair by the fireplace. Despite being early summer, it was Ireland and that still meant cool weather, especially given they were near the northwest coast. The fire offered a comfortable, draft-free place to sit in the stone behemoth of a building.

Sebastian glanced over the words in the paper, but he was focused more on the comings and goings. There were few at this hour of the afternoon. It was likely that many had fallen prey to jet lag and were napping in their rooms before the welcome dinner. Most of the people he saw in the lobby were wearing the uniforms of the hotel staff.

After about thirty minutes, out of the corner of his eye, he noticed someone approach the front desk. He turned his attention fully to the man standing there, realizing almost immediately that it was one of the few people on the trip he actually knew—Harper's ex, Quentin.

That made sense. Harper had mentioned that she'd been short on cash basically since college and she'd only dated Quentin a few years ago. If they'd been at all serious, there had to have been signs of her difficulties. Sebastian had noticed it in minutes. Quentin, of all people, should have been able to tell if Harper was broke. If not, maybe she'd confided in him and forgotten about it. And perhaps he might also know that her financial luck was about to change. It made sense. But would he be bold enough to try to get a piece of it?

Quentin stood nervously waiting at the counter for the desk clerk to return and, after a brief exchange Sebastian couldn't hear, turned and headed back toward the elevators empty-handed. He glanced around the lobby as he walked, an almost agitated expression lining his face. And then his gaze met with Sebastian's pointed glare.

He knew he could turn away. Try to appear more subtle in his appraisal. But at the moment, Sebastian didn't care if the bastard knew he was watching him. Let him know they were on to his sick game. Let him check the desk twenty times tonight. He was going to be disappointed. No matter what Harper wanted to do, she was right about one thing. There wasn't going to be any way to pull a hundred grand out of thin air in a foreign country.

It might even be a tricky thing for Sebastian to do and he had ten times that much cash in his checking account at any given time. Banks simply didn't like handing over that much money. There were too many checks and balances, wire transfers, international calls and such before they parted with it. Perhaps if they were in Monte Carlo where people parted with larger amounts in the casinos on a regular basis, but rural Ireland? Not likely. If Quentin was behind this blackmail plot, his timing was crappy.

Quentin quickly broke their connection with an anxious biting of his lip and turned his back to wait for the elevator. Within a few seconds it opened and he disappeared without looking back in Sebastian's direction.

Sebastian was so engrossed in watching his mark that he didn't notice someone approaching his chair.

"May I join you?"

He turned and recognized Harper's older brother standing there. Oliver and his wife, Lucy, had been introduced briefly to him on the bus, but they really hadn't had time to talk aside from some basic pleasantries. Sebastian expected that he had questions for the new boyfriend. Any brother worth his salt would when his little sister was involved, even if she was a grown woman. "Please, have a seat. I'm just trying to stay awake until dinnertime, so I could use some company."

Oliver chuckled and settled into the other wingback chair. He had a cut-crystal lowball glass in his hand filled with some ice and a dark amber liquor. "I know how that is. International travel messes with your internal clock. I'm hoping to eat a huge dinner, have a couple drinks and pass out at a reasonable hour. Whatever that is. I'm not sure if Harper told you, but Lucy and I have nine-month-old twins. Our sleep schedules haven't been reasonable in quite some time."

"I can imagine. I wouldn't be surprised if the two of you did nothing but sleep when a wedding event wasn't taking place." Sebastian hadn't noticed any children on the flight but Violet and Aidan's toddler, so he presumed they were all back in New York with their nannies and their grandparents. Sounded like the perfect getaway to relax, nap and have some alone time together.

And yet he was downstairs with Sebastian instead.

"Lucy is actually napping right now. I told her not to because it would screw up her sleep, but she told me to mind my own business and go downstairs." Oliver chuckled and sipped at his drink. "They're a sassy group of women, my sister included. I never thought

I'd be roped into all of it, and yet here I am. Do you know what you're getting yourself into, Sebastian?"

He smiled. He was pretty sure he was in over his head when he'd agreed to go on this trip and she'd kissed him in the department store. "If I didn't, I'm getting a good feel for it on this trip," he said. "It's been quite the experience so far and it's only the first day here. Being the odd man out allows me to sort of observe from the fringes, which is fine by me. To be honest, I don't spend a lot of time with people. Certainly not like this. My business partner, Finn Solomon, is the outward face of our company. I spend most of my time sketching out plans or tinkering with my latest ideas in the lab at work."

"I used to be that way. When I inherited Orion from my father, the company was a mess. Apple was king and PCs weren't cool anymore. Especially those old tower dinosaurs everyone had at work or in their closets. I sacrificed a lot of my personal life sitting with my engineers, trying to brainstorm new computer products that would make us competitive again. Now, of course, we're back on our feet and I'm able to shift my focus to other more important things, like Lucy and the twins. Say, have you been married before?"

Let the prying begin. Nice segue. "I haven't. I suppose I've been more focused on building our company, so I've never married or had any children."

Oliver nodded thoughtfully. "You know, all of Harper's friends have recently settled down and had children. After Violet and Aidan get married this weekend, Harper will be the only single one left."

"She's mentioned that."

"I suppose she feels some pressure to follow suit."

Sebastian narrowed his gaze at Oliver. "You're asking if Harper is barking up the wrong tree with me since I'm a thirty-eight-year-old workaholic bachelor?"

Oliver simply shrugged and sipped his drink. "Is she?"

"I suppose I'm getting to the age where I need to take the idea of a family more seriously, but until Harper, it hadn't really crossed my mind. I'm not opposed to it, no, but it simply hasn't been in the cards for me yet."

Her brother listened thoughtfully and nodded. "I was the same way until Lucy blew through my life like a hurricane. I didn't think I was ready for marriage or children, either, but she changed everything. It was like my eyes were suddenly opened and all I could see was her and our future together. Is it like that with you and my sister?"

That was something Sebastian didn't think he could lie about. It was easy to pretend to date and to be attracted to Harper because he was attracted to her. But to love her? To envision their future together? That was different and he had no doubt her brother could spot it if he fibbed. "It's only been a few months, but I think we're definitely getting to a more serious place. I care for your sister," he said.

And he did. He didn't want to see her get hurt, be it by him or Quentin or whomever that sleazy blackmailer was. That meant he cared a little, even for a woman he hardly knew. It was hard not to when he'd been drawn into her world and her problems so quickly. If Lucy was a hurricane, perhaps Harper was a tornado, plucking him from a wheat field and sucking him up into the swirling drama of her life.

"Listen, I don't want to do that stereotypical brother thing where I threaten you not to hurt my sister and wave around my shotgun. It's kind of cliché and not that effective, if Quentin is any evidence of that. I also don't own a shotgun. But I will say that you're the first man my sister has seriously dated in quite a while. I'm happy for you both, but I'm also nervous. She's kept this relationship quiet and the fact that she's suddenly announcing it to the world means she's feeling more comfortable with her feelings for you, whatever they may be. My sister is all sarcasm and sass on the outside, but all that is there as a barrier to protect the fact that she's really a marshmallow on the inside. She gets hurt easily."

Sebastian listened carefully. Even though he knew this relationship wasn't real, he took her brother's words to heart. He'd already been a witness to Harper's softer side—the side that was nervous about what other people thought of her and the part that was tied in knots over her secrets being exposed. She definitely had a soft underbelly. To be honest, seeing that part of her had endeared her to him more than he realized. She wasn't just the snarky single friend living the footloose and fancy-free life in Manhattan. She was more than that. Much more. And it made Sebastian curious to unearth more of her hidden layers.

Oliver glanced down at his watch and sighed before finishing off his drink. "Well, I'm glad we could have this little chat. I'd better head upstairs and wake Lucy so she has time to freshen up before dinner. I'll see you and Harper there in a little while."

"We'll see you later," Sebastian said with a wave. He watched Oliver disappear from the lobby and glanced back over at the hotel front desk. He hadn't been watching it for at least fifteen or twenty minutes. Anyone looking for the package of blackmail money could've come and gone and he'd missed it while chatting with Oliver.

Frustrated, he folded up the newspaper and decided to follow Oliver's suit. It was almost time for the welcome dinner in the great hall and he could use some time to change. With a sigh, he picked up his notebook and headed for the staircase to find Harper to report on what he'd seen, carefully leaving out her brother's little chat.

As far as he was concerned, Quentin should be at the top of the suspect list and he was going to keep an eye on him.

Five

Since everyone was tired, the welcome dinner was short and, for that, Harper was relieved. Aidan and Violet said a few words, thanked everyone for coming, and every couple was given a gift bag. Inside were some useful essentials: a schedule of activities, a map of the property and some authentic Irish chocolates.

Harper had difficulty focusing on any of the food or conversation. Her eyes kept running over each guest, wondering which one was expecting to be a hundred grand richer before bedtime. No one was watching her, no one was acting odd, and yet she could feel someone's eyes on her. Her gaze flicked over to Quentin. He seemed a little out of sorts tonight. He fidgeted with his food and didn't engage anyone, even his fiancée, in conversation.

After Sebastian had mentioned seeing her ex go by

the front desk, it had confirmed her suspicions that he might be behind this. He was the only one who made sense. He knew a little about her situation, or he had back when they dated. The question was whether or not he needed money badly enough to use it against her. She didn't know. A hundred grand wasn't a lot in the scheme of things. All she knew was that she hated being in the same room with him. She wanted to escape upstairs as soon as she could.

At the same time, as they got up to leave the great hall, Harper realized she was also dreading going back to the suite with Sebastian. When he'd returned to the room before dinner, she had thankfully already dressed for the evening. She'd been in the process of curling her hair in the bathroom as he'd entered their room. He'd gone about changing his clothes, paying no attention to the fact that Harper was in the next room with the door wide open.

She'd tried not to stare in the mirror at him as he'd walked around in his navy boxer briefs, laying out his outfit. She'd told herself that it was surprise, not desire, that had caused her to study his mostly naked body so closely. She'd expected the mad scientist to be soft through the middle from long hours at the lab and less-than-ideal eating habits, but he wasn't. His body was long and lean with hard muscles that twitched beneath tanned skin that extended far below his collar line.

How did he get a body like that working in his lab for long stretches of time?

"Ye-ouch!" she'd hollered, pulling her attention back to the blazing-hot curling iron where it belonged. She'd sucked at her burned finger and focused on finishing her hair, even when he'd come into the bathroom still in his underwear. He'd bent over the sink to splash water on his face and beard, then combed his hair back and was done. Men had it so easy.

"Could you put on a robe or something?" she'd finally asked. Despite her best intentions to ignore him when they were alone, she was sure to burn off a chunk of hair if he kept walking around mostly naked.

Sebastian had seemed startled and mildly insulted by the request at first, but had quickly retrieved one of the resort robes and covered up.

She'd thanked him and the tension between them eased. They'd finished dressing, gone down to the great hall and sat together throughout the meal, engaging in polite conversation with those around them. They'd smiled, leaned into each other, shared bites of food and were as lovey-dovey as they could stand to be until they were finally released for some welcome rest.

Now that she'd had an eyeful of what he was hiding under his suits, Harper wasn't sure how well she would sleep tonight. Not lying a mere inch or two from Sebastian for hours on end.

They bypassed the elevator and walked slowly and silently up the staircase together to their suite. About halfway up, Harper felt the brush of Sebastian's fingers against her own. She looked down and put her hand in his when she realized he was intentionally reaching for her. He was right. They should be holding hands. She couldn't let any awkwardness that happened behind closed doors impact the show they were putting on for everyone else.

If only touching him didn't unnerve her the way it did. His hand was large and warm, enveloping hers in a way that made heat radiate up her arm. By the time they reached their room, her blood was humming through her veins and she felt as if the silk pussy bow that tied at the collar of the Fendi blouse she'd chosen was about to choke her. She also felt flush in the otherwise cool castle. That could only be Sebastian's doing.

He let go of her hand long enough to open the door and let her step in ahead of him. He followed behind, pulling the door shut and fastening the privacy latch.

Harper wasn't the only one who was oddly overheated. As she untied the bow at her neck, she watched Sebastian slip quickly out of his suitcoat and tug his tie loose. She found her eyes drawn to the hollow of his throat as he unfastened his collar and continued down the line of buttons until a touch of dark chest hair was exposed.

Suddenly the thought of pressing a kiss against that part of his neck appeared in her mind. The warm scent of his skin, the stubble brushing her cheeks, the rhythmic thump of his pulse against her lips… An unwelcome tingle of desire surged through her whole body, making her belly clench and her breasts ache with longing in the confines of her bra.

When her nervous gaze met his, she found a questioning look in his eyes and a room that was abruptly very quiet. "What?" she asked before turning away to focus on kicking out of her pointy-toed heels.

Sebastian just shrugged and sat in a chair to pull off his shoes. "You were staring at me, that's all. I was waiting for you to say something. Did I get some shepherd's pie on my shirt?" He looked down at the pristine gray shirt.

She wished he was a mess. Maybe then she could ignore the building attraction between them. Instead, he'd been the perfect companion so far. Perfect aside from being too attractive, too nice and too supportive. A soft, pasty midsection would really help her control her libido right now, but she knew that what was under that shirt was anything but. "No. I just…got lost in my thoughts, I guess."

It was then that, with them both in states of partial dress, they found themselves at an impasse. Harper didn't know what to do next. She certainly wasn't about to tell him what was on her mind. If she stood there any longer, he'd continue to undress like before. She supposed she could gather up her pajamas and take them into the bathroom to change like this was a sleepover with a group of shy ten-year-old girls. Perhaps that would give him time to change privately, as well.

She turned to where her luggage was sitting open and started riffling through it. Thankfully she'd thought to pack pajamas that were less than intriguing. She had passed on the dog onesie—it was too bulky— but had chosen something just as unappealing. There was a piece of nice lingerie for show, but the rest was purely practical in nature. They were flannel, for the potentially cold Irish nights, and long-sleeved, to keep any glimpses of exposed skin to a minimum.

"Here," he said.

Harper turned her attention to Sebastian in time to see him deliberately taking off the rest of his clothes. "Um, what are you doing?" she asked, clutching her pajamas to her breasts for dear life as she realized what was happening.

"I'm getting this out of the way." He shrugged off his dress shirt and stepped out of the suit pants that had pooled at his feet. "We can't spend this whole week tiptoeing around each other and if you keep burning fingers on your curling iron while you sneak peeks at me, people are going to start asking questions. We're sharing a room. Sharing a bed. It doesn't matter what does or doesn't happen in the bed—we need to be more comfortable around each other. You said so yourself when we first agreed to this whole thing." Standing in nothing but those same navy boxer briefs, Sebastian held out his arms. "Take a good look. Get it out of your system. It's just the standard equipment."

Harper watched with confusion and curiosity as he displayed himself to her. His equipment was anything but standard. Her gaze flickered from his defined biceps to the chest hair across his pecs to the trail that ran down his stomach to the gray waistband of his briefs. She was tempted to glance lower, but he turned, giving her a look at his muscular back and curved rear end, as well.

"Well?" he asked with his back to her.

"Why are you so tanned?" she blurted out to her own embarrassment.

He turned around to face her with a smile. "You're staring at my ass but your only question is why I'm tanned?" He shrugged, unfazed by her question. "Okay, well, my apartment building has a rooftop pool. I swim a lot. It's one of my stress relievers. It's not enough, apparently, but it's what I do. I'm not big on going to the gym. It's boring."

"What do you mean it's not enough?"

Sebastian's lips twisted for a moment in thought and he shook his head. "Nothing. There's not enough stress relievers in the world when you're in my line of work, that's all." He looked down at his chest and back at her. "Seen enough?"

Harper nodded nervously.

Sebastian mirrored her nod and sought out a pair of lounging pants from his bag. He tugged them on and looked at her with a wry grin. "Now when you talk to your girlfriends about getting me out of my pants, you don't have to lie."

Harper smiled, still fiercely holding her pajamas as though they were a protective armor. It felt silly after that to hide in the bathroom to change, but was she brave enough to do it out here?

"Your turn."

Her gaze met his. "What?" she said with obvious panic in her voice. Did he honestly expect her to parade around mostly naked because he had?

He held up his hands to deflect the blowback. "I'm just kidding Harper. Relax."

Harper held in a nervous twitter of laughter at his joke. "Oh."

"It's nothing I haven't seen before, anyway," he added. "I'm sure it's nice and all, but I'm not about to hurt myself while I stare at you."

Harper didn't know if she should be relieved or offended. He'd told her before that she was beautiful, but at the moment he seemed as though he couldn't care less about catching a glimpse of her naked body. Maybe he was using reverse psychology on her, she couldn't be sure, but she had the sudden urge to take off her clothes and prove him wrong.

Against her better judgment, she went with the surge of bravery and decided to put him to the test. "That's good to know," she said. She set her pajamas on the edge of the bed and pulled her blouse up over her head. She paid no attention to Sebastian as she straightened the straps of her cream-satin bra and unzipped her pencil skirt. She let it pool to her ankles, bending slowly to pick it up off the floor and to give him all the time he might need to see her cream thong and firm ass. She'd spent a lot of hours in the gym working on that butt and he damn well better be impressed by it.

She wanted to turn and look at him. For some reason, she wanted to see naked desire and need in his eyes. She knew it was there—she could practically feel his gaze on her body. But she didn't dare look at him. She wasn't sure what she would do if she found what she was looking for. Would she act on it? Ignore it? As it was, they would both spend tonight aching for something they couldn't have.

Harper decided not to turn in Sebastian's direction. It was enough to know that he hadn't moved from his spot since she'd started undressing. She forced herself to step into the plaid pajama pants. She unbuttoned the flannel top and readied it to put on before reaching back to unfasten her bra. Before she could slip it from her shoulders, she caught a blur of movement from the corner of her eye and a moment later the bathroom door shut hard. The shower came on not long after that.

So much for being comfortable around each other and getting it out of their system, she thought. Harper continued to put on her pajamas with a grin.

It was only the first day and she could already tell this was going to be a miserably boring trip.

It was not at all what she had envisioned when they'd been invited to the glamorous overseas wedding of

Violet Niarchos and Aidan Murphy. Yes, sure, they'd flown on a snazzy chartered plane and were sleeping in a private Irish castle, but watching the Queen of England snore into her teacup would be more exciting than hanging around this rotting pile of bricks with a bunch of blowhard billionaires.

She'd heard the wedding coordinator talking to her assistant on the plane about the week's itinerary. It sounded like one boring event after another with no end in sight. The week promised "highlights" like a round of golf for the gentlemen, a tea party for the ladies and shopping excursions into the sleepy village by the sea.

Couldn't they have at least stayed in Dublin for a night? Every person who walked past her in the hallway was worth a bloody fortune and yet hadn't the slightest clue how to have any fun with their money.

If not for the little blackmail scheme she was running, the whole trip would be a waste of her time. So far, even that had proven fruitless as far as money went, but it had been something to do. Watching Harper squirm under the pressure of blackmail was nice, but it wasn't what she really wanted.

That spoiled little princess needed to shut up and pay up. She could afford it. It was one tiny fraction of the fortune she was set to inherit from her dear old grandfather. Harper hadn't worked for or earned that money. It was to be dropped in her lap just because she'd been born into a family that handed down multi-million-dollar trust funds just as easily as other people passed hazel eyes and freckles down to their children.

She might not have all the money now, but she would have it soon. In the meantime, Harper could easily get her hands on it. She could borrow it from one of her rich friends, her brother…even her new boyfriend was loaded. Basically anyone on that flight could hand over the cash without blinking. Harper just needed the right motivation to ask.

Harper didn't deserve twenty-eight million dollars. She didn't even deserve the twenty-seven million, nine hundred thousand that would be left after she paid the blackmail.

She deserved it. She needed it.

And she was going to get it before the week was up.

That was the longest night of Sebastian's life.

As it was, he'd stayed in the bathroom far longer than was necessary. After he'd showered and tried to take the edge off, he'd meticulously brushed and flossed his teeth, rinsed with mouthwash, washed his face…anything and everything he could do to kill time and wipe the image of Harper's near naked body from his mind.

She might as well have been naked. That tantalizing little thong left almost nothing to the imagination and with the creamy color that nearly matched her skin, the rest of it just blended away. He'd tried to play it cool. Act like the mature adult he thought he was when they'd started this little game. He'd gritted his teeth, tried to think of the most un-arousing things he could, and even closed his eyes for a moment or two. But he hadn't been able to keep his gaze away for long. When she'd moved to take her bra off, though, he'd known he'd had to go.

It was that or… No. That hadn't been an option.

Theirs was a fake relationship. Despite all the hand-holding, embraces and canoodling they did in public, it was all fake. They weren't in love. They hardly knew one another. When he'd signed up for this, he'd thought it wouldn't be that hard to pretend to be Harper's lover. Now he wanted it for real so badly he could hardly draw in the scent of her perfume without gaining an erection.

By the time he'd come out of the bathroom, almost all the lights were out and Harper had been in bed. She'd been lying on her side with her back to him, so he'd been able to get into bed, turn off the nearby lamp and go to sleep without having to face her again.

At least that had been the idea. Instead he'd spent most of the night tossing and turning. He'd felt anxious. Squirmy. Filled with nervous energy that he couldn't shake. He should have been exhausted after staying up all day to adjust to the time change, but it hadn't mattered. All Sebastian's body cared about was the warm, soft female lying mere inches from him.

He remembered seeing the light of dawn through the curtains right around the time he was finally able to doze off. The next thing he heard was the shower running. When Harper emerged from the bathroom—fully dressed, thank goodness—she sat in the chair and rifled through the welcome bag they'd received the night before.

"What's on the agenda today?" he muttered into his pillow with a gravelly, sleepy voice.

"Today they've chartered a bus into the nearby town of Sligo if anyone wants to go shop or sightsee. It leaves at ten, after breakfast is done."

"And when is breakfast?"

"About fifteen minutes from now."

Reluctantly, Sebastian pushed himself up and swung

his legs out of bed. "I'll be ready in ten," he grumbled as he stumbled into the shower and turned on the water.

He quickly washed his hair and body, cleaned up his goatee, and was ready to go in ten minutes, as he'd predicted. He was wearing a more casual outfit for a day in town, so the jeans and polo shirt had come together quickly. Harper was dressed more casually, as well. When she stood to leave, he couldn't help but notice her skinny jeans were like a second skin. They clung to the delicious curve of her ass and thighs, bringing back flashes from the night before that were not breakfast appropriate.

"Is something wrong?" she asked.

If he didn't want to embarrass himself, yes.

"No," he said and reached for a windbreaker in the closet. "I was just considering a jacket." He folded it over his arm and carried it in front of him as they headed downstairs to eat.

"Miss Drake?" a voice called out as they reached the lobby and headed toward the great hall.

They both stopped, turning their attention to the front desk where a clerk was looking their way. The woman had an envelope in her hand that looked eerily familiar.

Sebastian's empty stomach started to ache with the feeling of dread. It was a similar envelope to the one Harper had received on the plane. He wasn't sure why that surprised him. She hadn't met last night's blackmail request, so another note had arrived. He hadn't been in the lobby to see who had left it there. When he'd mentioned seeing Quentin loitering around the desk the night before, Harper hadn't seemed surprised, which had just reinforced his idea that he was the suspect to watch.

"I have a message here for you, ma'am," the clerk added in a thick Irish accent.

Harper knew what it was, too. They walked together to the front desk and she took the envelope from the woman's hand. It had her name written on it in the same nondescript block text. "Thank you," she said.

"Did you happen to be working when they left the note? To see who left it?" Sebastian asked.

"No, sir. I just started my shift. The previous clerk said it had been left at the desk early this morning while she was setting up the coffee station. She didn't see who left it, either. Is there a problem?"

"No," Sebastian said with a reassuring smile. "Thanks so much." He turned back to Harper, who was looking at the envelope with a face almost as white as the parchment. "Let's take that back upstairs," he suggested. "Breakfast can wait."

She nodded blankly and let him lead her out of the lobby. He glanced around, looking for someone loitering curiously in the area, but it was mostly empty. A couple he didn't recognize was looking at magazines in the corner, but there was no one else there. They were all likely in the great room gathering for their first authentic Irish breakfast.

Back in the room, he escorted Harper over to the love seat and sat beside her.

"You know, with everything else going on last night, I almost forgot I was missing the deadline. This morning, the thought hadn't even crossed my mind. How could I forget about something like that? And then I saw the envelope in her hand and I remembered what a mess I was still in. Now I don't want to open it," she said.

"Why not?"

"Because…it's not going to be good. He's going to be angry because I didn't pay the blackmail money. There's one of two things in this note—a second chance to pay or notification that my secret is as good as public knowledge by now. I could walk into the dining hall and everyone could know the truth about me."

"You won't know which it is until you open it."

With a sigh, she ran her finger under the lip of the envelope and ripped it open. She pulled out another small card, identical to the first, with the same block-style text inside. Harper held it up to read aloud.

"It seems your payment got lost in the mail, Harper. Yesterday was a tiring day of travel, so I'm going to be kind and give you another opportunity to give me what I want. This time, to make it easier, make it one hundred thousand euros in an envelope at the front desk by noon tomorrow. Don't disappoint me again.'"

Harper's hand dropped into her lap with dismay. "Great, now the price has gone up. When I looked at the exchange rate yesterday, it was in the euro's favor. He's now asking for something in the neighborhood of a hundred and twenty thousand dollars in the name of 'convenience.' I mean, why not?" She giggled, bringing her hand to her mouth just in time to stifle a sob. "I couldn't pay the hundred grand, so two days later, naturally, I should be able to pay that and more."

Sebastian wrapped his arm around Harper's shoulders and pulled her tight against him. She gave in to the embrace, burying her face in his chest and holding on to him. He hated seeing her upset. He wasn't a very physical person by nature, but if he got his hands on her blackmailer, he wasn't sure what he would do. At the moment he wanted to choke the guy until tears ran down his cheeks like Harper's did.

"What am I going to do?" She sniffled against his polo shirt. "He's not going to go away. I don't have the money. I don't know what to do, Sebastian."

He sighed and stroked her hair as he tried to come up with an answer. He wasn't sure there was a way out of this that wouldn't be painful somehow. "Do you trust any of your friends enough? Lucy or Emma maybe? Your brother perhaps?"

"Trust them enough for what?"

"Enough to ask them to help you with this. To give you the money. Just a loan until you get to your birthday and can pay them back."

Harper pulled away and shook her head. She wiped the tears from her cheeks, leaving black smudges of mascara that he wanted to reach out and brush away.

"I can't do that. I just can't."

"You don't think they'd give it to you?"

"No, they would. Each and every one of them would in a heartbeat," Harper explained. "That's why I can't ask. I'm not going to abuse their friendship like that. Besides, they'd want to know what it was for. They'd worry that I was in some kind of trouble."

"Aren't you?" he asked.

"Yes, but not trouble I want any of them to know about. This whole thing is so embarrassing. Really, even if I wasn't at risk of losing my inheritance, I wouldn't want anyone to know about the financial trouble I'm in. I'm an accountant. It just looks so awful."

Sebastian gently stroked her back, considering his options in this situation. Initially he hadn't been in favor of paying the blackmail, but this wasn't going to go away. This person was going to get the money or ruin Harper's life in the process. "What about the bank?" he asked.

She looked up at him, confusion creasing her brow. "What do you mean?"

"What about seeing if the local bank would lend you the money? When we go into town today, we can stop at a bank and see what options you have."

"Not many," she said. "Without collateral, getting that much money would be nearly impossible. If by some chance they did agree to loan me the money, it would be at an outrageous interest rate."

"Not necessarily," Sebastian said thoughtfully. "What if I cosigned?"

Harper sat back against the arm of the love seat and looked at him with an expression he couldn't quite read. "Are you serious?"

He shrugged. "Yeah."

"That's really sweet of you to offer, Sebastian, but I can't ask you to do that. It wouldn't be right."

"Why? I have no intention of paying a dime of the money back. It's all on you. And if you don't pay it when your inheritance comes through, I'll see to it that there are unpleasant consequences for you, if it makes you feel better about it."

She blinked a few times as though she were trying to process his offer. "You'd really do that for me?"

"Of course," he said. "You're my girlfriend. Don't

you think the blackmailer would think it suspicious if you couldn't come up with the money somehow and yet your boyfriend is a millionaire?"

Sebastian wasn't sure what the reaction would be, but he certainly wasn't expecting her to throw herself into his arms. Before he knew what was happening, Harper's lips were pressed to his once again. Just like at Neiman Marcus, she was enthusiastically thanking him with her mouth. Unlike at Neiman Marcus, this time there wasn't a crowd of onlookers to keep the kiss PG-rated.

If he was honest with himself, he'd been wanting this kiss since that one had ended. Not one of the quick pecks she gave him when they were out in public, but a real kiss. One where he could taste the cool mint-toothpaste flavor on her tongue and let his hands roam until they discovered that under today's long-sleeved T-shirt she was wearing a lace bra.

The kiss intensified as his palms cupped her through her shirt. Harper moaned softly against his mouth and moved closer to him on the love seat. It would be so easy to pull her into his lap, whip the shirt off her head and bury his face between the creamy breasts he'd only glimpsed the night before. But he wouldn't. Not now.

As much as he didn't want to, Sebastian forced himself to pull away. This wasn't the time or place for this to happen. If he and Harper ever transitioned from a fake relationship to a real one, he didn't want it to be because she was emotionally compromised or felt indebted to him.

He rested his forehead against hers as he took a cleansing breath and chuckled to himself.

"What's the laugh for?" she asked.

"I was just thinking that I would've offered to co-sign yesterday if I'd known I'd get that kiss in return."

Harper grimaced and shook her head with mock dismay. "Let's get back downstairs. We don't want to miss the bus to Sligo."

Six

"Wipe that anxious look off your face."

Harper clutched her purse to her chest and frowned at Sebastian. "I can't help it," she argued. "I don't like walking around with this much cash."

"You're not walking through downtown Manhattan. You're riding a bus with friends through the Irish countryside. We'll be back at the castle in a few minutes. No one on the bus is going to mug you, I'm pretty sure."

She could only sigh and shake her head, diverting her attention out the window to the passing scenery. Ireland was a beautiful country with rolling, emerald hillsides, misty valleys and wild, gray seas. She wished she was able to enjoy it. Harper had always wanted to go to Ireland but never managed to make the trip before. But now that she was here, all she could think about was the twenty-five thousand euros in her Birkin purse and the bastard she was about to give it to.

"Maybe B. Mayler is on the bus. Ever think of that? Maybe he followed us into town."

Sebastian turned to look over his shoulder at the people on the bus. "I doubt it. Besides, he wouldn't need to steal it from you. You're about to give it to him outright."

He was probably right. She hadn't seen Quentin on the bus or in town. She half expected to see him sitting in the lobby when they arrived, waiting with baited breath for her to leave the package at the front desk, especially after Sebastian had seen him at the desk the night before. She hated to tell Quentin that he was going to be disappointed.

Twenty-five thousand euros. Not a hundred thousand. That was all the bank would give her even with Sebastian's signature on the loan. If they'd had more time...if she'd had better credit, more collateral...if Harper'd had ties to Ireland... Their reasons for limiting the amount of the loan had gone on and on. She supposed she should be happy to have gotten this much. She was a quarter of the way there. Maybe it would keep the blackmailer happy until she could get more.

Looking into her purse for the twentieth time, Harper checked to make sure the bundle of bills was still there. It was in a white envelope, labeled as directed, and included a note that explained this was all she could get until she returned to the United States. She intended to leave the package at the front desk as they went in. Then, maybe, she would be able to take a deep breath for the first time since she'd spied that envelope on her plane seat.

Or perhaps not.

As they pulled up the curved gravel driveway of Markree Castle, she closed her bag to make sure the envelope wouldn't fall out. Sebastian stayed close by her side as they exited the bus and walked into the hotel.

Despite their situation, it was nice to have him be there for her. He hadn't signed up for any of this drama when he'd agreed to come on the trip as her boyfriend. He'd been promised a free vacation and instead he'd been roped into a blackmail plot. And yet he hadn't complained. He'd been her sounding board, her shoulder to cry on and, at the moment, her personal bodyguard. Harper didn't know how to thank him for everything he'd done so far. If she'd come on this trip alone, she wasn't sure what she would've done.

They stopped at the desk long enough for her to hand over the package with instructions for the desk clerk. She slipped it into a blank mail slot on the back wall and went to answer the phone as though it was nothing to her. Harper supposed it was. Just something left for a guest. Who would imagine it was filled with thousands of euros in cash?

"Let's go upstairs," Sebastian suggested. "We need to get away from the desk so he can come pick it up."

Harper didn't argue. She just took his arm and let him lead her away. It felt good to cling to him, to have the strong support of his body against her own. It meant so much to have him there for her. It had been a long time since she'd had that in her life. When so much of her day-to-day existence was a lie, it was almost impossible to let people in. Even her best girlfriends, the people who knew her better than anyone, didn't know the whole truth about her.

As they stepped inside their room and he closed the door behind them, she realized how lonely she had been. Even when she had been with Quentin, something had been missing. She was holding part of herself back from everyone, never letting anyone completely in.

But Sebastian knew all her secrets. And he was still there with her. At least for now.

Harper didn't expect him to stay around after the end of the trip. He had a life to return to and so did she. But they had the here and now together and, for her, that was enough. She just needed to feel like she wasn't going through this by herself. She wasn't lonely when he was around. She didn't have to pretend to be someone she wasn't. It was such a relief to be able to let her guard down and just relax into who she really was for the first time in forever.

She turned to look at Sebastian. His large, dark eyes were watching her from across the room the way they always did. He constantly seemed to be in silent study of the world around him. Of her. Perhaps it was the engineer in him, taking things apart and putting them back together in his mind. Figuring out how things worked. What made them tick. What made her tick. The idea of him instinctively knowing just how to push her buttons was enough to make her need to slip out of her suddenly too warm jacket.

He was one of the most intense men she'd ever encountered. And now, in this moment, she wanted to lose herself in that intensity.

"Sebastian."

It was all she said, yet she knew her tone conveyed so much more to him than just his name. He bit thoughtfully at his full bottom lip as his gaze narrowed at her. At last, he started moving toward her at an unhurried pace. Their gazes never broke away from one another as he came nearer. And even when he was close enough to reach out and pull Harper into his arms, he didn't touch her. He just studied her, taking in every inch from her dark ponytail to the cobblestone-scuffed deck shoes she'd worn into town.

This was her move to make. Their relationship was set up with parameters she'd defined. If they were going to cross a line, she had to be the one to do it. And that was fine by her.

Her lips met his before she could lose her nerve. Their kiss this morning had been proof that there was more between them than just some arrangement. Excitement and gratitude had overridden her good sense then, but the kiss had been about anything but saying thank you. The current running beneath the surface was one of mutual attraction, undeniable chemistry... they had just been holding back out of respect for the agreement they'd made. This relationship was supposed to be all for show, right?

But all that went out the window when he looked at her the way he did. Touched her the way he did.

"Make me forget about all of this," she said in a desperate whisper against the rough stubble of his cheek.

Sebastian didn't hesitate to give her what she'd asked for. Within seconds her shirt was over her head. His hungry mouth traveled down her chin and throat to bury in the valley between her breasts. He nipped at her delicate skin with his teeth even as he unclasped her bra and cast it to the floor.

The sensations were so overwhelming, all Harper

could do was close her eyes and try to take it all in. His hands moved quickly to cover her exposed breasts. She groaned as her tight, sensitive nipples grazed his rough palms. His fingertips pressed into her flesh, squeezing and kneading her breasts.

The moment he drew one tight bud into his mouth, Harper's head fell back and she cried out to the ceiling. His silky, hot tongue bathed her skin, sucking hard and then biting gently with his teeth until she gasped. She gripped his head, trying to pull him closer as she buried her fingers in the dark waves of his hair. She couldn't get close enough.

Then he pulled away.

Sebastian stood fully upright for a moment, his hands encircling her waist. He held her steady there as his dark eyes studied her face. He seemed to take in every detail, from the curve of her lips to the scar across her brow where she'd fallen out of a bunk bed as a child.

Harper suddenly felt self-conscious as she stood there, topless and exposed to his scrutiny. What would he see if he looked that closely? She wanted to turn off the lights, to cover up, pull away before he found something he didn't like about her body.

Then he shook his head and said, "Beautiful," under his breath and she tried to put those worries aside to be the beautiful woman on the inside that he saw on the outside.

With his firm grip on her, he pulled her across the wooden floor to their four-poster bed. He pushed her back until she was sitting on the edge. Harper eased back just as he moved forward, planting his left knee and fist into the soft mattress beside her. Hovering over her, he used his right hand to trace faint circles across her stomach.

It both tickled and turned her on at the same time. She tried hard not to squirm under his touch, but her body couldn't stay still. She ached to move closer and pull away all at once. Then he moved down and brushed his fingers over the button of her jeans. With a quick snap, they were undone and he pulled the zipper down to the base. He probed under the fabric, tracing over the lace that protected her center.

Harper gasped as he grazed her most sensitive spot once, twice, then a third time, more forcefully, making her back arch up off the bed.

Sebastian's gaze fixed on her. Ever the engineer, he studied her expressions and her every reaction to his touch. With a satisfied smirk, he eased back and hooked his fingers beneath her jeans. He slid them over her hips and down her legs, throwing them to the floor.

His hands replaced the denim, sliding back up her legs and gliding over every inch of her skin. His mouth followed in their wake, leaving searing kisses along the insides of her ankles, calves, knees and inner thighs. When he reached her panties, Harper expected him to pull them off like he had with her jeans. Instead he grasped the side with his fist and tugged hard until the pieces came off in his hand. He threw the torn strips of fabric away.

"That's much better." With nothing else in his way, he pressed her thighs further apart and leaned in to lap his tongue over the newly exposed flesh.

The sensation was like a lightning bolt through her core.

"You're buying me new panties," she gasped.

"Those were twenty-five dollars and I can't afford to replace them."

"Fine," Sebastian said. "I'll buy. You three pairs. For every one. I destroy." With each pause in his speech, his tongue flicked over her again.

"Are you planning to rip them all?"

"It depends." He spread her legs wider and moved his mouth more furiously over Harper until she was once again squirming beneath him.

"Depends on what?" Harper gasped and gripped the blankets beneath her in tight fists.

"On whether or not they get in my way."

Harper made a mental note to keep her nicer panties in her luggage. That was her last coherent thought.

At that moment Sebastian slid two fingers inside her. He thrust them deep, positioning the heel of his hand to grind against her clit. His whole hand started moving and she began to unravel. The combination was like nothing she'd ever felt before. She found herself yelling out, gasping and crying, even long before her release. The sensations were almost overpowering.

Her orgasm came fast and furiously. She wasn't prepared for how hard the pulsating waves would pound her body. She shuddered and rocked against his hand, shouting with the power of her release until it had nearly zapped all her strength. It took all she had to reach down and grab his hand, pulling it away from her. She couldn't take any more. Not quite yet, at least.

Harper closed her eyes and collapsed against the mattress. Her skin was pink and flushed, the butterflies still fluttering inside her. She swallowed hard, noting her raw throat as she gasped for breath. She wasn't entirely sure what she'd expected from Sebastian, but it hadn't been that. She'd never experienced an orgasm like that in her life. It was intense. Overwhelming. Amazing. And as soon as she recovered, she wanted to do it again.

Sebastian's weight shifted on the bed and she heard him walk into the bathroom. She opened her eyes when she heard him come back in. He had gotten rid of his clothes and replaced them with his pajama pants.

Bending down, he scooped her into his arms and placed her properly onto the bed. He crawled in beside her and tugged the blankets over them both.

Harper was surprised. She didn't think they were finished. She was great, of course, but she thought for sure that he would want some for himself. Maybe he didn't have protection with him. She'd have to be sure to correct that before they got together again.

Instead, he rolled onto his side and wrapped his arms around her, pulling her into the warm nook of his body. It was unexpected, but perhaps exactly what she needed.

"What are you thinking about?" he asked.

"Not a damn thing," Harper said. She could barely string together a coherent sentence at this point.

"Good. Mission accomplished," he said.

"You know what I've noticed?"

Sebastian clung to consciousness long enough to make a thoughtful sound in response to Harper's question. "Mmm?"

"I've realized that I really don't know anything about you, but you know everything about me."

The question was enough to jerk him from the comfortable nap he'd almost settled into. Apparently the post-coital bliss he'd induced in her was short-lived and her mind was spinning again. With his eyes wide open now, he sighed. "That's not true. We met up before the trip and talked about each other for the cover story."

Harper snuggled against his chest and let her fingers twirl through his dark chest hair. "Yes. We talked about a few things, but you were pretty light on details. You know all my deepest, darkest secrets and all I know is that you went to MIT."

"There's not much more about me to tell," he said. It was a lie, but the one he preferred people to believe. "I had a very boring, uneventful life before I went to college and met Finn. Then we started a business, invented some stuff and got rich in the process. My life is still boring, I just have more money. Unlike you, there's no secret dramas, no trust fund stipulations, no blackmail plots. You're not missing out on much with me, I promise."

Now it was Harper's turn to make a thoughtful sound. Eventually she stilled and her breathing became soft and even against his chest. Of course, she had riled him up and fallen asleep, leaving him lying in bed with a brain no longer interested in sleep.

Part of him felt bad about lying to Harper mere minutes after giving her an orgasm. She had been brutally honest with him about her life, but that was out of necessity, not out of a willingness to share her past with him. He'd been sucked into her blackmail plot or he was certain she wouldn't have told him, just like she hadn't told anyone else. He was just there. And he was okay with that. She just shouldn't expect him to reciprocate.

It wasn't because he had huge skeletons in his own

closet. His uncle Joe had gotten a DUI for driving his riding lawnmower to the gas station drunk to get more beer. That was the closest his family had come to brushes with the law. No scandals. No secrets. They were just the one thing that he couldn't be once he'd found himself dropped into the world of Manhattan society against his will—poor.

Harper had been angry with him initially for not telling her that he was rich. It was her presumption that he wasn't—he hadn't said anything either way. He typically didn't. Sebastian wasn't the kind to present himself like the usual power-hungry Manhattan CEO, so most people wouldn't think he was, much less believe him if he insisted otherwise. Finn was the suave one: well-dressed, well-spoken, well-traveled. He reeked of money and prestige. No one ever questioned that he was the president of BioTech.

Sebastian flew under the radar and he liked it that way. He didn't like the way people changed around him when they found out he was rich. All of a sudden people acted like he was more important and things he said were more interesting. He'd go from being mostly ignored to receiving invitations to play racquetball at the club. He didn't play racquetball and had no intention of starting. It was all perception. His wealth shaped how people saw him.

And the same would be true if his rich friends found out he'd come from a dirt-poor background.

At the moment he was sleeping under the same roof as some of the most powerful business owners and billionaires in Manhattan. When he'd been introduced as one of them, they'd welcomed him with open arms. He was good enough for Harper, he owned his own company…he must be good people. But would they respond differently if they knew he was fifteen years removed from what they considered to be poor white trash? That his parents would be living in the same trailer he'd grown up in if he hadn't bought them a house with his first million?

Harper had money troubles of her own, but even at her poorest, she had more money than his family'd had growing up. He'd had to bust his ass to earn scholarships and get through college to build a career and wealth of his own. None of it had been given to him by his daddy or grandpa or anyone else.

While he'd been sympathetic to her plight when she'd told him about blowing her first two-million inheritance, a part of him had winced internally at the thought of it. Finn had some family money that helped them get started, but it was nowhere near enough. What could Sebastian have done if someone had handed him two million to get BioTech off the ground? They could've gotten a decent facility up and running instead of working out of a garage the first year. They could've gotten their first major product into production years earlier.

And she'd blown it on purses and shoes.

Harper had obviously grown up a lot in the years since she'd made those mistakes. She'd not only managed to support herself, but do a good enough job at it that no one questioned that she wasn't still rich. But with that big balloon payment looming in her future, he had to wonder if she would be back to her old habits.

It would take longer to blow through twenty-eight million, but she could still do it. Then what? There would be no third payment to bail her out again unless some rich relative died.

Or she married well. To a rich CEO perhaps?

Sebastian sighed and looked down at Harper as she slept peacefully on his chest. He didn't want to think that way about her. She hadn't seemed at all like the typical Manhattan gold digger. But she certainly had seemed a lot more interested in him once she'd realized he was rich and not just some wheelchair salesman. Yes, he could easily revive the glamorous lifestyle she had once lived. Since things between them had accelerated so quickly, a part of him worried about her motivations.

She'd been completely in love with that creep Quentin only two years ago. A guy who might very well be blackmailing her right now. She herself had said she didn't have the greatest taste in men, and choosing Quentin certainly seemed like a style over substance choice in his opinion.

That said, she genuinely seemed attracted to Sebastian. She hadn't asked anything of him, even though they both knew he could pay off that blackmail and put an end to it all. If it would ever end. She'd barely agreed to let him cosign the loan. And yet part of him was still concerned about what Harper was after.

He didn't mind getting physically closer to her. He was happy to. Holding her warm, soft body in his arms was one of the best things to happen to him in a long time. He actually wished he could've taken this afternoon further, but he knew putting the brakes on when he had was the right choice for now. He'd felt his heart racing uncomfortably in his chest as she'd come and had decided he needed to stop there. He'd promised to help her forget her problems and he'd done that.

The doctor had told him he would know if he was feeling well enough to indulge. It had been almost a week since his attack, so hopefully that would be soon. But that was about as far as he was willing to go with Harper. At least for now. There were too many unknowns, too many balls in the air for him to let this fake relationship develop past much more than a simple vacation fling.

Once they were back in New York, he would return to his lab, she would inherit her fortune and they'd likely go their separate ways. He didn't have time for a relationship and she wouldn't need his help any longer. Things would fall apart. So planning for the worst, Sebastian intended to keep his distance.

opened right up, revealing the relatively tidy space. She took her time looking around at the antique furniture and heavy velvet drapes. The room was much nicer than the one she was staying in, but she wasn't one of the bride's best friends like Harper was.

After the courier she'd hired picked up the package at the front desk and brought it to her in the castle's east gardens, she'd been certain her plan was a success. Then she saw the note inside and counted only a quarter of what she'd been expecting. It was a lot of money to be sure, but not enough.

Harper seemed to think that she was the one in control of this situation. That she could just not pay, for whatever reasons she could come up with, and everything would be okay. That was not the case. That meant taking her threat up a notch.

She'd only intended to leave a note in the room. She'd wanted to invade Harper's space and unnerve her by showing what she could do if she wanted to. But once she was there, she realized she had an opportunity to make this a more lucrative visit and create a huge impact at the same time. She opened the largest piece of luggage and dug around inside. Most of the clothes were hanging in the closet, so all that was left in the bag were some intimates and a Louis Vuitton jewelry roll tied up with a leather cord. Bingo.

She unrolled the bundle, looking over the neatly organized pieces of jewelry in the different pockets. A few looked like nice costume jewelry, but in one pouch she pulled out a pair of diamond stud earrings that were at least one carat each. She slipped them into her purse, following with a necklace with a fat, pear-shaped sapphire pendant. Last, she pocketed a diamond-and-ruby tennis bracelet and an aquamarine-and-diamond cocktail ring. All nice, but somehow she'd expected more from Harper. Maybe she'd left her pricier pieces at home this trip.

In the other piece of luggage, Sebastian's she assumed, she found a fancy pair of gold-and-emerald cufflinks in a velvet box and an old pocket watch. She wasn't a jeweler, but she knew enough to estimate that she'd made up for a good chunk of the money Harper had shorted her. It was a start, at least. She'd have a jeweler back in the States appraise her haul later.

Harper seemed to think there was no way she could come up with the money, but she just wasn't putting her mind to it. Just flipping through the clothes in the closet, she spied a couple designer pieces that would fetch a pretty penny on Poshmark. The Hermès Birkin purse she was carrying the other day would, too. There was a waiting list to get one of those bags. Even the case she kept her jewelry in was worth at least a couple hundred dollars.

Harper had a lot of expensive things. There wasn't a single designer piece in her own closet, but then again, she wasn't pretending to be rich. Having these things was all part of Harper's ruse. Of course, if she could get her hands on stuff this nice just to fake out her friends and family, she could get the money, too.

Part of her wanted to blow the top off Harper's whole lie just to expose how shallow she was. What a horrible thing it was to be poor! She was just trying to make it by until that next big payment from granddad, then everything would be okay again. In their lifetimes, most people would never see the amount of money she'd already blown, never mind what she was set to inherit later.

There were worse things than being poor in this world. Perhaps being shallow? Being a liar? Maybe even a thief? She laughed at that thought. She didn't look at this as theft. She was just an instrument of karma in this scenario. If she got a tiny piece of the pie in the process, that was just a bonus.

She turned around and looked at the tidy, elegant room. Housekeeping had already come for the morning and left chocolates on the pillows. It hadn't been a part of her original plan, but she decided on the spot that it could use a little redecorating. Just to make the place look lived in, of course.

When she was out of breath and the room looked like it had been hit by a tornado, she took the white envelope out of her pocket and left it on the nightstand.

She had officially turned up the heat on Miss Drake.

They'd spent a long afternoon touring the Irish countryside and Sebastian had enjoyed it. It was a quiet, peaceful country to just sit and soak in the atmosphere. A good choice for a vacation location and he was sure his doctor would approve. Outside Dublin, most of the towns were small and laid back. No honking taxis and aggressive panhandlers. Just old historic sites and friendly people, all with stories to tell.

Despite the peaceful scenery, having Harper in the seat beside him on the bus had the opposite effect. The nearness of her kept his pulse fairly high. Every now and then he would get a whiff of her perfume. She would lean in to him to say something, touch his knee and playfully kiss him. At this point, the lines of their relationship were so blurry, he didn't know if she was really kissing *him* or if it was all for show. Though if people were suspicious of their relationship, it was a little too late to care. The wedding was tomorrow. They would be back in the US before long.

So did she mean it?

Sebastian tried not to overthink it. Instead he turned back to his notebook and worked on a sketch he'd started at the abbey. It seemed an odd place to get inspiration for medical equipment, but there had been a statue in the museum that was wearing some kind of armor. The shape of how it fit to the knight's leg had got him to thinking about prosthetic and robotic legs in a whole new way. That was all it had taken for him to lose all interest in old churches and to turn his focus back to work.

"You're not even listening," he heard Harper say.

Snapping out of the zone, Sebastian looked up. "What?"

"You're a million miles away. Did you hear a word I said?"

He shook his head sheepishly. "I didn't. I was focused on my work."

"I thought so. What is that?"

He sighed and looked at the rough sketch. It would take a lot of refinement for the doodle to become a cutting-edge piece of equipment, but it was a start. "One day, it may be BioTech's latest design for a robotic prosthetic. This one is for the leg."

She looked at the sketch thoughtfully. "Is that the kind of thing you usually work on?"

He shrugged. "It varies. Our very first product, the one that put us up with the big boys, was a prosthetic arm. Looking back at it now, it seems like such a crude design, but it changed everything for patients at the time. Lately we've been using 3D printing to develop custom fits for patients. Insurance wouldn't pay for something like that, so most people couldn't afford a customized fit until now. That's made a huge difference in comfort for people who've lost limbs."

"Do you work a lot with soldiers?"

"Yes. We also work with accident victims or people born with various birth defects. That's only part of what we do there. My latest project is for paraplegics. If I can get a successful prototype finished—one that can be produced affordably enough—it could change the lives of thousands of people that are wheelchair bound. This sketch is part of that."

There was a long silence and when Sebastian turned to look at Harper, he realized she was staring at him, not his sketches. "What?" he asked.

She smiled and reached out to brush a chunk of dark hair from his eyes. "I've never seen you like this."

"Like how?" He looked down to take inventory of himself self-consciously.

"I've never experienced your passion for your work. I guess I thought you were just another guy making a buck on medical research, but you really seem to care about what you're doing. Your work is amazing."

"Thank you," he responded awkwardly.

It always made him uncomfortable when people gushed at him about his research. He didn't do it for the feel-good factor. He did it for people like his brother who faced a lifetime lived with physical limitations. If he could finish the exo-legs, it meant he would have accomplished his biggest dream. Seeing his older brother walk again would mean he'd finally succeeded. The money, the success, the praise...it was all nice, but that wasn't what he wanted. He wanted to see the look on his mother's face when she saw her oldest son walk across the room unassisted. To him, that was worth sacrificing most of his life. Unfortunately he'd pushed too far and almost sacrificed all of it.

"So what inspired you to go into this line of work?" she asked.

He'd been waiting for that question. That was a slippery slope in conversation and Sebastian wasn't ready to go there. Not with reporters and not with Harper. He had a prepared answer for those times, however. He'd done several interviews and never wanted to bring his brother or his past into the discussion. It wasn't because he was embarrassed to talk about his brother's accident or his family situation. It was more that he wanted to maintain their privacy as well as his own. He didn't need the headline claiming he was a "rags to riches" success driven by his poor brother's tragic accident. That simplified the story far too much.

"I was always interested in robotics and engineering," he began his practiced story. "When I met up with Finn, he was in medical school and we got the idea to combine our specialties and start a company together after graduation. It was easy to develop a passion for the work when you see how it can impact people's lives."

"I imagine it is. I'm a corporate accountant for Jonah's company. There's no passion there, but I'm good with numbers so I got a finance degree. We're a video game company, though. It's hardly important work."

"It's important work to the people that love to play those games. Every job is critical in a different way. Finn says I'm a workaholic, but when you're doing something that can change someone's life, how do you justify walking away from your desk for a moment? Especially for something as trivial as a vacation?"

"I guess it's about balance. You don't want to burn out. But look—here you are on a vacation. Sounds like that's a big step for you."

Sebastian chuckled to himself. She had no idea. "It is. I haven't been out of my labs this long since we started the company ten years ago."

"So how were you able to do it now?"

He tensed in his seat. What was he going to say? A doctor-enforced break? Not the answer he wanted to give. He was supposed to be a successful guy. He didn't want to show weakness to Harper or any of the other people on this trip. Like a pack of wild animals, they could easily turn on the weakest member. He didn't want to give any of them the ammunition to come for him. Not his background, not his health, not his fake/real relationship with Harper. If he let out too much about himself, he might be the next one blackmailed.

"You gave me no choice," he said with a laugh. "A beautiful woman walks up to me in a department store, asks me out and offers me a free trip to Ireland. How can any red-blooded man pass that up?"

Looking up, Sebastian noticed they had reached the hotel. He was relieved to end the conversation there. "Looks like we're back."

Everyone gathered their things and shuffled back

into the hotel. The arrival couldn't have been better timed. He was more than happy to stop talking about himself. All he wanted to do now was to go upstairs, take a hot shower and get ready for dinner. Tonight they were hosting some kind of authentic Irish dinner show at the castle with traditional music and dance. It sounded interesting enough.

"I'm ready to take off these shoes," Harper said as she slipped her key card into the door. She took two steps and stopped short, sending him slamming into her back.

"What's wrong?"

Harper pushed open the door and revealed the mess that had once been their hotel room. Their things were scattered everywhere. Furniture was overturned. It was awful.

"Don't touch anything," he said. "We've been robbed."

"Don't touch anything?" Harper asked. "What are we going to do? Call the police?"

"That was my thought."

Harper walked into the room and picked up a familiar white envelope sitting on the nightstand. "Think again. If we call the cops, the blackmailer will expose me for sure."

With a sigh, Sebastian slammed the door shut and walked in to survey the mess. "So what does it say? I take it he wasn't pleased by the partial payment."

"It says that he's taken a few things to make up for the missing money. That was just a punishment, though. He still expects a hundred and twenty thousand dollars before the wedding reception ends." She looked up with despair in her eyes. "What about the twenty-five thousand euros he's already got? It's like it didn't even count. That or he's just jacking up the fee every time we miss a deadline." She dropped her face into her hands. "This is never going to end."

Sebastian walked over and sat beside her on the mattress. "It will end. He can't string this along forever. You're going to turn thirty and once you inherit, there's nothing to hold over your head. Or he exposes you and there's no money to be had. But it will end." He wrapped his arm around her shoulders. It wasn't the best pep talk he'd ever given, but it was something.

He didn't know what else to say as they sat and looked at their destroyed hotel suite. It must have taken quite a bit of time to do it, but given they'd been gone for hours, the blackmailer had had all the time in the world.

"Did you bring anything valuable?" he asked.

"Just a few things. Mainly pieces I was going to wear to the wedding." Harper got up and sought out her overturned suitcase. "My jewelry roll is gone. Oh, wait…" She spied it in the corner and picked it up. She poked through a couple pockets and shook her head. "He got all the good stuff. That sapphire necklace belonged to my mother," she said, tears shimmering in her eyes.

Sebastian cursed and stood to go to her. "We can call the cops. We don't have to mention the blackmail. You'll need the report for your insurance claims."

"What insurance?" she chuckled sadly. "You're talking like I have the money to insure all this stuff. I don't. It's gone. It's all just gone. Probably forty thousand dollars' worth of jewelry, easy. Did you bring anything?"

Sebastian hadn't really thought about his things. He hadn't previously been a target of the blackmailer, but he supposed if they wanted money, they'd get it from anywhere. "Not much," he said. Looking around, he found the box with his cufflinks for his tuxedo. It was empty. Figures. The only other item he had with him was his grandfather's pocket watch, but it wasn't worth anything. He carried it for sentimental value.

He dug around in his stuff, flinging pillows out of the way, but found that it, too, was gone. He turned a chair right-side up and sat with a disgusted huff.

"What did he get?" Harper looked at him with wide eyes of concern.

"My great-grandfather's pocket watch," he said. "He was a train conductor. It's not worth a dime to anyone but me. I can't believe the bastard took it."

Harper groaned. "Oh, no. I'll replace anything you lost once I get my money," she offered. "I know I can't replace your grandfather's watch exactly, but I'll do whatever I can. I'm so sorry to have dragged you into this whole mess."

"It's not your fault," Sebastian said. "But we've got to find a way to put an end to it all. Maybe I just need to give you the money."

"Sebastian, no," she said, crouching at his knee. She looked up at him with a dismayed expression. "I can't ask you to do that. You've already done too much."

He shook his head. "I don't want to pay him. He doesn't deserve the damn money, but it might be the only answer we have. But if we do pay him," he said with angrily gritted teeth, "I want all our stuff back."

* * *

"So what do we know about this Josie?" Lucy asked in a hushed voice over a delicate china plate of tea sandwiches.

They were at Violet's bridal tea, a ladies-only event. All the men, Sebastian included, had gone to play a round of golf, followed by some day drinking that would likely run until the rehearsal dinner. This was one of Harper's first real opportunities to sit with her friends without Sebastian or the other guys since they'd arrived in Ireland.

Violet was at another table near the front, being adored by all the ladies in attendance, leaving Harper, Lucy and Emma to sit in the back corner and gossip as they often did. They all shrugged in response to Lucy's question, Harper included. She didn't know, or really care much about Quentin's new fiancée. She had bigger, more pressing worries, but she was interested in why the others were so concerned.

"I hadn't met her before the trip, but I had heard about her through the grapevine. To hear it told," Emma said as she gripped her teacup, "the engagement was quite the surprise to everyone. Given his current situation, I think a lot of people felt that Quentin might have chosen a woman with a fatter bank account and better connections. As far as I know, Josie is a broke nobody. She's a secretary for a financial firm or something. Not exactly what I was expecting. Of course, all that could've happened after he proposed and then he was stuck with her."

Harper perked up in her seat at Emma's story. "Given his current situation? Stuck? What do you mean by 'all that'?"

Emma and Lucy shared knowing glances before turning back to Harper. "We hadn't said anything because bringing up Quentin in conversations always seemed to put you in a bad mood."

"Yes, well, talking about someone's ex is hardly a way to perk up their day. Unless it's bad news. Is it bad news?"

Lucy nodded. Her dark eyes lit with excitement. "Apparently he was cut off by his dear old dad."

Harper sat back in her seat, her jaw agape. That certainly was news. Quentin was an attorney, but he was a long way from being the successful hot shot he pretended to be. Most of his money had come from his family. When they were dating, she recalled him getting a ten-thousand-dollar-a-week allowance from his father. He'd been twenty-eight at the time, giving Harper a run for her money when it came to being spoiled.

"He's the low man on the totem pole at his law firm," Harper said. "Without his allowance, he would be in big trouble. He couldn't afford his apartment, his car...he certainly couldn't afford the giant engagement ring I've seen her sporting, either."

"Exactly," Emma said.

"Do we know why he got cut off?" Harper asked.

Lucy shook her head. "I haven't heard anything specific, but you know he had to have done something his dad really wasn't happy about to get cut off."

"So why would someone in his position propose to a woman that won't be any help with that situation? There are plenty of rich, single women in Manhattan that he could've chosen instead. He could've even come crawling back to you," Emma said.

"Not likely," Harper said. Quentin knew Harper didn't have any money or he might've tried. She couldn't tell the others that, though.

"What's so special about her?"

"I don't know. He loves her, maybe?" Harper replied with a sarcastic tone.

"Love? Quentin? Come on, now." Emma snorted. "If he was capable of that, he would've married you years ago. Maybe she's from an important family or one of his clients' children. No, my bet is that his father disapproves of the engagement and cut him off when he found out Quentin proposed. Unless she's got more to offer than meets the eye, I think he's searching for his relationship escape hatch. Once this wedding is over, he's going to drop her like a rock to get back in daddy's good graces. You just watch."

"Why would he propose to a woman his father didn't like?" Lucy asked. "Could she be pregnant?"

The three turned to where Josie was seated sipping tea. Her dress was fairly tight, showing no signs of a baby belly. "I doubt it," Harper said.

"I wonder if he just wanted to be engaged to someone at the wedding to make Harper jealous and it ended up backfiring on him."

Harper turned to Emma and frowned. "That's silly. Who would make up a fake relationship just to make someone else jealous?" The irony of the words were not lost on her.

"Maybe not jealous. Maybe he just didn't want to come here and face you on his own."

"He hasn't even spoken to me the whole trip. I doubt he's given me much thought at all."

"Well, you may be right, but I think it gives him the

perfect motive to pick a random girl to be his fiancée for a few weeks."

Harper lifted her teacup and sipped thoughtfully. Being cut off by daddy also gave her the one piece of the puzzle she'd been missing—the perfect motive for Quentin to blackmail her.

Eight

Sebastian was exhausted from a day golfing with the others but keen to get back to Harper to tell her everything he'd overheard during the trip. Between eighteen holes and half a dozen beers, mouths had loosened among the gentlemen. In addition to getting to know them all better, he'd picked up some stock tips, improved his swing and gotten some more dirt on her ex, Quentin.

As the bus pulled up in front of the castle, he spied Harper walking out toward the east gardens. When they unloaded, he trotted off after her, catching up just as she reached the intricate hedges that outlined the borders. She sat on a stone bench that overlooked the formal pattern of flowerbeds in bright summer colors that contrasted with the lush green of the grass.

"Harper!"

She turned and looked over her shoulder at him. She was wearing a pretty, pale pink, eyelet sundress with a matching sweater. "Hey there, Arnold Palmer. How did the golf go?"

He strolled the rest of the way toward her to catch his breath. He needed to do more running, apparently. "Awful," he said as he dropped down beside her on the bench. "I couldn't tell them I'd never played before, so I had to fake it and claim I was rusty from working too much."

"You've never played golf? What kind of CEO are you?"

Sebastian chuckled. "The kind that doesn't take clients out to schmooze on the greens. That's Finn's job. I work. But I have played golf. Just not this kind. I'm used to the windmills and the alligators that swallow your ball if you putt it into the wrong hole."

"Miniature golf. You've played Putt-Putt. Yeah, I'd say that's a little different."

"I'll tell you, though. Once I got the ball near the hole, I was an excellent putter. Just took me five swings over par to get that close."

Harper winced and laughed. "Wow. Lose any money?"

He shook his head. "I'm not that stupid. There was no way I was betting on my game. I did offer Quentin a wager, though. I bet him a thousand dollars that he'd shank his next ball into a sand trap."

She arched her brow curiously. "And?"

Sebastian reached into his pocket and pulled out a roll of hundred dollar bills. "I think I jinxed him. He basically shot it straight into the sand dunes and couldn't get out. Completely rattled the guy. I didn't feel guilty about it, though. If he's your blackmailer, then this thousand may have come from the money you paid him yesterday. If that's true, then I'm glad to steal some back." He handed the cash over to Harper.

"What is this for?" she asked, looking at the bills uncurling in the palm of her hand.

"For whatever." He shrugged. "It's not my money, so you can light cigars with it for all I care. Pay it to the blackmailer. Pay it on the loan. Get a really expensive manicure. Save it for a rainy day. Whatever you want. Just spend it knowing that I took it from Quentin. That should make it all the sweeter."

Harper closed her fist around the money and nodded. "It will," she said before slipping it into the little wallet pocket of her cell phone case. "Anything else interesting come up this afternoon?"

"Lots of man talk. Mostly bluster without substance. It got a little heated about the Yankees once alcohol got involved. The groom's face turned as red as his hair when someone said something about the Mets being a better team. I was smart enough to stay out of that. I don't know enough about sports to comment intelligently."

"Really? You didn't play sports in school?"

Sebastian frowned. "No. That wasn't my thing," he said. He supposed it might've interested him if he'd had the time. Maybe the swim team. But the fees to participate in school sports had been too high and all his free time had been taken up by working to help support his family. He hadn't had the typical frivolous youth, but Harper didn't know that. "I did learn something interesting about Quentin, though."

Harper turned toward him on the stone bench. "Me, too. But you go first."

"Okay. While we were talking, someone mentioned that Quentin was in some legal hot water. Apparently he'd tried to flip some real estate and used shoddy contractors to save money. The people that bought the place took him to court and the judge sided with them, awarding them a settlement to correct some of the repairs. Guess for how much?"

"A hundred thousand dollars?"

"Bingo."

"That is interesting. It certainly gives him a reason to come after me for exactly that much money. Especially after what I learned about him at the tea party."

"What's that?"

"His father cut him off, financially. We're not sure if it's because he disapproves of the fiancée, or maybe because of his legal troubles, but he isn't getting any more money from his father. I can tell you that's huge. He's probably hurting for cash right now. Even that thousand-dollar loss to you today likely stings."

Sebastian only shrugged. "He should've turned down the bet, then. He's too cocky to think he will lose."

"That is Quentin for you. Looking back, I know I dodged a bullet with that one."

"I'm sure you did. For all your dating angst, I hear you're quite the catch. All the gentlemen I spoke to think rather highly of you," Sebastian added with a smile.

Harper blushed with embarrassment and pushed a stray strand of dark hair behind her ear in an endearing way. He liked the way she was wearing it today. It was down in loose waves, almost like wild morning-after hair. It made him think about how it had cascaded across the pillows the other afternoon as he'd pleasured her. When he'd touched it, it had felt like silk between his fingertips. He wanted to touch it again.

"Do they now?" Harper said. "What did they say?"

"Well, they all congratulated me for winning you over. They said you were an amazing woman and that I would be a fool to let you slip through my fingertips."

Sebastian knew their words to be true before the men had confirmed it. Harper, however, seemed dumbfounded by the whole conversation.

"Really?"

"Yes, really."

"Even Quentin?"

Sebastian nodded. "Even Quentin. I don't know if it's all part of his game or not, but he said there were times when he knew he'd made the wrong choice letting you go."

Harper gasped. "I can't believe it."

"I don't know why. You're smart, beautiful, funny, sweet…"

"Quit buttering me up."

"You tend to lie a lot, though," he added with a smile. "Of course, they don't know that. They did mention that you have expensive tastes and might be costly to keep, but that you were worth it."

Harper laughed aloud at the final observation. "That sounds more like I was expecting to hear. How funny. Who knew golf with the boys could be so enlightening?"

It certainly had been for him. He'd already been dreading the end of the trip and their run as a couple, but his chat with the other men had made him wonder if maybe he shouldn't push harder for something more with Harper. Something beyond the physical. He'd been worried about letting himself get too close, but perhaps in time it might be possible. If he let himself do it. If he could take a step back from his work and allow life to take its place. Balance had never been his strength. He was balls-to-the-wall, all or nothing. Here, a relationship was easy because work wasn't interfering. Back home, the relationship would interfere with his work.

And that was only if Harper was open to the possibility. Now that he'd filled her head with compliments about how great a catch she was, he might not be what she wanted. He was a great stand-in for a boyfriend in a pinch, but would she want him once they were back in the States again? Maybe only if her grandfather cut her off.

"I guess the men's golf game is just as big a gossip cesspool as the ladies' tea," Harper said with a smile. "Did my brother say anything embarrassing?"

"Not much. He'd already said his peace to me a few days ago. The first day we arrived, actually."

Harper's eyes got big as she stiffened on the bench. She put her hand on him, squeezing his forearm. "What? No. What did he say?"

Sebastian chuckled. "Nothing too embarrassing, just basic big-brother stuff. I think he was just worried about you. He wanted to make sure my intentions were honest. He gave me a little insight into you, too."

"Like what?"

"Like, I'm not telling you," Sebastian retorted.

"So unfair. You've got all the insight into me and

you're this puzzle box I can't get into." With a sigh, Harper pushed up from the bench.

"Where are you going?"

"Back inside to get ready for the rehearsal. I'm a bridesmaid, you know."

Sebastian stood with her. Before she could get away, he wrapped her in his arms and pulled her close to him. "I forgot to say how nice you look today."

Harper smiled. "Thank you. You don't need to lay it on so thick, though. I don't think anyone is watching us out here together."

She seemed to think that every word, every caring gesture, was part of the game when it wasn't. How was he supposed to know if anything she said or did with him was genuine? That orgasm was genuine enough, but everything else? He couldn't be sure. Perhaps the idea of something real between them was a bridge too far.

But for now, he was going to go with it.

"I don't really care," he said, dipping his head and capturing her lips in a kiss.

As rehearsed, Harper marched down the rose-petal-strewn aisle in her lavender bridesmaid gown clutching a bundle of purple-and-cream roses with dark purple freesia and ranunculus in her hands. She was the last of the bridesmaids, with the rest of the wedding party already waiting up front with the minister.

Today, the Markree Castle gallery was acting as the chapel where the wedding was taking place. The long hall was lined with wooden paneling and pale blue-green walls. As she made her way down the long stretch of chairs that lined the aisle, she looked up to the pitched wood-beam ceiling and the intricate stained-glass windows that adorned the far end of the chapel, taking in their beauty.

Turning to the left, she lined up with Emma and Lucy to await the arrival of Violet in her wedding finery. She glanced over at the groomsmen across the aisle. They all looked handsome in their black tuxedos and lavender ties. Even little Knox had a matching tux. Aidan had managed to comb his wild red hair into submission for the special occasion. He was practically beaming with his eyes laser-focused on the back of the hall for the arrival of his bride.

The musical crescendo started and all the guests stood. The doors opened and Violet stepped through on the arm of her father. Even knowing what the dress looked like on Violet, Harper still felt the magnificence steal her breath as everything came together so beautifully.

The Pnina Tornai gown from Kleinfeld's was a beautiful but relatively plain gown from the front, allowing Violet's beauty to shine. It was a strapless, white ball gown with a crystal belt and corset top that molded to her perfectly. Her neck was as long and graceful as a swan's with her hair up and a simple diamond-and-pearl choker at her throat. In her hands, she carried a magnificent hand-crafted brooch bouquet made of silk rosettes in different shades of purple and covered in Swarovski crystal pins in two dozen different styles. Dripping from the teardrop-shaped bouquet were strings of pearls and strands of crystals.

But that was just the beginning. Harper heard the gasps of the guests as Violet passed and the back of the dress was revealed. That was where the beauty of the gown shone. From the waist down, the dress was a waterfall of large, silk roses that cascaded to the floor several feet behind her. The moment Violet had put on the dress at the bridal salon, they'd all known it was the one. Few other dresses could stand up to the grand venue like this one could.

As she looked out, Harper spotted Sebastian in the crowd. He'd chosen to sit on Aidan's side since he had fewer guests attending.

He was looking incredibly dapper in his tuxedo. He claimed he hardly ever wore it, but it fit perfectly and suited him well. The only thing missing were his cufflinks that had been stolen. She had gone that afternoon to Oliver's room and borrowed a pair, claiming Sebastian had forgotten to pack his own.

Unlike everyone else in the church, whose eyes were on Violet, Sebastian's eyes were on Harper. When he realized she had turned his way, he smiled and gave her a wink before looking over to Violet with the others as she stepped up to stand beside Aidan.

Harper handed her bouquet off to Lucy so she could straighten Violet's train and veil. Once they were perfect for pictures, she took the very heavily jeweled bouquet so Violet could hold Aidan's hands during the ceremony.

Once the service began, Harper looked down at the beautiful arrangement in her hands and the reality of the moment finally hit her. She was the last of her single friends. Practically, she'd known that. Violet and Aidan had been engaged for a while as they'd planned the event, so it's not like it had snuck up on her. But until that moment, she hadn't allowed herself to really grasp what it meant.

She was on the verge of thirty, hardly an old maid, but seeing the last of her friends pair off made a wave of sadness wash over her. Why hadn't she found someone like they had? She should be happily engaged and ready to start her life with someone, and yet here she was, basically bribing a man just to pretend to be her boyfriend at the wedding.

Her gaze drifted back to Sebastian. He was sitting in the chair, listening attentively to the service. She was so thankful he was there with her for this. Yes, it was because she had asked him to be, but she wondered what would've happened between them if things had gone differently. If he had asked her to dinner instead of her asking him on this trip…if there had been no wedding and they'd decided to go for drinks after they'd met at the store…would they have become real lovers instead of ones just for show?

In that moment she wished they were in a real relationship. Not just because she didn't want to be alone, but because she found she really cared for Sebastian. He was smart, handsome, thoughtful and kind. He was there for her when she needed someone. There was a part of her that was extremely susceptible to being treated the way he treated her. That part of her wanted to fall head over heels for him.

The other part didn't know where they stood.

Yes, they had crossed the line of their fake relationship that afternoon in their room, but their ruse had muddied the water. Was their attraction real or did they just think they were into one another because they spent all day flirting and pretending to be a couple? She was pretty certain that her draw to Sebastian was authentic. The moment she'd laid eyes on him outside

Neiman Marcus, she'd been attracted to his dark eyes and strong jaw. She'd wanted to know more about him instantly.

Honestly, after spending a week together, Harper found that she still wanted to know more about him. Mainly because he wasn't opening up to her the way she'd hoped. In all their conversations there had been plenty of chances for him to tell her about his childhood or where he'd grown up. His time in college. Anything outside of work. But that was really all he spoke about. His work was his life.

She knew Sebastian was passionate about his job, but she couldn't help but feel that there was more to him that he wasn't sharing. Intentionally. That worried her. Not because he was keeping potentially damaging secrets that would run her off, but because he didn't think he could open up to her.

If he didn't think he could share with her, what would happen once they returned to New York and didn't have a wedding packed full of events to get through? Would he call her? Would he want to kiss her again? Or would he return to his lab and disappear into his tools and toys the way he had before the trip?

She didn't know the answer. And that uncertainty scared her. Perhaps because no matter what the answer was, she knew it was already too late for her. Those dark eyes and that crooked smile had already captured her heart.

Maybe it wasn't being the last single friend that was troubling her today. Being single hadn't really ever bothered her before. Maybe it was knowing that, yes, she wanted a romantic moment like this for herself, but that she wanted it *with Sebastian*. She wanted him to be the man to whom she recited her vows to love, honor and cherish. She was upset because she knew deep down that she would never have this moment with him.

The loud sound of applause jerked Harper out of her thoughts. She turned to the altar in time to realize that the wedding ceremony had ended. Aidan and Violet were sharing their first kiss as husband and wife.

"Ladies and gentlemen, may I present for the very first time, Mr. and Mrs. Aidan Murphy!"

Violet turned to Harper to get her bouquet and face the crowd of wedding guests. Harper moved behind the bride to straighten her dress and veil one last time before Aidan scooped up Knox in his arms and they marched down the aisle as a family. Once they departed, she took her bouquet from Lucy.

Lucy followed the bouquet with a tissue she'd tucked away in her bra. "Here," she said, despite fighting tears of her own. "Don't mess up your makeup before the photos."

It wasn't until that moment that Harper realized she was crying. But it wasn't because of the beautiful service—it was because she knew she was right about her future with Sebastian. She dabbed her eyes, took a deep breath and pasted a smile on her face for the cameras.

No matter what, she still had a wedding reception to get through.

The new Mr. and Mrs. Aidan Murphy walked down the aisle together, holding their adorable toddler. Both of them were beaming with happiness and it took everything she had to not scowl at them as they went by. She put a fake smile on her face and clutched her program as the rest of the wedding party followed in their wake.

First was tech heiress Emma and her rebellious, gaming CEO husband, Jonah. The two of them were so beautiful together that she already hated their daughter. She was still a baby, but she would no doubt grow up to be a Victoria's Secret Angel or something. Behind them was the formerly poor but incredibly lucky Lucy, who'd managed to inherit half a billion dollars from her boss, then married her boss's nephew, Oliver, with his computer empire. She wished she'd had that kind of luck, but she'd learned she had to take control of her own destiny.

Last down the aisle was Harper on the arm of a groomsman that must be a friend of Aidan's because she didn't know him. She'd only studied the people with enough money to matter on this trip. This guy didn't matter. None of these people really did. Once she got her money, she was pretty sure she'd never see the likes of most of them again. That is, unless she uncovered another scandalous tidbit to make some more money off of them.

The guests at the wedding stood and started filing out of the gallery toward the dining hall for the cocktail reception. After thirty minutes of that overly romantic ceremony, she needed a drink. Maybe two. Or four by the time dinner rolled around. This was going to be a long night.

They were headed back to the States soon and she could feel time was running short. Time in Ireland. Time with all of these people. Time to execute her plan and make off with the money she needed.

The blackmail payment was supposed to be at the

front desk before the reception ended, but she wasn't holding her breath. Every other deadline had passed with disappointment. Why would this one be any different?

She wanted her money. She didn't want to have to pull the trigger and expose Harper. That wouldn't do either of them any good. No, Harper was being obstinate, insisting she couldn't pay when they were surrounded by people who could just write a check for that amount if they wanted to. Harper only had to ask. But she wouldn't.

Harper was going to ruin things for her. So that meant that she had no choice but to ruin things for Harper.

Nine

Sebastian spun Harper on the dance floor and then pulled her tightly against him. Dinner had been excellent, but he couldn't wait to take Harper out for a spin. He wasn't much of a dancer, but it was the only socially acceptable way he knew of to hold her body against his in public.

"You really look beautiful tonight, Harper. Have I said that yet?"

"No," she said with a smile, "but thank you. You should know, though, that I'm just a bridesmaid, so I can only be pretty. At a wedding, only the bride can be beautiful. It's the rules."

He leaned in to her and the scent of her floral perfume tickled at his nose, putting his nerves on high alert. It made him want to pull her closer. Or better yet, to tug her off the dance floor and head upstairs to their hotel room. His medical restrictions on sexual activity should be over now. He'd take it slow just in case, but he needed to indulge in Harper at least once before all of this came to an end.

Sebastian pressed his lips to the outer shell of her ear. "Well, don't tell Violet, but I think you're the most stunning woman here tonight. I don't care who the bride is. You take my breath away even when you're wearing that ugly purple dress she picked for all of you."

When he pulled away, he could see Harper blush before she glanced down to look at her dress with a critical eye. "You don't like my dress? I like it. I mean, I like it for a bridesmaid's dress. I wouldn't wear it to the Met Gala or anything, but it's pretty enough."

He didn't know what one would wear to the Met Gala, but he was pretty sure this pale purple frock with flowers on the shoulder wasn't it. "To be honest, I think you would look much prettier without it."

Her brow arched in suspicion. "I think you just want me to be naked."

Sebastian shrugged. "If you want to look your best, my vote is for naked."

"Just like a man," she groaned. "No respect for the power of fashion."

That was true. For all his money, Sebastian didn't know one designer from the next, nor did he care. He'd be just as happy buying all his clothes at Target, if Finn would let him. He was more about function than style most days. He couldn't even tell you the name of the designer he was wearing right now. It was someone important. Finn had made sure of that. But without slipping out of his jacket to look at the name sewn inside, he had no clue.

What he did know was that the tuxedo was getting hot. Or maybe it was dancing so close to Harper that was overheating him. Looking around, he spied a door that opened onto a courtyard.

"You want to get some air? It's getting a little warm in here."

Harper glanced around the room for a moment and nodded. "Sure. I think we still have a little time before they cut the cake."

Sebastian took her hand and led her off the dance floor. They made their way around a few tables before they reached the door that opened up to the courtyard. Out there, half a dozen small bistro tables and chairs had been set up. Each table was decorated with a floral arrangement and a flickering pillar candle protected from the breeze with a tall hurricane glass. At the moment, no one was outside, giving them some privacy.

He stepped over to the stone wall that separated the patio from the gardens beyond. It was a clear, cool night with a sky full of stars. He couldn't imagine this many stars existed if he lived in Manhattan his whole life. He'd only seen this many on nights in Maine as a kid. Even so, it hardly held a candle to the beauty of the woman standing beside him.

He hadn't just been flattering her earlier, it was the truth. It would be so easy in a moment like this—with candlelight highlighting the soft curves of her face and stars reflecting in her eyes—to let his guard down and fall for Harper once and for all. The music and the moonlight seemed to be conspiring against him tonight, wearing down his defenses. This week was supposed to be relaxing and yet he'd spent the entire trip fighting with himself.

He hadn't expected any of this when he'd agreed to come to Ireland. Yes, he'd thought he would spend a few days holding hands with and kissing a beautiful woman overseas. He'd never imagined that he would be tempted to take their fake relationship seriously and open up to her. That he might look forward to returning to New York and spending time with her instead of rushing back into his lab at the first opportunity.

If he had, he might not have taken the trip. His work was at such a critical point. Could he risk taking time away to build something serious with Harper? He wasn't sure.

"Ahh, this feels good," Harper said. "Normally it would be cold, but it got so hot in the ballroom."

"Maybe it's all the champagne," Sebastian offered.

"Or maybe it's the pressure," she said with a sigh.

"Pressure? What kind of pressure?"

Harper leaned her elbows against the patio wall to look out at the garden. "The reception will be over soon and my time is running out. That means the blackmailer is going to realize he isn't going to get any more money out of me. He won't have any choice but to expose my secret. I wonder how long he'll wait. Will he reveal the truth tonight? Wait until the morning and ruin my flight home? Maybe wait until we're back in New York and have something printed in the paper so everyone, not just the wedding guests, finds out? I wish I knew how it would happen so I could brace myself for it."

Sebastian had been enjoying the romantic evening with Harper and pondering a future with her, and all the while her mind was on her troubles instead of her company. Perhaps he'd better put those thoughts aside before he regretted them. "And here I thought you might be enjoying the wedding reception."

She shook her head sadly and straightened up. "I wish I could. This was supposed to be a great trip and a special wedding for one of my best friends. Instead it's been nothing but a waking nightmare where everyone has Irish accents. I really just want to get on the plane and go home so I can get started dealing with the fallout."

Sebastian took her hand in his. She felt so small and delicate in his grip when she was speaking in such a defeated tone. "You're going to be okay, you know."

"What do you mean?"

"I mean that no matter what happens, you're a strong, independent woman. You've made the best of your situation before and you'll continue to make the best of it, regardless of what the blackmailer does. He might feel like he's in control of your fate, but he's really not. How you handle your situation is entirely up to you."

Harper studied his face for a moment and nodded. "You're right. And I think I'm going to start handling the situation right now." She turned away from him to head back into the reception.

Sebastian reached out and grasped her wrist before she could get away. "Wait. What are you going to do?"

She took a deep breath and straightened her spine. "I'm going to confront Quentin and put an end to this."

"Quentin? May I speak with you privately for a moment?"

He hesitated, looking at his fiancée before whispering into her ear and nodding to Harper.

Harper hadn't had any discussions with Jessie or Josie or Jamie—whatever her name was. She wasn't interested in chatting with her ex-boyfriend's new fiancée. It was hard enough to look at the glittering diamond rock on her ring finger and not think about the bare finger on her own hand. The only difference lately was that when she imagined a man down on one knee proposing, there was only one face that came to mind.

And it sure wasn't Quentin's.

He finally disentangled himself from his fiancée and followed Harper out into the hallway. "What's this all about, Harper? Josie doesn't really like me talking to you, to be honest. The sooner I'm back in the reception, the better off I'll be."

Harper couldn't care less about Quentin's fiancée and her jealous streak. "This won't take long. All I want to say is that I can't give you any more money, Quentin."

She'd hoped that her blunt confrontation would catch him off guard and he might give something away. Instead he stopped short and narrowed his gaze at her. "What are you talking about, Harper?"

She crossed her arms over her chest. "Oh, cut it out. I'm tired of playing these games, *B. Mayler*. I've given you all the money I can get my hands on right now. You've stolen jewelry from my room and that will have to suffice until—"

"Wait," Quentin said, holding up his hands. "I haven't stolen anything from your room. I don't even know where your room is in this place. And what money? Seriously, Harper, I have no idea what you're talking about."

Her ex's tone gave her pause. It was a sincerely confused voice and it matched the expression on his face. "You're being sued, right? And your dad cut you off, didn't he?"

A ruddy blush of embarrassment came to his cheeks. "How did you hear about all that?"

"It's a small world. But I know it's true, so don't pretend you don't need the money."

"Sure, I could use some money. I wouldn't have dropped fifty grand on Josie's ring if I knew my dad was going to cut me loose a few weeks later. He doesn't like Josie, but I'm sure he and I will work that out. And the lawsuit is no big deal. My attorneys are handling it. But I don't know what my problems have to do with you."

"You're going to stand there and tell me that you're not the one that's blackmailing me?"

"What? No, I'm not." His eyes widened in concern and he leaned closer to speak in a softer voice. "Someone is blackmailing you?"

The concern in his voice might as well have been a punch to the gut. Harper didn't know what to say or do, but the truth was plain as day when she looked into his clueless face: Quentin was not her blackmailer.

So who the hell was?

"You know what? Just forget I said anything," Harper said. "Go back inside before Josie gets upset."

Quentin hesitated for a moment and then nodded, silently returning to the reception hall.

Harper was relieved to see him go without a fight, but the relief was short-lived.

From the very first blackmail message, she'd been fairly certain that Quentin had been behind it. He was the only one with the slightest inkling of her financial difficulties. When they'd dated and she'd finally opened up about her problems, he'd actually coached her on some financial planning. They'd even used the same financial advisor. But no one else, until she'd told Sebastian, had known.

Maybe she was fooling herself. Maybe everyone saw through her ruse and was too kind to say anything. They just let her carry on as though no one was the wiser. If that was the case, then anyone could be the blackmailer.

Harper stood at the entrance to the reception hall and watched everyone enjoying themselves inside. Violet and Aidan were cutting the cake while a crowd gathered around them. Flashes from cameras and the *awws* of bystanders drew everyone to the corner where the towering confection was on display. A few people were sitting at their tables, chatting and sipping their flutes of champagne.

Some people she knew better than others, but who was capable of blackmailing her? Of ransacking her room and stealing both her and Sebastian's things? She didn't even know where to begin looking for a new suspect.

"Miss Drake?"

Harper turned her attention to the waiter who had come up beside her. He had previously been carrying a silver tray of champagne flutes, but now his tray held nothing but the miserably familiar white envelope.

"I have a message for you," he said. "It was left at the front desk."

Of course it was. "Thank you," she said with a sigh and accepted the letter. She supposed she should open it and see what the latest threat entailed. The money was due by the end of the reception. There was only an hour or so left in that and she was pretty sure that both of them knew she wasn't paying it. So what was the point?

She slipped the envelope into the front of her bra to read later. Maybe. What did it matter in the end? She wouldn't have the money. Unless the blackmailer was bluffing the whole time, her news was going to come out sooner or later.

When she'd first told Sebastian about the note she'd received on the plane, he'd told her that one of her courses of action would be to expose the truth before anyone else could. To take the power back from the blackmailer. At the time, the idea had been out of the question. She would be throwing everything out the window if she did that. Now she wondered if that hadn't been the best policy all along. Perhaps if she spoke to her grandfather and explained her situation, he would understand. Or not. Perhaps he would cut her off and that twenty-eight million would vanish into thin air.

So what?

It seemed like a ridiculous thought to have. It was a life-changing amount of money. She'd been scraping by for years waiting for the day that money would arrive. But now that she stood there, she realized that things hadn't been so terrible. She had managed just fine. She had a good job at FlynnSoft that paid well and offered amazing benefits like a gym, a no-cost cafeteria and coffee shop, and insurance for minimum premiums and co-pays. Her beautiful, large apartment was paid for. The fees and insurance were high, but she paid them every year without fail.

No, she didn't have all the latest fashions. Her high-end pieces were either relics from her previous spending days or lucky thrift store finds. She had learned over the years how to get by without keeping up with the Joneses. If she told the truth about her situation to her friends and family, the pressure to shop and spend money with them would likely go away. No one had ever treated Lucy any differently when she'd been the poor one in the group. After she'd inherited half a billion dollars and married Harper's rich brother, she was still the same old Lucy.

Perhaps she could be the same old Harper. Just a little less flashy. She'd spent the last eight years just trying to get to her thirtieth birthday when perhaps she needed to be happy that she had made it all this time on her own. If she wasn't pretending to be something she wasn't, she could make changes to make her life easier. Maybe she could sell her flashy apartment for something more reasonable, then pocket the profit into savings. She could sell some of her designer clothes that she never wore anymore.

The realization that she didn't need her grandfather's money was a profound one for her. Suddenly it was as though a great weight had been lifted from her shoulders. She didn't know who her blackmailer was, but she was about to stick it to them. The one thing they couldn't have counted on was the spoiled heiress Harper Drake having the nerve to go it on her own.

Straightening her spine, Harper marched into the reception hall with a feeling of purpose. Cake was being distributed and the happy couple was sharing a piece at their table near the front. The band was playing a soft instrumental piece and the dance floor was empty for the moment. This was her chance.

She snatched a flute of champagne from a passing server and climbed the steps of the stage. Several people had made toasts to the couple from this perch earlier. Violet had only had bridesmaids since she said she couldn't choose a maid of honor from her three best friends. Harper could easily be the next one from the wedding party to make a toast to the happy couple.

The stage band saw her approach and eased out of the song they were playing so she could offer her good wishes to the bride and groom. She nodded and waved to them, taking the microphone from the stand and walking to the edge of the platform.

"Hello, everyone. I'm Harper Drake and I've known Violet for many years. Our families knew each other growing up, but we really got close when Violet and I went to Yale together and joined the same sorority. Pi Beta Phi sisters forever!"

The crowd laughed and applauded. "It's true. There, I made best friends for life. Not just Violet, but also Emma and Lucy, who is now my sister-in-law. Over the last few years, I've seen each of these beautiful, smart, wonderful women find love and happiness. I could not be happier for all of you. And tonight, I want to raise a toast to Violet and Aidan. May your lives together always be as magical as the fairy-tale wedding where it started."

She raised her glass and the room applauded and joined her in the toast. Harper didn't leave the stage, however. She waited for the applause to die down and continued. "Tonight, in this room, are some of the most important people in my life. So I wanted you all to hear the brief announcement that I'd like to make. No—I'm not engaged or pregnant, so let's just get that out of the way," she said with a smile. "I actually want you all to know that I've been lying to you.

"Every day for the last eight years or so, I have gotten out of bed and lived a lie. I have carried on with my life as though nothing has ever changed, but the truth is that I am broke. Flat broke. It seems silly in retrospect to lie about something like that, but my pride got in the way. No accountant wants to be seen as a poor money manager and that's what I was. I was spoiled rotten and when the well ran dry, I didn't know what to do."

Harper sipped her champagne and took a moment. Her eyes stayed focused on the tapestry on the back wall. She feared that making eye contact with someone might make her start to cry and she didn't want to do that right now.

"You're probably wondering why I'm up here telling you this. It's because someone found out about my lie—someone in this very room—and they've been using it to blackmail me. You see, if my grandfather found out I wasted all my money, I would lose the rest of my inheritance. So they've harassed me throughout this entire trip. They've taken thousands from me I couldn't afford to give, ransacked my hotel suite and stolen family pieces that can never be replaced. They've demanded money that I can't pay. And I won't ever pay it because my inheritance is basically out the window at this point.

"So I'm up here tonight to tell all of you the truth and to apologize for misleading you. And also to tell my blackmailer, whomever he or she is, that they can kiss my ass. Thank you."

She put the microphone back in the stand and made her way off of the stage as quickly as possible. She had done what she'd had to do, but she wasn't sure if she was ready to face the backlash yet. The room was unnervingly quiet, but eventually the band started to play again.

"Harper!"

She heard someone shout her name, but she didn't stop. She couldn't stop. She just wanted to get out of the ballroom as quickly as she could.

Harper made it out of the party and down the hallway before she felt a warm hand clamp down on her wrist. She stopped, spinning on her heel to find Sebastian standing behind her.

"Let me go, please," she said. "I just want to go back to our room."

He looked at her with his big, dark eyes and nodded. "That's fine. But you're not going without me."

Ten

Alone in their suite, they took their time getting undressed. There was no sense of urgency pressing them on. Tonight, she knew, they were going to savor the moment. It was their last night together and an emotionally heightened one after everything that had just happened downstairs.

"Unzip me please," she asked, presenting her back to Sebastian and lifting her hair.

He had already slipped out of his jacket and tie. He approached her, gently taking the zipper and sliding it slowly down her back. Harper could feel his fingertips grazing along her spine as he traveled down to the curve of her lower back. His touch sent a shiver through her whole body. She closed her eyes to savor the sensation of his warm breath against her skin.

His large, firm hands cupped her shoulders, pushing the one floral strap down her arm. With little effort, her dress slipped to her waist and then pooled at her feet in a puddle of lavender chiffon.

She heard his sharp intake of breath and realized he had discovered her lavender lace boy shorts. She had strategically chosen them for several reasons. First, was how they would wear beneath the dress. Second was that the cut highlighted the curve of her butt nicely. And last, they were replaceable when Sebastian tore them.

She felt his fingers grip the clasp of her strapless bra and then it fell to the floor with the rest of her clothes.

"Looks like you dropped something," he said.

Harper glanced down at the floor and realized that the note from the blackmailer she'd tucked into her bra had fallen out. She bent to pick it up and held it thoughtfully in her hand. "Another love note," she said.

Without hesitation she walked across the room to the fireplace and tossed it inside. The flames immediately started to blacken and curl the corners, then the whole thing was engulfed in the orange blaze. Although she hadn't intended it to be a symbolic gesture, it felt like one now. Consequences be damned, she was done with her blackmailer.

"Now, enough of that interrupting my trip." Harper turned back to Sebastian and approached him. She started unbuttoning his dress shirt, feeling immediately calmer and content as her hands ran over the chest hair hidden beneath it. "I don't want to think about anything but you and me right now."

She pushed his shirt over his broad shoulders and then wrapped her arms around his neck. Her lips sought his out tentatively. When they met, she molded against him, pressing her breasts into the hard wall of his chest to get as close to him as she could. "Make love to me tonight," she whispered against his mouth. "I want you. All of you."

Sebastian kissed her tenderly and then pulled away. There was a hesitation in him she didn't understand, but she shoved her doubts away when he said, "Whatever you want, darling."

His words made her smile. She hooked her fingers into the loops of his pants and tugged him over to the bed. Harper sat on the edge, bringing his waist to her eye level. There, she unfastened his belt, unbuttoned and unzipped his tuxedo pants, and slipped them down with his briefs.

She reached out for him then. He was hard and ready for her without even touching. She wrapped her fingers around his soft skin and stroked gently until she heard him groan. She moved faster, leaning in to flick her tongue across the tip.

"Harper!" Sebastian nearly shouted, grasping her wrist to still the movement. "Wait a minute," he said. "Before we... I don't have anything."

Harper leaned over to the nightstand and pulled a small box of condoms out of the drawer. "I picked these up when we were in town one day."

After their last encounter, she'd wondered if not having protection had put the brakes on things and she hadn't wanted to run into that problem again.

The breath rushed out of his lungs all at once. "Oh, thank you," he groaned. With that worry off his mind, Sebastian seemed to become more engaged. He pressed Harper back against the pillows and covered her body with his.

She loved the feel of his weight holding her down, the scent of his cologne and skin teasing her nose, and the heat of him warming her chilled body. His lips and hands were all over her, leaving no inch of skin unloved as he moved lower and lower down her body.

His fingers brushed over the lace barrier between them. To her surprise, he eased them from her hips and tossed them to the side. "I like those," he said when he caught her surprised expression. "If I ruin them, you can't wear them again."

Harper laughed, but the sound was trapped in her throat when his fingers dipped between her thighs and stroked her center. Instead it came out a strangled cry as he knowingly teased the right spot. When his finger slipped inside her, Harper's inner muscles clamped down and both of them groaned aloud.

"I wanted to take my time with this," he said, shaking his head.

She reached for the condoms and handed him the box. "We can take our time later. I want you right now. I'm ready."

"So am I." He didn't hesitate to tear open the box and grab one of the foil packets from inside. Within seconds Sebastian had the latex rolled down his length and in place.

Harper shifted her legs to cradle him between her thighs and slid her hips lower.

He leaned forward, bracing himself on his elbows.

Harper lifted her knees to wrap them around his hips, but he stopped, leaning down to kiss her instead. "Thank you," he whispered.

"For what?"

"For this week. I know I was supposed to be helping you, but I needed this time away almost as much as I need you. So thank you for that." Sebastian kissed her again and this time he pressed his hips forward and entered her, ending any further conversation.

Harper gasped against his lips as Sebastian filled her. She gripped his face in her hands and kissed him hard even as he eased back and surged forward into her again. She was surprised by the stirring of pleasure deep inside her. It wasn't something she expected based on past experience, but there was something about the way he moved. A tilt of his hips, maybe, that made every stroke more amazing than the last in a way she couldn't even describe. It was just like Sebastian to have mastered the mechanics of sex.

It was so intense, she had no choice but to close her eyes and hold on. She clung to his bare back and lifted her hips to meet his every advance. Her cries grew louder and louder as her release built inside her and she couldn't hold back any longer. She shouted his name as the dam broke and the rush of pleasure surged through her.

He thrust harder then. Previously his movements had been controlled and measured in a way that was distinctly Sebastian. He seemed to be taking his time and yet ensuring every stroke made the maximum impact. As her orgasm started to fade, she realized the calculated Sebastian was giving way to a man on the edge.

He thrust hard, again and again, until he finally stiffened and groaned in her ear. He held perfectly still for a moment, his eyes squeezed tightly shut. Then he collapsed beside her on the mattress, his breath ragged with strain.

Harper curled up against his side, resting her head on his chest to listen to his heartbeat, which was faster than she expected. They lay together like that until both his breathing and his pulse had slowed to normal. At that point, he seemed to relax. He wrapped his arm around her and placed a kiss against her forehead.

"Everything okay?" she asked, lifting her head to look up at him.

"Yes, we're good," he said. "Great, actually."

Harper chuckled and lay back. "I'm glad. I've been fantasizing about this moment all week."

"Really?" Sebastian laughed. "I'm sorry to make you hold out so long. I figured you had other things on your mind. Speaking of which, you were really amazing tonight."

"Well, thank you. I aim to please."

Sebastian swatted her bottom playfully. "That's not what I meant. I was talking about the reception. It took a lot of guts to get up there and take control of your situation. I was really proud of you."

"Oh," she said in a sheepish tone.

"What prompted it? You went to talk to Quentin and the next thing I know, you're on stage."

"I spoke with him, but it was apparent that he wasn't involved. That scared me. I had no idea who I could be dealing with and I decided it wasn't worth hiding any longer. You had been right from the beginning—exposing myself was the only way to take back my power. But I don't want to talk about that anymore. It's taken up this whole trip and I want to put it behind me. Tonight I'd rather talk about you for a change."

She felt Sebastian stiffen in her arms at the mention of talking about him. "Please," she added. "Tell me something I don't know about you. Like why you decided to go into medical technology. What inspired you? And I don't mean whatever practiced answer you put together for the company web site. The truth. What happened?"

He'd spoken about combining his engineering skills with Finn's medical expertise before and it seemed a winning combination, but there was still more to it. She could tell. No one dedicated themselves to their work like that without a reason. A personal reason.

Sebastian sat thoughtfully for a moment. The silence was long enough for her to worry he might not answer. But then he began.

"I was a shy, nerdy sort of kid. I liked to tinker. My older brother, Kenny, was more outdoorsy. He was always riding his bike or skateboarding. He stayed active."

Harper felt anxiety start to tighten her shoulders. She should've anticipated that this conversation wouldn't be a cheerful one. With his type of work, inspiration likely came from some kind of tragedy. She wanted to kick herself and yet, in the moment, was so grateful he was sharing, she would happily listen to any story he told.

"His best friend in high school ended up getting a four-wheeler for his birthday one year. My brother had graduated from high school at that point and he and a couple friends had gone camping somewhere to ride the ATV and hang out for the weekend. I don't know the details of what happened, but Kenny ended up rolling the four-wheeler. He was wearing a helmet, thankfully, but the ATV landed on top of him and crushed his lower spine. They were so deep in the woods, they couldn't land a helicopter out there to get him, so they had to carry him out on a gurney until they could reach an ambulance, which drove him to a place where the helicopter could pick him up."

Harper grasped his hand in the dark as he spoke, squeezing it tightly.

"The accident severed his spinal cord. He was eighteen and doomed to be a paraplegic for the rest of his life. I saw the toll his accident took on him and on my family. It was my hope that doing the work I do, someday I could develop something that would help him. One of the projects I've worked on for years has been a mechanical exoskeleton that would allow Kenny to walk again."

"That sounds amazing."

"It does. But so far, it's been the one thing that has eluded me. I have the technology together. I have a prototype that works in the lab. But my goal is to create something anyone can afford. Not just for rich people or ones with good insurance. That is going to take more time. That's why I work so much. For Kenny. And all the other Kennys in the world."

Harper had asked the question and now she knew the answer. In that moment she almost wished she hadn't. Now she knew just how important his work was to him. It was personal. It was his first love. Unlike Quentin, who used his work as a cover for affairs, Sebastian was truly a workaholic. It made her wonder if that meant there would never be any room in his life for anything—or anyone—else.

It was then that she realized that she was fighting a losing battle with him. No matter what happened between them, she could never fully have Sebastian in her life. She would be better served by keeping her feelings to herself and moving on once they arrived home.

There was someone out there for Harper. Someone who would love her, treat her well and let her be the most important thing in his life. Unfortunately that man just wasn't Sebastian West.

"Ladies and gentleman, welcome to New York. The current time is nine thirty in the evening."

Sebastian perked up in his seat after the wheels hit the ground and the pilot announced the long flight was finally over. He wished he'd been able to sleep on the way back and have it go as quickly as flying over, but that wasn't the way it worked.

Instead he'd spent most of the flight watching the television in the lounge with several other wedding guests. Harper had been…quiet…since they'd left Ireland. He wasn't sure what was wrong. Things had to be looking up. The blackmailer was out of business, they didn't have to pretend to be dating any longer, they were back home…life could return to normal.

Even Sebastian was relieved to know he only had a few days left on his leave before he could get back into the office. He might not burst through the door like usual, but he had a lot of exciting sketches in his notebook and he was ready to get to work on the prototypes as soon as possible.

Perhaps Harper wasn't interested in things returning to normal. Going home meant facing the consequences of her actions with her grandfather. Even Sebastian had to admit that he wasn't quite ready for their fake relationship to come to an end. But she hadn't voiced any interest in continuing. Perhaps he had read too much into their physical connection.

They were two of the last people off the plane. Most everyone had their drivers picking them up in black, luxury sedans, so the parking lot of the small airport emptied quickly. By the time they collected their bags and went out to where they'd parked, Sebastian found it was just the two of them.

"So now what?" he asked, setting down his luggage beside his car. Although he rarely drove it in the city, he had a blue BMW that he traveled back and forth to Maine in from time to time.

Harper set her bag down and sighed. "I've got an Uber coming to get me."

"That's not what I meant," he said. "I meant with us."

She crossed her arms over her chest in a defensive posture she'd never taken with him before. "I don't know. The week is over. Thank you very much for being my boyfriend on the trip. You were very…thorough."

"Thorough?" He couldn't keep the irritation from his voice. "Is that what you call it?"

"What else would you call it, Sebastian?"

There was a tone in her voice that he couldn't pinpoint. He wasn't sure if she was daring him to admit that it was more than just for show or not. Did she want him to profess his undying love and beg her to be his girlfriend for real? Or did she just want him to lay out his feelings so she could stomp on them? The way she'd pulled away from him today made him unsure.

"I sure as hell wouldn't—"

"Your time is up, Miss Drake," a woman's voice interrupted him.

Both Harper and Sebastian turned their attention to the shadowy figure standing in the dark, empty parking lot outside the airport.

The person took a few steps closer into the beam of an overhead light and Sebastian could finally make out who was standing there.

He didn't know her name, but he recognized the woman as Quentin's fiancée. And more importantly, she was aiming a gun at Harper.

Without thinking, he took a step forward and put his arm out to shield Harper. "What the hell are you doing pointing a gun at people?" he asked.

"Josie?" Harper asked from over his shoulder. "What's going on?"

"Surprised?" The woman smiled but it came out more like a smirk. "I bet you didn't suspect little old me for a second, did you? Of course not. You haven't given me a second thought this whole trip. I wasn't important or rich like the rest of you. I was just the disposable arm candy."

That was true. Sebastian had hardly paid any attention to the younger woman who'd always seemed glued to Quentin's side. To be fair, he hadn't really known many of the people on the trip, but Josie had been a silent, ignorable presence. Harper hadn't even known the woman and she knew everybody.

If that was true, how had Josie managed to get hold of such personal, private information about Harper?

"You're the one blackmailing me?"

"Guilty," Josie said without moving the gun a centimeter. It was still fixed on Harper, even if it had to go through Sebastian to get there.

"I don't understand," Harper said, pushing his arm out of the way. "How did you find out about my trust conditions? Did Quentin tell you?"

Josie shook her head. "All Quentin provided me was access to you. The rest I got on my own. If you'd bothered to speak to me this trip, you might've discovered that I work for your financial management firm. I know everything about you, Harper, including the provisions of your trust. I just knew a spoiled diva like you would've blown it. It only took a little digging to find out what I needed to know. Honestly, it was too easy."

"Why would you do this to me, Josie? I've never done anything to you."

"Aww, it wasn't personal, Harper. It's just about the money. It could've just as easily been any one of you."

"It was personal to me. Ransacking our room? Taking my late mother's necklace, his grandfather's watch—that was personal. I've spent the last week tied in knots because of you. And for what? Just some money?"

"You say that just like a rich person. You've gotten good at fooling everyone. Yes, I just did it for some money. That's enough for most people, although I have to admit I haven't gotten much cash out of the deal. I've spent this whole trip trying to get my point across with you, but nothing seems to be working. I've threatened you, stalked you, raised the price, promised to expose you, and here I stand with mere pennies of what you owe me."

"I don't owe you anything. Nobody owes you a

damn thing. Everything you've gotten was taken by force."

"And everything you've gotten was given to you on a silver platter. All you have to do is give me the money and I'll be on my way."

"You of all people know that I won't have any money until after my birthday. How can I pay you what I don't have?"

Sebastian wished he could think of something to do. Like some smooth kung-fu move to kick the gun out of Josie's hand and then wrestle her to the ground. But he was an engineer. At best, he could outthink her. If he could get his heart to stop pounding so loudly so he could focus.

"Like you couldn't get it if you needed it with all your rich and powerful friends. Violet spent more money on the rehearsal dinner alone than I was asking for. To tell the truth, I feel like I've been accommodating. I doubt there are many other blackmailers out there that would've given you as many chances as I have, Harper. But I'm done being nice. I need the money and I need it now."

"Why would I pay you another cent?" Harper asked. "It's all over, Josie. It's been over since the wedding. Everyone knows my secret. You can't blackmail me with it anymore."

She nodded. "That's true. That's why I brought along the gun. This isn't so much a blackmailing anymore as an armed robbery. I want my money."

"Why do you need money from me? You're marrying Quentin. His family has plenty of money. A hundred thousand is nothing to them."

"And I'm nothing to Quentin," Josie replied with

narrowed eyes. "It turns out he was just using me to make you jealous. He proposed and brought me on this trip just because he knew it would bother you. He never expected daddy to cut him off in the process. Now that the trip is over and he sees you're in love with someone else, he's dropped me like a rock and gone crawling back for forgiveness. So the money is more important than ever, actually."

Sebastian watched the heated discussion continue to volley between the two women. He curled his hands into fists at his sides as frustration and anger built inside him, but he felt an unpleasant tingling sensation running down his left arm. It forced him to shake out his hand in the hope it would go away.

It didn't.

The women continued to talk, but he found he couldn't focus on their words any longer. He felt the panic start to rise in him. Yes, Josie was holding a gun on them, but this was a different kind of panic. A familiar one. He was getting dizzy as he tried to focus on the two small figures standing in front of him. He reached out for Harper to steady himself before he stumbled.

"Sebastian!" Harper said in a startled voice. "What's wrong? Are you okay?" she asked.

He wanted to answer her but he couldn't. His chest was suddenly so tight he could barely breathe, much less speak. As the vise tightened harder on his rib cage, he realized that this wasn't just some random panic attack. This was another heart attack—a stronger one than last time.

The doctors had warned him to take it easy. And he'd tried. He'd done as best he was able and yet here he was—looking into the eyes of the woman he loved and wondering if it was for the last time. Was it done? Had he lost his chance to say all the things to Harper he'd been too afraid to voice? Could he say enough in time?

"I love…" He gasped and hunched over, unable to finish. His hand slipped from her shoulder and he heard her scream as his knees buckled beneath him.

Blackness enveloped Sebastian and he was unconscious before he hit the hard pavement.

Eleven

"Harper?"

Harper sat up from a dead sleep, making the best she could out of the recliner in Sebastian's hospital room. Still groggy, she wiped an unfortunate bit of drool from her chin and looked around. That's when she realized that Sebastian was awake.

She leaped from the chair to stand at his bedside. "You're up," she said with a smile.

"I guess. I feel like I've been hit by a truck." He brought his hand up to his face, dragging all his IV tubes along with it. "What happened? Where am I?"

Harper was surprised but relieved that he didn't remember the last few days. It had been a roller coaster of tests, bloodwork, scans and, finally, a stint placed in one of the arteries to his heart. He'd been out of it most of the time. Harper had just sat by his bedside waiting for the next bit of news from the nurses and doctors caring for him.

"You had a heart attack at the airport," Harper explained. "You've been in the hospital for a couple of days."

Sebastian frowned as he looked around, taking inventory of his body. "Why does my wrist hurt?"

"That's how they went in to put a stint in your chest."

He put his hand against his chest and shook his head. "Wow."

Harper sat on the edge of the bed. She'd been filled with a mix of emotions over the last few days that she'd never expected—and never wanted to experience again. First was the fear of being shot by a vengeful and bitter Josie. She'd never anticipated being confronted with a weapon like that and had hardly known how to respond. When Sebastian collapsed, Harper had reacted and rushed to his side, forgetting all about Josie. She wasn't sure how long her blackmailer had stood there with the gun, but eventually Harper looked up and Josie was gone. Apparently she hadn't wanted to hang around for the fire department and ambulance to arrive.

Since then, she'd hardly given that situation any thought. The fear of suddenly losing Sebastian before she could tell him how she felt had taken its place in her mind. All the way to the hospital, she'd sat in the back of the ambulance, racked with guilt at thinking she'd put him in a dangerous situation that had almost killed him. Then days of anxiety waiting for the results of all his tests.

Finally, and most recently, she was angry.

That was the most surprising emotion, but the one

she couldn't shake. The night before, the doctor who had been treating Sebastian had come in with another man he introduced as Sebastian's cardiologist. They'd spoken to her about his ongoing condition like it was something she was aware of. They'd discussed how this was more serious than his previous attack. Two weeks away from the office wouldn't be enough this time.

As they'd continued, it became harder for her to keep a neutral expression on her face. Harper hadn't wanted them to know she had no idea what they were talking about. But the more they'd talked, the more things about Sebastian had started to fall into place.

Like why the workaholic could drop everything and take a trip to Ireland. He wasn't *allowed* to work. Not after his last heart attack had driven him to the floor of his lab less than two weeks ago.

Two weeks ago he'd had a heart attack and he hadn't said anything about it. He'd acted like nothing happened and got on a plane with her to Ireland. The truth of it made her mind spin. What if something had happened in Ireland? That castle had been out in the middle of nowhere, literally hours from Dublin. How long would it have taken to get him to a hospital with a state-of-the-art cardiac care unit?

If he had told her, at least she could've known to watch for the signs. Or when he'd collapsed, she would have known what it was and been able to tell the 9-1-1 operator and the EMTs he had a heart condition. As it was, she'd just sat helplessly, crying and saying, "He just collapsed," over and over in despair and confusion.

Talking to his business partner hadn't made her feel any better. Finn was listed as his emergency contact and medical power of attorney, so he'd been called into the hospital the minute they'd arrived. He was the one who had authorized the tests and cleared it with the hospital for Harper to stay even when she wasn't family. She was indebted to Finn for that alone, much less the information he'd shared with her while he was there.

"The doctors said you're going to be okay. But you've got to take it easy. You'll probably be discharged tomorrow. Finn has set up a nurse to stay with you at your apartment."

"I don't need a nurse," he argued.

"Finn says, and I agree, that you lost your ability to make decisions in this arena when you had that second attack. You're not going into work. You're getting a nurse to make sure you're taking all the medications and eating well. You're supposed to register for a cardiac rehabilitation program to help you rebuild your stamina and design an exercise regime to keep this from happening again. You have to do it all, to the letter, or you're going to have another attack. You might not bounce back the next time."

Sebastian opened his mouth to argue with her and then stopped himself. "Okay. You're right."

Harper had practiced what she'd wanted to say to him a few times in her mind. She wasn't sure it would come out right, but she had to try anyway. "It's been a long couple of days in this hospital, Sebastian."

"I bet. Weren't you wearing that outfit on the flight home?"

Harper looked down, but she knew he was right. She hadn't gone home. She had ventured down to the gift shop for a toothbrush and some other toiletries to get her through, but other than that, she hadn't left his side. Their suitcases and everything in them had been left behind at the airport where they'd run into Josie. In the ambulance, she'd called Jonah and he'd gone back to pick up their things for them. He and Emma had offered to bring her whatever she'd needed, but she hadn't wanted to be a bigger imposition than she'd already been.

"It's been even more stressful for me because it came out of the blue. Young, healthy thirty-eight-year-old men do not just drop to the ground with a heart attack, Sebastian."

She watched as his jaw tightened. "I didn't think it was important."

"Important?" she cried. "You didn't think it was important to tell me that you were recovering from a heart attack? That you were supposed to be recuperating? I didn't need to know that because *it wasn't important*? We had sex, Sebastian. That could've killed you."

Sebastian sighed. "I didn't want you to treat me like I was fragile. I'm not fragile. The sex didn't kill me. Not even close. And if that woman hadn't tried to kill us, I probably wouldn't even be here right now."

"That's not what the doctor said. He said that you were supposed to schedule a heart catheterization while you were off from work to check for arterial blockages. Not only did you not schedule it, you left the country instead. You could've died, Sebastian. Right there at my feet. And I wouldn't have had the slightest clue as to what was happening to you or why because you didn't tell me."

"I thought I had it handled. I didn't want to worry you when you had your own problems to deal with."

"If it were only that, I might buy it. But it's more

than just your heart condition, Sebastian. Yes, you kept something so important a secret from me, but you haven't opened up to me about anything else, either."

"I told you about my brother."

She nodded. "Only as it pertained to your work and your inspiration. You never share anything about your past, your feelings. You just won't let me in."

That was the crux of it: how could he possibly care about her—really, truly care about her—if he was shutting her out like this?

It was then she realized that maybe this was a problem of her own making. This wasn't supposed to be a real relationship, despite how far they'd gone off the rails. They weren't supposed to confide in each other, get physical and fall in love. She was the one who'd broken the rules and fallen for him. She'd poured her heart and soul out to him and gotten nothing in return. So this was really a mess she'd made. She couldn't be mad at him for sticking to their agreement. He didn't love her. And she had to be okay with that.

But she didn't need to stay around and witness the evidence of her foolishness any longer. If she stayed, she would say something she would regret and she didn't want to agitate him any more than she already had when he was in this fragile state.

"Where are you going?" he asked as she stood and scooped her purse up from the floor.

"I'm going home."

"Why?"

Harper stopped and looked at him one last time. "Because the wedding is over," she said. "Thanks for pretending to be my date this week. I couldn't have gotten through it all without you."

He sat up in the bed and reached for her. "Wait. Are you coming back?"

She moved toward the door, finally shaking her head. "Why would I? Now I know you're going to be okay. You're in good hands. Goodbye, Sebastian." She slipped out the door before he could respond.

Dashing down the hallway, she rushed into the nearest elevator to keep from changing her mind.

"Mr. West, you have a visitor," Ingrid called from the living room.

Sebastian had heard the phone ring a few minutes earlier and assumed it was the front desk. They were the only ones who called the house line. That meant he either had a delivery coming up or a visitor. He'd already received some flowers from his parents and a plant from work, so he'd figured there might be a guest coming upstairs. He had gotten out of bed, put on some real clothes and straightened his disheveled appearance in anticipation of company.

Looking in the mirror was rough. His goatee was getting long and the rest of his beard was starting to fill in with coarse, almost black hair since he hadn't shaved since in Ireland. He needed a haircut, too, as the dark waves were getting wild and fighting his comb to stay standing straight. His eyes were bloodshot and he was bruised and scabby from the elbows down from the hospital using him as a human pin cushion.

It really was a lost cause. A brush through his hair and a swig of mouthwash was the best he could do on short notice. He wanted to look somewhat put together just in case it was Harper.

He'd had a couple visitors since he'd gotten home

from the hospital—his family had even driven down from Maine to see him—but the only person he really wanted to see was Harper. So far, she had eluded him.

He made his way down the hallway to where his home health aide, Ingrid, was waiting on him. She smiled and gestured to the couch where someone was sitting. It was Finn.

Damn.

"Don't get too excited to see me," Finn said in a dry tone. "I wouldn't want to put too much strain on your heart."

Sebastian made his way over to his recliner next to the couch and settled into it.

Ingrid brought them both bottles of sparkling water and then disappeared into the kitchen to give them some privacy.

"Sorry," Sebastian said. "I was hoping you were someone else."

"Harper, perhaps?"

"Yes." There was no sense in trying to deny it.

"Has she been by to see you since you left the hospital?"

"No." It had been several long, lonely days without her smiling face and sassy attitude.

Finn frowned at his partner. "That seems odd. Are you sure that she's okay? She wouldn't leave your side for a moment at the hospital."

Sebastian didn't remember most of his time at the hospital, but knowing she'd been there, so dedicated to making sure he was okay, made him feel better. He'd never had someone like that in his life before. And yet he'd managed to ruin it the moment he'd woken up. "Yes, well, once she determined I was okay, she left and said she wasn't coming back. I was just being optimistic that she'd changed her mind."

"What did you do?" Finn said in his usual accusing voice.

Sebastian shrugged it off. "I suppose I deserve that," he admitted. When things went wrong around the office, it was typically Sebastian's doing. He'd overload the breaker and cause a building-wide blackout. He'd set off the smoke alarm with his latest project and sent everyone marching out to the street while the fire department searched the building. Honestly, there were times where he wondered why Finn wanted to be his business partner. Or even his friend. But sometimes you had to overload the breaker to achieve greatness.

"She was sick with grief when I saw her at the hospital the first time. That woman loves you and cares about you very much. If she isn't here with you this very moment, you screwed up pretty badly."

"Okay, yeah, I screwed up," he said. "I didn't tell her about…well, anything. Including my heart condition. She said I was shutting her out. I guess I was."

"Why would you do that? She's by all accounts an amazing woman. I know her family, too. You don't drive a woman like that away when she loves you, Seb."

"I don't know why I did it. I guess it's just all I know how to do. I'm not a relationship guy. I'm an engineer. A pioneer in medical technology. I don't know how to be that and a man in a serious relationship. Is it even possible to be both at the same time?"

Finn chuckled and shook his head. "You'd better figure it out or you're going to be a lonely old man. I can't have you coming to my house for the holidays every year for the rest of your life. Eventually you're going to become our creepy uncle Sebastian."

"You're the one that invited me to your family Thanksgiving," Sebastian pointed out in a bitter tone.

"Of course I did. Otherwise you would've been at the office working. Or sitting at home eating who knows what with a plastic fork. If you're going to shake up your life, you've got to make a lot of changes."

Sebastian was used to his fair share of lectures from Finn—it was one of the side effects of working with a doctor—but for the first time in his life, he was actually listening to what his partner had to say. "Okay, fine. Fix me, Yoda. I'm a ball of clay in your hands. Turn me into a pastier, hairier but more charming version of you."

Finn ran his palm over his shaved head and twisted his lips in irritation. Fortunately he was used to Sebastian after years of working together. They were very different, but they complemented each other well. Sebastian's inventions wouldn't have been nearly as successful without Finn there to guide and market them. And Finn probably would've settled into some nice, boring dermatology practice on the Upper East Side if he hadn't had Sebastian pushing him to do more important things with his life.

"You've got to take better care of yourself, for one thing."

Sebastian couldn't help rolling his eyes. "Thank you, Dr. Obvious. But not all of us can be hunky Shemar Moore look-alikes with chiseled abs and muscular thighs like tree trunks."

"You think looking this good is easy?" Finn quipped. "It takes a lot of work. I'm at the gym five days a week. While you're getting junk food delivered to the office, I'm drinking protein smoothies or bringing in grilled chicken breast and kale salad for lunch. Life is a series of choices. You've just got to make better ones."

"You sound like my nutritionist," Sebastian grumbled. He'd already met with her and had his first cardiac rehab appointment. Basically he'd just walked on a treadmill while they'd done an EKG and monitored his blood pressure. It would get harder from there. As for the nutritionist, she'd decided to sign him up for a meal delivery service while he was recuperating. There was going to be a lot of lean protein and vegetables he couldn't recognize in his future.

Finn crossed his muscular arms over his chest. "I might know what I'm talking about, Sebastian. I *am* a doctor, you know."

"I know. And listen…" Sebastian leaned forward and rested his elbows on his knees. "For all my blustering, I am taking this all to heart. I know this is serious and I'm changing. I want to change. At this rate, I won't live long enough to be your kids' crazy uncle Sebastian, and I know that. I've always had this drive in me and succeeding was more important than anything else, including my own health. But you were right."

Finn held up his hands to halt the discussion. "Wait. Repeat that please. I want to cherish it."

Sebastian smirked at his partner. "You were right, Finn! Anyway, I'm trying to be serious for a moment here. My work is important, but I'm not helping anyone if I'm too sick to continue. I can't sacrifice my life, my health or my relationships to make my inventions a reality. There's more to life, and I realize that now. I realized it the instant I hit the ground."

He shook his head, thinking back to that night as he'd stared down the barrel of Josie's gun and felt his chest tighten like a rubber band was wrapped around him. "It was the scariest moment of my life. As I went down, I looked at Harper and realized what was happening and how serious it could be. My life could've been ending. In those few seconds, all I could think of was that I'd never told Harper that I loved her. I was going to die and she was never going to know. I tried, but then I passed out."

Finn listened silently, a pained expression on his face. "That sounds horrible. Why didn't you tell her the first chance you got at the hospital? It might've changed everything for the two of you."

"I don't know. I've kicked myself over how that whole thing played out. I was so disoriented at first and before I could get my bearings, she was laying into me about keeping secrets. I instantly went on the defensive and then she was gone. But she was right, I wasn't telling her things. I have so much I need to share with her. But I need to start with how much I love her. That's the most important part."

"Wow," Finn said. "It's true. You've really fallen hard. I can see it in your face when you talk about her. I wasn't sure I'd ever see the day you looked up from your notebook and noticed someone other than a client. And to fall in love… If you can fix this, you might beat me to the altar. Maybe I can be your kids' crazy uncle Finn."

"Shut up," Sebastian groaned. "You've got women

lining up outside your apartment. If you could just pick one to keep, you'd be married in no time."

Finn laughed. "Probably so. If you're serious about wanting to marry Harper, maybe I'll catch the garter at your reception. You never know what can happen then."

Sebastian's expression instantly sobered. "I am serious about marrying her. I'm serious about all of this. I want to get my health in order so I can go to her and feel confident that I'm not selling her damaged goods. Then I want to tell her how I feel and, hopefully, she feels the same way. If she does, I'm going to propose right there on the spot. Time is too precious to waste. I don't want to give her the chance to slip away from me again."

"If you're really planning to propose, I know a good diamond guy. I could give him a call and have him bring some pieces here to the apartment."

That was a relief. Sebastian didn't even know where to start when it came to that. He couldn't name the four Cs if his life depended on it. "Set it up. I've still got to talk to her father and ask permission, but I want to move forward on everything. I want it all in place when the time comes."

"Sure thing." Finn picked up his phone and typed in a few things. "I'll have him text you."

"Perfect. It feels like everything is falling into place. I just have one more little thing to do first."

"What's that?" Finn asked.

"I have to figure out where Harper lives."

Twelve

"Come in."

Harper took a deep breath and turned the knob that led to her grandfather's study. She had been fearing—dreading—this moment since she was twenty-two years old. Now here she was, a woman of almost thirty years, and she felt as nervous as ever.

It was easy to be brave in Ireland when she'd been thousands of miles away from the consequences of her poor choices. With Josie having disappeared and the blackmail behind her, Harper knew she had to face her grandfather and the reality she'd avoided all this time. She had to tell him she was broke. Odds were that he'd probably already heard the news by now, but she'd wanted to tell him in person as soon as she had the chance.

"Afternoon, Grandpa."

The elderly man looked up from his desk and smiled at the sight of his only granddaughter.

"Harper! What a surprise! You're looking lovely, as always. For a moment I thought it was your mother standing there. You certainly have come to look so much like her as you've gotten older."

Harper gave him a hug, ignoring the tears in his eyes as they both thought about the woman who'd been taken from them too soon. As she sat, Harper realized that she was older now than her mother had been when she died. It was hard to believe. Life could be so unfair sometimes. It made Harper feel foolish for wasting all her emotional energy on such silly things when her mother had been facing her own death and leaving her children behind at the same age.

"To what do I owe this visit?" his asked. "I didn't expect to see you before your birthday. The big one is coming, isn't it?"

Harper smiled and nodded. "Yes, I'll be thirty."

"I suppose you'll have a big party to celebrate with your friends. Blow some of that inheritance on expensive champagne?"

She winced and shook her head. Considering everything that had happened over the last week, she hadn't planned anything. Turning thirty was depressing enough. Add that she was now going to be single and broke going into her thirties and she couldn't gather up much reason to celebrate. "Not exactly. That's why I came by to see you today. I needed to talk to you about my trust fund."

"Can't wait until the end of the week for the money?" he asked with curious gray eyes. "I suppose I could loan you a few dollars until then."

"No, Grandpa," she said, reaching out to stop him from pulling out his wallet. "I'm not here to borrow money. I'm actually here because I needed to tell you something."

His brows went up in surprise and he eased back into his leather chair. "Okay. What is it, Pumpkin?"

She took a deep breath, trying to figure out how she was going to tell him the truth. Pumpkin had screwed up. She'd thought that losing out on the money would be the hardest part, but she was wrong. Telling her grandfather what she'd done was far worse. The sun had risen and set on Harper as a child as far as he was concerned. He would be so disappointed.

"I'm broke, Grandpa."

He narrowed his gaze at her, visibly trying to piece together what she meant by that. "Broke, you say?"

"Yes. I've been keeping it a secret all these years because I was embarrassed and I didn't want to lose the rest of my trust fund. But I'm coming clean. I blew all the money when I was in college and I've been faking it ever since."

"So all these years…you never once asked for money. Your father didn't have any. How did you get by?"

Harper shrugged. "Like everyone else. I worked hard. I saved every dime I could instead of blowing it like I would've in the past."

"But no one knew the truth? Not even your brother?"

"No, I didn't tell anyone. Not Oliver, not Daddy. I didn't want anyone to know, especially you."

"If that's the case, why are you telling me this now, Pumpkin?"

Now it was her turn to frown. "Because I should be

honest. You added the provision that said if I misman-aged the first payment, I wouldn't get the second. And I blew it. I wanted—no, needed—to tell you the truth, so you can have your financial manager do something else with the money. I've forfeited my share."

Her grandfather reached for the candy bowl on the edge of his desk. He grabbed a soft caramel and handed a second one to her. For as long as she could remember, he'd always had caramels in his study. He unwrapped the candy and chewed it thoughtfully. Harper could only hold on to hers. She was waiting for his response. The rebuke. The disappointment. For him to announce that he was donating her inheritance to a charity.

But he didn't. He just chewed his caramel and watched her. Finally he said, "Something else is wrong. What is it?"

"You mean aside from throwing away twenty-eight-million dollars?"

He nodded. "That's just money. Something else is bothering you. Something more important."

Sebastian. Could that be what he saw? "I've just had a rough week, Grandpa. Nothing has been going my way, be it my love life or anything else. Someone tried to blackmail me and they stole Mama's sapphire necklace when I didn't pay them in time. The guy I love lied to me and I don't know what to do. Really, losing the money is just the latest thing to come up. I'm not having a big birthday celebration. I don't feel much like celebrating."

"Tell me about this man. You said he lied to you."

She nodded. "He kept me in the dark about so many things in his life. I worry that he can't open up to me. Why would he keep things from me?"

"Why would you keep your friends and family in the dark about your own situation, Harper? I imagine you'll find the answers to your questions about your gentleman in your own motivations."

"I was embarrassed. I didn't want anyone to know I could be so stupid. They might treat me differently." As she said the words aloud, she realized her grandfather was probably right about Sebastian and his secrets. Would she have treated him differently if she'd known he was physically fragile? Perhaps. Was he embarrassed that he'd let his drive get in the way of his health? Probably.

Since they'd started out as a week-long fake romance, there'd been no reason for him to tell her those things. Honestly, if she hadn't been blackmailed, she wouldn't have confessed her own truths to Sebastian. Why would she expect him to do the same?

They had a lot to learn about each other. A week wasn't nearly enough time to peel back all the layers and expose the secrets shared with only the most intimate of partners. She'd overreacted out of fear, she knew that now. Seeing Sebastian lying on the ground surrounded by EMTs…the sirens, the wires, the shouting… It had been all so unexpected, so scary. Josie and the gun hadn't been important anymore. All that had mattered was Sebastian.

She'd almost lost him in the moment and she hadn't understood why. Then she'd turned her back on him and walked away—losing him for certain—just for doing the same thing she'd done her whole life.

She was a fool.

"Harper, why do you think I added that provision to your trust?"

She turned back to her grandfather and shook her head. "To scare me straight? I was a spoiled little diva. I'm sure you didn't want me to make the same mistakes as Daddy did."

"That's a little harsh," he said. "You just didn't know what it was like to go without. You didn't grow up poor, like I did, so you didn't have the appreciation for it. That wasn't your fault. But you have it now, don't you?"

Harper chuckled bitterly. "Most certainly. I kick myself every day for wasting what I had. I think about what I could've done differently. If I'd been smart or industrious like Oliver…"

"You don't have to be like your brother. He's one of a kind, and so are you. Let me ask a different question. If you were to have a second chance and someone handed you that two-million dollars over again, what would you do?"

She didn't even have an answer at first. "That's hard to say, Grandpa. I'd probably go wild and pre-pay my co-op fees and utilities for the next year. Stick the rest in the bank for a rainy day."

Her grandfather's old, weathered lips curled into a smile. "Okay then." He reached across his desk for his cell phone.

Harper was confused by his response. "Okay what?" she asked.

"Okay, it's time to call my estate manager and discuss releasing the rest of your trust fund."

"What do you mean, *release it*?"

He reached out and patted her hand. "Happy birthday, Harper. I'm satisfied that you've grown into the mature, responsible woman I've always known you could be. And as such, you're about to be twenty-eight-

million dollars richer. Now go find this man you're
in love with and plan a proper birthday celebration."

Sebastian walked into the lobby of Harper's building as though he were approaching the X on a trea-
sure map. Finding where she lived hadn't been an easy
task. To ask for it from her friends was to admit he'd
never been to her home before—an incredibly suspicious fact considering they were dating. But without
any other options, he'd had to confess the truth about
their fake relationship to Emma when he'd hunted her
down at FlynnSoft. But it was only when he'd told her
that he was hopelessly in love with Harper, for real,
that she'd given him the address for Harper's building.

He was in the process of signing in at the front desk
when he heard a voice from over his shoulder.

"She's not home."

Sebastian paused and turned to find Harper standing behind him with a full bag of groceries in her arms.

"That's a shame," he said. "I really wanted to talk
to her about something important."

Her blue-gray eyes searched his face for a moment.
"Something important, huh? Well, maybe I'll let you
up and you can wait for her. I'm sure she'll be interested in hearing what you have to say for yourself."

Ouch. Okay. "I'd really appreciate it."

Harper smiled and headed toward the elevator with
him in her wake.

Sebastian hadn't been sure what kind of reception
he would receive after the way they'd parted at the
hospital. So far, it had been pretty neutral, but he was
going up to her apartment. She could've just turned
him away. That was something.

Running into his arms and kissing him would've been another option, but he may not deserve that. He had a lot of apologizing to do before hugs and kisses would be on the agenda. Her semi-frosty reception proved that much.

When they stepped into her apartment, Sebastian got his first real dose of what Harper's life was like. It was a nicer place than he had—a remnant of her old life—decorated with some familiar and inexpensive IKEA pieces. As she set her groceries in the kitchen, he noticed a nice bottle of champagne and a couple pouches of ramen noodles. He supposed she had learned balance over the years.

Sebastian hovered awkwardly at the entrance of the kitchen as she put away her groceries. He was waiting for the invitation to talk, but she hadn't given him one yet. He wanted to sit and look her in the eye, not try to apologize while she was distracted with chores.

Finally she folded the paper sack and looked at him. "Do you want a drink? I want a drink."

"I'm not really supposed to," he admitted. He really wanted one—it would ease the tension—but he was working on a new healthy lifestyle. Day drinking two weeks into the plan would doom him to failure. "Some water would be great, though."

She eyed him for a moment before she nodded and pulled two bottles of water out of the fridge. She handed him one and pointed to the wall. "Let's head into the living room. People always congregate in the kitchen and I hate that."

Sebastian backed out of her way and followed her lead into the open and airy living room. She had comfy couches, a few nice pieces of art he recognized and a decent-size, flat-screen television on a shelf. There was a wall of books on one side of the room and a wall of windows on the other. From where he was, he could spy a glimpse of green—Central Park—a few blocks away.

"Have a seat," she said as she settled onto the couch.

He opted for the oversize chair just to her right, facing her. Their knees almost touched as they sat, but he kept his joints to himself for the moment, no matter how badly he wanted to touch her. "Thanks for talking to me, Harper."

She shrugged and opened her water. "The last time I saw you, you were on death's door. I was hoping to hear you were doing better."

"I am," he said proudly. "I've been going to cardiac rehab three times a week and they've started me on a new lifestyle program that will make me more mindful of what I eat and how much rest I get. It's made a huge difference already."

Harper listened to him talk but nothing more than a casual interest lit her eyes. "I'm glad to hear that."

"Me, too. Going forward, I know I can't let my work overtake my life. I want more than a career and a string of patents under my belt. I want a life, too. A wife. Maybe a family."

That got her attention. She sat more upright in her seat, her brows knitting together in thought. "That's a big change for a workaholic bachelor. What's going to keep you from losing yourself in your work again and this time ignoring your new family instead of just your health?"

She didn't think he could change. "I'm not going to ignore you, Harper. I couldn't possibly."

"I didn't mean me," she said. "I just meant in general. Old habits die hard. Like keeping secrets. Trust me, I know."

"I'm sorry I lied to you. It wasn't that I didn't trust you with the different aspects of my past. I was just… embarrassed. You understand that, don't you?"

"Of course. But I told you everything, Sebastian. You told me almost nothing."

"If you hadn't been blackmailed by Josie, would you still have told me? Or was it only out of necessity?"

The self-righteous expression on her face softened a little. Her gaze dropped to the cap of her water bottle as she fidgeted with it. "And then I find myself clutching your unconscious body in the middle of a parking lot, screaming. When the ambulance arrives, I can't tell them your medical information. I can't say if you have a history of cardiac problems. I know literally nothing. You could've died and there was nothing I could do to help."

"I shouldn't have put you in that position. I never dreamed it would happen again or I would've said something."

Harper nodded. "I understand we started off with the whole fake relationship thing, but that's over. The wedding trip is over and now this is real life, Sebastian. Real feelings. We're not playing a game any longer. I need to know the truth."

"About what?"

"About *everything*. I want to know everything you've been keeping from me before I can consider continuing this relationship."

"Right now? You just want me to lay out my whole life story right now?" He had an engagement ring burning a hole in his pocket. He was desperate to hear her say yes and move forward, but Harper wasn't having it.

She sat back against the couch cushions, making herself visibly more comfortable. "Do you have somewhere you need to be, Sebastian? Work, perhaps? It's a Saturday, but who knows with you."

"No," he insisted. "There's nowhere I need to be but right here, right now. I'll tell you whatever you want to know if it will make you feel more comfortable in loving me. Because I love you, Harper. I've never let myself love a woman before. I'm not sure I'm going to do things right, but I can't help how I feel. I'll do anything you want me to if it means you'll tell me that you love me, as well."

Harper's jaw dropped at the first mention of the word "love" and stayed there until he was done speaking. "Well, why don't you start from the beginning? You've never said much about your family or where you grew up. Just about your brother's accident."

Sebastian nodded and sat back in his seat, ready to tell her whatever she wanted to know.

"I grew up poor," he said. "And so we're clear, not the kind of poor you've been. I mean dirt poor. Oldest-trailer-in-the-trailer-park poor. I never owned a new pair of shoes until I went to college and bought them myself. Until then, every bit of clothing I'd ever had was my brother's hand-me-down. My parents did everything they could to get ahead in life, but there was always something on the next horizon ready to knock them back down.

"When my brother and I were old enough, we worked to help make ends meet. Kenny worked at the burger place near our high school. I liked to tinker and helped my dad with fixing the car and such, so I ended up working at a shop that fixed old lawnmowers and small engines. If I could, I'd mow people's lawns after I fixed their mowers, too, for extra cash. Every penny went to my parents. For a while, we were doing okay. My dad got a promotion, my brother graduated from high school and started working full time. Then he had his accident."

Harper was watching him speak so intently, he wondered if she was even breathing. He shook his head and sighed. "We had insurance, but Kenny fell off the plan when he graduated. He didn't have any at work yet, either. There was a little coverage from the owner of the ATV, but it wasn't nearly enough. He spent my entire senior year in hospitals and rehabilitation centers. The bills were crippling. My mom had to quit her job to stay home and take care of him, making it worse."

"How awful," she whispered.

"I was determined to do more than just rebuild lawnmowers my whole life. I wanted to make something of myself so I could help my parents and my brother. That's what drove me. I worked as much as I could after his accident, and the only money I ever kept for myself was enough money to apply to MIT and take my entrance exams."

"How are they now?" Harper asked.

Sebastian finally found a reason to smile.

"They're great. With my first million, I bought my parents a real house in Portland that was near the doctors and specialists Kenny sees regularly. It's nice, but not too big for them to maintain, and it's fully wheelchair friendly so my brother can get around. I bought them an accessible van and I send them money every month to help take care of things. My dad continues to work out of pride, but he should be retiring in a few years."

Harper smiled and reached out to put a hand on his knee. "I'm glad to hear it."

"We've all come a long way. It took a lot of hard work to get there. I don't regret it or the toll it took on my health to get there. I just know I need to do better going forward."

"I can understand why you did what you did. To start with nothing and build a company like yours is amazing. I bet you look at someone like me, who squandered a fortune, and resent the hell out of it."

Sebastian shook his head. "I don't. Everyone comes from a different place, but that makes them who they are. You made your mistakes and you grew from them. You owned them. I'm not sure I'd be strong enough to stand up and do what you did at the wedding. Even with the money I've made, giving up almost thirty-million dollars is heartbreaking."

"Well, actually, it turns out that I didn't."

He frowned at her. "What do you mean?"

"I spoke with my grandfather. I came clean about the whole thing. He decided I'd learned my lesson and gave me the money anyway. That's why I bought the champagne. Today is my birthday. My grandpa wanted me to throw a big party but I wasn't ready for all that after what happened in Ireland. I thought I might have a little celebration by myself. Would you like to join me?"

Sebastian smiled. "I would." He wouldn't have more than a sip since he was trying to be good, but he would certainly toast to her birthday.

They got up and went to the kitchen where she

poured two champagne flutes. Back in the living room, they sat, this time both of them on the couch together.

"Happy birthday, Harper," he said, raising his flute. "I'm glad I was able to be here today to celebrate with you. I wasn't sure if I would have the chance to tell you that. Or any of the other things I said to you today. Thank you for giving me the chance."

Harper smiled and clinked her glass against his. "Thank you. This isn't how I imagined my birthday, but it couldn't have been better, really. I've learned a lot about myself the past few weeks. Without Josie trying to blackmail me, I might not have realized that I could get by on my own. Or that I didn't need money and fancy cars to define me. I also wouldn't have realized how important you are to me, too."

Sebastian's heart stuttered in his chest and this time it had nothing to do with his clogged arteries. He set his untouched drink on the coffee table. "I'm sorry I didn't know it was your birthday today. I would've brought you a present." He reached into his pocket. "Instead, all I have is this."

Her gaze locked on the blue box and her jaw dropped once again. "What…" Her voice trailed off.

"I told you before that I love you, Harper. And that I'm ready to find some balance in my life. But what I left out was that I want to find that balance with you. Just you. Life is too short to hesitate, and I can't risk losing you again."

Sebastian slid off the couch onto one knee and opened the box to display the emerald-cut halo ring inside. "I promise that I won't keep secrets from you anymore. I promise I will never make my work seem more important than you or our family. You are the most important person in my life, Harper. I never knew I could love someone the way that I love you. Please do me the honor of being my wife, Harper Drake."

He looked at her in time to see her eyes flood with tears. "Yes," she whispered with a smile that spread from ear to ear.

Sebastian slipped the ring onto her finger and squeezed her hand in his. They stood and she leaped into his arms. He pulled her tight against him and kissed his fiancée for the very first time.

This was the start of their future together. A future he almost didn't have, but that he would cherish with Harper for as long as he could.

Epilogue

"Merry Christmas, everyone!"

Harper heard the commotion at the door and rushed out of the kitchen to see who had arrived. She was excited to host her first Christmas with her family and Sebastian's family all together.

Sebastian was hugging his mother as she came through the door. His father was right behind her with arms full of presents. And in the back was Kenny. *Standing.*

With the help of Sebastian's exoskeleton prototype, his brother moved in a slow but steady pace through the doorway with a wide grin on his face. He looked almost as happy as Sebastian himself.

Nothing could match his excitement. This was the culmination of his dream. The best Christmas gift he could ever give his family. She knew watching Kenny walk across the room and sit by the fireplace unaided was the greatest present Sebastian could ever receive.

It was his sketches from Ireland that made the difference. He didn't realize it at the time, but once he returned to his lab, Sebastian had a breakthrough. She could tell it pained him to come home at a reasonable hour each night when his mind wanted him to keep pushing, but his goal had still been achieved in the end.

The two families were introduced and everyone gathered with drinks and appetizers in the living room. Harper was just about to return to the kitchen for more eggnog when Sebastian caught her eye.

He reached under the tree for a gift and gestured for Harper to follow him down the hallway to their bedroom. "I wanted to give you this now," Sebastian said once they were alone.

"Now? It's only Christmas Eve."

"Please open it."

Harper sighed and accepted the beautifully wrapped present from her fiancé. He'd already given her such a beautiful engagement ring, she felt guilty accepting a present from him. She opened the golden foil lid and found a collection of sparkling items wrapped in tissue paper.

A sapphire necklace. A ruby tennis bracelet. Diamond earrings. An aquamarine cocktail ring. Emerald cufflinks. An old pocket watch.

It couldn't be.

Harper's eyes grew wide as she looked down at the gift and back up at Sebastian. "This is my mother's jewelry. And your things, too. Josie stole all of this. How on earth did you get it back?"

Sebastian grinned even wider than he had when

his brother had successfully walked through the front door of their apartment. "Well, it turns out that our little blackmailer went after someone else to make some cash. Instead of paying, they went straight to the police. All these items were found in her apartment when she was arrested. The cops contacted me last week because the jewelry matched the description in the police report we filed."

She picked up the pocket watch and looked at it in wonder. Harper had thought she might never be able to replace this special piece for Sebastian. "They said they couldn't find Josie."

"Apparently that wasn't her real name. But after she tried to blackmail Quentin—"

"My ex, Quentin?" she interrupted in surprise.

"Yep. When he got the threatening letter, he remembered what happened to you and led the cops straight to her door. Turns out her name is Amanda Webber. I hope she looks good in orange."

Harper smiled and handed Sebastian his great-grandfather's watch. "Merry Christmas, my love."

"Merry Christmas, Harper."

* * * * *